FLYING WITH AMELIA

FLYING

WITH

AMELIA

ANNE DEGRACE

McArthur & Company

Toronto

First published in 2011 by
McArthur & Company
322 King Street West, Suite 402
Toronto, Ontario M5V 1J2
www.mcarthur-co.com

The author is grateful for permission to use an excerpt from
Manual for Draft-Age Immigrants to Canada by Mark Satin.
Reprinted by permission of House of Anansi Press.

LIBRARY AND ARCHIVES CANADA CATALOGUING IN PUBLICATION

DeGrace, Anne
Flying with Amelia / Anne DeGrace.

ISBN 978-1-55278-979-7

I. Title.

PS8607.E47F59 2011   C813'.6   C2011-904290-8

 Canada Council   Conseil des Arts
for the Arts   du Canada

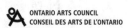 ONTARIO ARTS COUNCIL
CONSEIL DES ARTS DE L'ONTARIO

The publisher would like to acknowledge the financial support
of the Government of Canada through the Canada Book Fund
and the Canada Council for our publishing activities. The publisher
further wishes to acknowledge the financial support of the Ontario Arts
Council and the OMDC for our publishing program.

Design and composition by Ingrid Paulson
Author photograph by Tam Forde
Printed and bound in Canada by Solisco Printers

10 9 8 7 6 5 4 3 2 1

For my children, who are making their own stories

FLYING WITH AMELIA

ACROSS
THE ATLANTIC

·1847·

|||

WE COUNT THE days by making scratches in the rough wood of our berth, as if we are in prison, and prison it is, even if freedom lies at the end—if end we reach. The ship heaves and rolls, creaks and sighs, as do we all: one hundred and seventy-six souls below decks. We are but one family: Daniel and I, our four children, and my sisters—Catherine, eighteen, and Sally, two years her junior—amid so many others. The children fall asleep against us, and we, sometimes, against each other, like a pile of barn cats but not so well fed—although a cat would do well in this hold. It would need to be a big cat indeed so as not to be devoured itself by the rats.

Fanny, awake, leans against me, her body hot and damp, as the others sleep. We have been talking, remembering the ginger tom that could sometimes be seen sitting on our wall of an early morn. I hold Fanny curled in my lap, Finn and Henry sleeping with their small heads against my skirts, and whisper about that big old tomcat. I wonder aloud what he's doing now, and if he misses us. Eliza, who thinks herself too old for such tales (herself the eldest at just seven years), pretends not to listen, but I know she does. For the telling of stories makes the time pass.

WHEN I FIRST saw the hold in which we were to travel across the Atlantic, I thought: as bad as things were in Waterford, this is worse. Rows and rows of rough berths lined with a bit of straw, trunks and cases now doing duty as tables, and everywhere, families trying to sort themselves into cramped quarters the like of which we could not have imagined. At first it was something of an adventure for the children, who ran about between the rows, but that changed within hours of sailing, as the roll of the sea made us all sick, with buckets soon full and nothing to be done about it.

That first day I watched as Daniel spoke with the husband and father of the family whose berth is next to ours. Each berth is barely long as a man is tall, and as wide as that again. We were assigned two berths for our family: two berths between the eight of us, and my heart fell at the thought of it. And yet the Murphys next to us were given just one berth for two parents and six children, the oldest son almost as big as his father.

I looked over at Martha Murphy, standing with her children around her, and looked away, torn between being the good Christian I wanted to be, and knowing that the journey is long, and space will be precious. There was nothing to be said once arrangements are made, as Daniel's word is final. The youngest Murphy girls—twins Jane and Agnes, and two-year-old Bridget—would share our upper berth with Sally and Catherine. Daniel and I and the children would share the lower. Martha and Paddy Murphy would now share their berth with their three older boys.

"It's the right thing, Mary," Daniel told me quietly, and I nodded. Now, the distribution of human bodies is fairer. And fair my Daniel is, which is a fine quality, and the one that makes me love him most. He was fair enough to pay passage for Sally and Catherine, and it means the world to me.

We had to say goodbye to Da, who would not leave his Eire. True enough he urged us all to go, as Mama would have done were she still with us, God rest her soul. There was never a sadder day than that, and it pains my heart to think of it. Da stayed in Waterford where our cousins have taken him in. We said goodbye and then made the trip to Dublin, and from Dublin to Liverpool across the cold Irish sea, to huddle together in the hold of a ship we prayed might be seaworthy while we waited for the hatch to close, and the journey to begin.

As we settled in on that first day, Martha Murphy caught my eye and her thin smile was grateful, as she knew as well as I the value of this gift. Now, I wonder: would I have been so charitable, had I known?

||||| ||

THE DAYS HAVE been fine, and we spend as much time as we can above decks. The children play with others, but the rules are clear: there's to be no running about where a child might fall through the rail, and in any case, the crew keeps us to our area, for there is much to be done to keep us on our course.

I watch Eliza, hoping she will find a playmate among the children. She is a serious child, especially since she saw her father cry in pain when the accident happened, and understood our talk as we sold one thing, and then another, to pay for the doctor. She stays close by, and is a help with her brothers and sister, but I would that she would play just a little.

At night we must stay below decks—the Master's rule— and last night there was a fiddle and a pennywhistle and someone had a pan and a wooden spoon, and there was dancing. Two young men from the crew came down and brought with them three barrels of beer—the Master could not have known—struggling down the ladder, and with help from the reaching arms of our men below. For they are Irish like ourselves, and when they heard the music they wanted to join the fun.

The lads danced with the ladies, and the children dance amongst themselves, and before long the beer was gone, for it was not so much amongst so many men. But the presence of it made them merry just the same, and the women for seeing the men cast their worries aside for a bit.

And now it is night again, and the once-calm sea is calm no more, and there'll be no dancing tonight.

||||| ||||| |||

THE HATCH HAS been closed two days, the better to keep us from drowning as the storm-ravaged sea sweeps the decks above, but it's hard to imagine a fate worse than drowning in our own foul mess. Not a fortnight into the voyage and so many sick with the dysentery, and worse. The straw does nothing to stop the contents of stomach or bowels from seeping through top bunk to bottom for those too weak to reach the buckets, which in any case overflow and will not be emptied 'til the storm abates. The stench is not something I will soon forget, the dank air close with the heat of unwashed bodies. Some have the Ship's Fever, with the aches and chills and pain and sores, and I hold the children close and pray.

Sometimes I hear Martha do the same. She is a frail thing, with skin so white as to look like china, and eyes too big for her face. But she has a lovely smile, and better teeth than my own. She worked as a serving girl in a big house, she told me, until the mistress died and the master's new wife brought her own people. When she told me, she sounded wistful, but I'd not want a life in service such as that. My Daniel had his own shop, and worked for no master.

My sisters and I are Murphys too, like the family who shifts and whimpers in sleep nearby—or at least, a Murphy I was until Daniel McGrath took me for his wife. And so we have a name in common if we are not related in some way, as most of Ireland is, I suppose. It's something to have, this bond, however small, as we voyage in this heaving, tossing, stinking, ship across the Atlantic to what we hope will be a better life.

Most on the ship have had passage paid by their landlords, who'd sooner see them gone for a few pounds' passage than have to look at them starving on the land, the rent unpaid, potatoes black in the fields. We were near as hungry as the rest of them, with starvation not so far ahead. It's a terrible thing to have a hungry child and not a crust to give him.

"We'll go while we have our health, Mary," Daniel said. "There's nothing for us here." He'd received a letter that day from his brother Niall in Newfoundland, and indeed it seemed that in such a place we might make a life.

"Tell us about Ginger Tom," whispers Finn now, his dirty thumb in his mouth, and I do, because it will help pass the night until, the Lord be with us, the day is fine tomorrow and we can go above decks, wash ourselves in seawater as best we can, and let the sun fall upon us. The pitch has subsided, now, the worst of the storm passed.

"Well, he was a big old cat," I begin, and my Daniel reaches over and rests his good hand on my head where it lies, warm and comforting. I feel something crawl beneath his fingers, then feel his fingers in my hair, searching for pests to pinch, knowing there is no point but doing it just the same.

"How big?" Finn's eyes are wide in the dim light from the swinging lamps as he turns his head around to see me, and I smile just a bit, for the cracks in my lips make it hurt to smile more.

"Bigger than you," I tell him.

"Bigger than Eliza?"

"Oooh, twice as big," I tell him, and I can feel Eliza shift; she's listening, even if she won't let on. She seldom speaks these days, and now I wonder when I last heard the voice of my oldest daughter, who has shrunk into such a sad wee thing. "He grew so big the mice weren't near enough to keep him."

"What did he eat?" Fanny, now. She has Henry curled in her lap, and she whispers so as not to wake him, even though around us are the sighs and groans of people and the creaking beams of the ship. From far above comes the crack of sails in the wind, and across the hold a pennywhistle plays a mournful tune. It is eerie quiet of late, as it was not when we began this voyage eight days ago. The children no longer play, and with the rough seas and the sickness, no one has the will to sing or dance as we did in the first days, when we were happy to be on our way at last, and, despite our hardships, full of the promise of a new life.

Daniel, beside me, scratches at his own hair with the two remaining fingers of his right hand. Whatever will we do in the new world? "Pigs," he says, and it takes me a moment to remember the story I was telling.

"Pigs?" I hear a small laugh from below, and it's Catherine. I am grateful, again, for Daniel being the kind of man he is, buying passage and provisions for my sisters as well as us with the sale of the blacksmithy and the money Niall sent from St. John's. The sound of Catherine's laugh warms me.

"Pigs," Daniel continues. "That Mr. Ginger started hunting the pigs, right under Lord Richbugger's nose, for who would think an old tomcat would be stalking such a thing as a pig? He began with just a small pig, mind you. Just to start." Below, the shift and sighs of Catherine, Sally, and the Murphy girls, and in Fanny's lap Henry stirs, waking.

As Daniel tells the tale of how the ginger cat got the pig despite the best efforts of its foolish owner, in my mind's eye I can see the fields of Eire, the green, gentle-looking hills belying the misery of those who toiled upon them. In Waterford we were a little better off than the tenant farmers: we had two small rooms, and a shack for the smithy, there on the edge of town. When our own small plot of potatoes turned black we'd already got wind of the blight and the hunger that followed, but oatmeal could still be had in trade: a wagon refitted for someone with more than ourselves, a bit of work here and there. And then came the accident.

". . . and, being such a good old kitty, he brought the tender piglet—carried it he did over his shoulder like a sack o' spuds—to the McGrath home, for wee Henry had been kind to old Tom Ginger all the while, as Henry always loved God's creatures. Don't you, Henry?"

"Yes," says Henry.

9

"And all of the children—Henry and Fanny and Finn and Eliza—danced a jig, and Mama made a grand feast for us all."

From the berth beside ours, in the darkness, I hear a soft cluck of disapproval.

"You should not be talking so. It makes us all hungry," whispers Martha.

"All the better to dream," I tell her, "for sure enough dreams are all we have."

She doesn't answer. I'm not angry with her; I know that gnawing longing as we all try not to think about the hole we feel inside. In the darkness I can hear her sigh, and then her steady breathing. She is sleeping, and for that I am envious.

||||| ||||| ||||| ||||| ||

THERE IS LITTLE left of the provisions we brought with us. They said the trip would take twenty-one days, but I heard two of the crew talking, a couple of the mates—not so much older than young Tom Murphy—saying that the storm which kept us shut up those two long days took us well off course. The water we have to drink is brackish, but there is enough, yet. We have food for a day or two more, and the portions will be thin, sure. After the accident, and everything we had gone to pay the doctor, we knew hunger, but not like we know hunger now.

The hatch opens, and light and air stream in from above, the salt air sweet, and Daniel takes his knife and carves one more mark in the wood. Another day, and we are all still here.

Henry cries as I splash him with the cold water, but it's a fine day and the sun is warm, and if we stay sheltered from the wind it will dry him soon enough. Daniel is talking to Paddy Murphy, and there is a seriousness to their faces, and all at once I realize that Martha is not above decks. It's

Catherine and Sally washing the Murphy girls, not Martha. Colum and Liam splash seawater at one another, but there is no joy in it.

I search for Tom, at thirteen the eldest Murphy boy. When I saw him first, when this voyage began, he was a good-looking, freckled lad, just growing into the man he will someday be. He is leaning on the rail, his head down, thin and pale and small.

"Tom?" I touch his shoulder.

"Leave me. Leave us," he mutters, his voice flat. "There'll be no help for us."

Eliza has the wee ones in hand. I go below, and there I find Martha with the fever, and she does not see me at all.

||||| ||||| ||||| ||||| ||||

YESTERDAY, MARTHA MURPHY died. I heard the wail, and though it was hard to fathom as human, I knew it to be Paddy. Afraid as I was for myself and my family, I smoothed her hair and straightened her dress and Daniel alerted the crew; three dead were taken up this morning from the hold in canvas slings that served as coffins as they were slipped overboard, with a prayer to the Virgin for their safe passage to heaven. I did my best not to think of the dark water or the things that dwell there.

There is more room, I suppose, in the Murphy berth now.

Sally and Catherine keep the Murphy girls with them, and Paddy has the boys, and we keep our children close, but there is no escape from filth and disease, the smell and the sorrow. The Murphy boys have taken to Catherine as well, and I suppose that with their mother gone a woman's touch is a comfort. I see Tom, his chin on his hands, listening to every word. Like Eliza, he's spoken little of late.

Catherine's picked up the Tale of Ginger Tom, spinning broader and broader yarns to the delight of all. Catherine was a storyteller from the moment she could talk, for I was six years when she was born, my mother having lost two between, and I remember well. I sit above and listen, and when the ship begins to sway with the swells that speak of stormy weather, I let her voice wash over me as I try to keep my stomach in its place. There is nothing for it to give up, anyway.

Daniel has used most of what little money we brought to purchase biscuits and water from the Master's stores, paying terrible prices for hard things made of flour and sawdust. Some have weevils, and I tap them out so the children will not see. Paddy Murphy has traded the family broach that Martha had treasured so. We share our food, the Murphys and the McGraths, as if we were one family. It is not so everywhere in the hold, where one desperate moment of thievery led to murder two nights ago. The Ship's Master is a cowardly man, and has left us to ourselves.

We are still days from port.

I look in the faces of my children for the healthy, happy things they once were. I wonder at my own face. Daniel and I seldom look at one another, so painful is the sight. And yet, we are better off than many. There are still a few biscuits from the Master's cupboard, stored now in the tin I keep tightly closed, nestled amid the foul straw. There is still water in the jug.

"Feel the sway, Bridget?" I hear Catherine ask, her voice drifting up, weary-sounding, from below. "We're in a cradle, we are, like babes, and that's Old Tom Ginger, rocking us off to sleep."

"Tom Ginger is here?" asks Agnes sleepily, awakened by the voices.

"'Course. He came with us, didn't he? To see we made it safe ashore."

"Will he sing us a lullaby, then?" Bridget asks.

It's quiet for a bit, and then Catherine lifts her voice quietly in song, a gentle crooning, and across the way, through the darkness, I hear Paddy Murphy begin to cry.

||||| ||||| ||||| ||||| ||||| ||

THROUGH THE LONG days and nights there is nought to do but think. There are some who live on the edge of madness, for they have lost loved ones, and no longer believe that this will end, believing instead they have been consigned to purgatory. Last night a squall sent the ship pitching so wildly I feared we would not see the light of day again, and in that time I heard sins confessed I am only glad my children couldn't understand. When the swells subsided we were left in the darkness and stench with the ghosts of our sad admissions and our pitiful thoughts.

This night is gentler. Beside me sleeps Eliza, who has not uttered a word for two days, now. I put my head down to hers, whisper in her ear: *All will be well, my darling, you'll see*, but she turns her head away, and I can't tell if she hears me or has turned in her sleep. On the other side is Daniel, and I can see in the dim light that his eyes are open, and that he is thinking just as I am.

At first we talked about what things we might do to earn a living on shore. Niall has learned the craft of fishing, and has told Daniel there is work for him there. Niall does not know about the runaway horse that bolted down our lane and through the smithy, nor how Daniel, when he tried to catch the animal, caught his hand in the tangle of its traces to be crushed under the weight of the great, terrified beast as it tried to fight its way to freedom. Daniel's hand—its

crushed and broken bones healed as well as could be hoped—
is good for little. Can a man fish with one hand?

Now, we don't talk about how we will live or what we will
do. Like Eliza, we barely talk at all. I know his hand pains
him, but he doesn't say. But with no words spoken, I know
what he says to me now, as he turns his face towards mine.

||||| ||||| ||||| ||||| ||||| ||||| |||

WE HEARD THE shouts from above at dawn; land! And crawling
up from below we emerged into the light, all of us shades of
brown, blinking like vermin caught in sudden light, smiling
with all of our grey and wobbling teeth.

Land.

Below us, the stinking hold, thirty-three marks scratched
into the wood of our berth. I think about the ones lost, the
ones we leave behind as we turn our backs to the sea and our
faces towards the distant shape on the horizon that is our
future.

Land.

Behind us, in Ireland, our fathers and grandfathers,
mothers and grandmothers, and the countless bones of our
ancestors. Ahead of us, in this new country, our dreams, the
dreams that our children, and their children, have yet to
dream. We stand at the rail, all of us together. Young Tom
Murphy catches my eye as if to say: Aye, we made it; now
what? And if he asked it aloud, I'd not know what to tell him.

Sally holds Henry in her thin arms, and I think I should
take him from her, so weak she's become, but she holds him
firm enough and smiling, she is. On the faces around me,
looks of wonder, or joy, or something like fear. It's a curious
thing, but I can feel the hearts of us all beating just now.

Catherine holds Bridget Murphy by the hand, and I catch Paddy not looking at the land ahead, but looking at my sister, his wife not two weeks gone, and yet it's as if lifetimes have passed for us all. I look at Catherine and I think: she won't need to change her name, then, will she? And then I laugh, because there is so much to think about, and I'm thinking of this.

"Will Tom Ginger be there?" Fanny asks, and Eliza, standing alongside, looks down, her small face serious, and I wait to see if she will answer.

"Of course he will," she tells Fanny after a moment. I lay my hand on her head.

Henry reaches his hands out to his Papa, and Daniel takes him from Sally and holds him close, then catches my eye over the top of his small head.

Around us are the others who've survived. One hundred and seventy-six began this journey thirty-three days ago, and now, how many stand on this deck? I lost count of the dead taken up. Perhaps forty or more, hopeful souls whose earthly bodies will not know land again. I can feel the swell of emotion around me, the swell of the waves beneath, and at my back, the whisper of what we've left behind.

Land.

I am full of hope, and I am terrified.

STATIC

·1901·

IT WAS A pounding on the door that started it off, and the call from the other side: any mummers 'lowed in? and I turned to see Mum there with her eyes bright and her smile wide, and my dad hauled open the door with a ho ho! The first one caught me up and picked me right up off my feet, saying: 'es a big one 'e is, better get the pot boiling. I tried to see who it was but he had the sheet over his head and tied at the neck with a striped muffler and with his voice all disguised— well, it might've been Mr. Kelly but I was laughing too hard to say anyways.

And then the fiddles started up and the kitchen was full of rubber boots all stomping and spinning, men dressed as ladies and ladies dressed as men and my mum and dad dancing with this one and that one, and then finally with each other. There was the smell of beer and the screech and wet wool from melting snow. One had mitts on his feet and the thumbs flopped around like fish, jigging across the kitchen floor like live things.

I think and I think and it seems like that was the last time I recalls laughing in our house. Because right after was when the accident happened. And somehow the drinking followed, and Mum said she could cope with the accident but not the drinking and after a while there was not laughing nor dancing nor even talking. And 'tis near time for the mummers to come again, and it'll be a cold kitchen they comes to.

IT WAS AT the butcher's I first heard about the job. I was there getting bones for the dog, or at least that's what I told Mr. Walsh, who wiped his big hands on his bloody apron and then started piling bones onto a pile of newspaper and wrapped them up with twine. Then he looked at me with his bald head and jowls making him look some old bulldog himself, and told me about the Eyetalian, a *scientist* he said, setting up a laboratory up by Cabot Tower, might need someone to sweep up and be useful.

"What are ye, twelve, Willie b'y? Could be something for your pocket."

I knew he meant money to help out at home, but wouldn't say. Folks in St. John's don't. Everyone's got hard times and good times, and nobody says a thing either way. Once I heard Mrs. Kelly say about us that "it's a good thing they just got the one," because between them they could hardly keep me fed. Most families have seven or eight kids who run in packs and stick up for one another. I had no brother to stick up for me, and no sister to defend, and I heard my mum say once to Mrs. Kelly that 'twas a disappointment. I didn't know if 'twas me she meant, or that there was no babies come after. I suppose it turned me quiet. If folks were thinking I didn't amount to a hill of beans, well then I supposed they must be right.

Back home I put the package of bones in the root cellar, because sure enough we have no dog, then made myself scarce before Mum found me something to do. Some would say I should've been in school, but I never cared for it much. And I used to help Dad jig cod and dry and salt it before the accident, and nobody minded much that my desk was empty most days—not the priest, nor the teacher—because lots of kids were out. You can't do schooling when your stomach's growling with the hunger, anyways.

The notion of a job, 'specially a job with a foreigner, sounded good to me, because St. John's folks don't have much to pay but a foreigner was likely rich. So I thought I'd best get up there 'fore some other bugger got there first and took my job.

The walk up the hill from the Battery was a miserable thing, with the wind off the harbour like ice, but it was the walk past Deadman's Pond that set my heart to pounding. For it was on the rocks above they'd set the gibbet to hang the bodies of the poor fellas who was executed, to hang there until they rotted and then be packed in a barrel with some rocks and rolled over the cliff and into the pond below. They say the pond just goes on and on, no bottom at all, and that it was the ghosts of all those hanged men reached up their bony hands and pulled down two sisters out skating one winter just like this one, grabbing their ankles through a hole in the ice. So between the wind and the cold and my heart a-pounding, I was fair wore out by the time I got there.

I could see nobody in the tower at first when I'd made my way up the hill, and I walked around her twice looking for what I imagined a foreign scientist might look like, but I didn't see a soul. So I finally asked a man in work clothes coming out of the old Fever Hospital, a place that gave me

the shivers, so gloomy it was, but I went up to him anyways
and asked if he might know. And he did!

"Look for the fella looks like a for'ner," the man told me. "I
seen 'im, with two other fellas, mustaches like nothing you
ever seen, b'y. He dresses like a for'ner, too, right fancy." And
he stumped off down the hill, probably to his dinner, which
made my stomach growl just thinking of it, and me with none.

I found Mr. Marconi in a dark wee room, oil lamp so dim
I missed it the first time, which is when I realized I wasn't
likely to get rich after all. He was alone—the two other fellas
somewheres else I figures—unpacking wooden crates. Inside,
packed in sawdust, were things I couldn't make out. Looking
around the room I saw there was a stove with a bit of smoky
wood burning, and a cot in the corner. He looked up at me
from where he crouched, caught in the light from the one
salt-washed window, and he looked at me like he didn't see
me, like he was coming up for air from the bottom of the
harbour. He wasn't so much bigger than me, and not so
strong, but his clothes were better and he looked like someone with the learning. He stood up, and I saw his coat was
no coat for a winter in St. John's. I told him why I come.

"Yes. I could use an extra pair of hands," he told me, holding up his own, blue with the cold. His speech was funny,
but his English was good. "Come tomorrow. We start early.
The days are so short."

FOR THE FIRST two weeks I swept up, pushed crates into place
to be tables and benches, brought in firewood, and tried to
stay out of the way when Mr. Marconi and Mr. Paget and Mr.
Kemp fiddled with wires and coils and tubes and whatnot.
Every so often Mr. Marconi would walk out to where the hill
looks across the pond t'wards England. He would walk while

the wind howled off the Atlantic, and more than once I thought he'd be blown fair away and that would be the end of my job. And that would be a sad thing indeed, because before I go home each day I get two pennies, big and brown and warm in my palm as I run down the hill.

Sometimes I'd get to hold something—a pinching tool or a wire or clamp. Mr. Marconi would tell me: "Stop fidgeting, William. Stand still, now," and I'd stand as still as I could, pressing my boots on the plank floor as if I'd glued them together and to the boards at once so as not to move an inch. I s'pose I wanted him to find a use for me more than sweeping and wood chopping, even if I couldn't make sense of the marks on the papers he has spread out on the table, all lines and arrows and letters, or what it means when the needle on the dials would go like the weathervane on our shed.

Mr. Marconi paid no attention most times, like I's one of the mice runs up and down the walls. But after I'd helped him he sometimes put a hand on the shoulder, and I'd feel good because lately there hadn't been much of that at home.

It was January last when Dad fell down a well shaft when he was out shooting hare; said he couldn't even see any house left nor figure why anyone would've ever built in a scrub bog never mind dug a well in all that peat, but there it was under him and down he went with one leg rammed into a crack between a couple of rocks and broken in three places. I heard my mum say to Mrs. Kelly that "my own grandfather came over from Ireland short the use of one hand and struggled they did, my mother told us time and again. And now here's my John, one leg useless and Lord knows what's to become of us now." I remembered my Granny Eliza: a grumpy old thing who'd tell me what a lucky lad I was, making me feel bad for wanting a sweet. My own mum sounded a bit like her, then.

There's no sweets for me now that it's most of a year gone with Dad hobbling around with a cane and not good for much says Mum, especially when he spends what money Mum earns, doing the laundry and the sewing, on the screech or whatever it is Donny Cummings is making this week in his back shed. What Dad don't know is that Mum's been hiding away some of her sewing money. I seen her putting coins into the English marmalade jar she's been saving since one of the mummers left it last Christmas, filled with whisky when he came and empty when he left, and she could hardly return it since she wasn't supposed to know it was Duncan McCurdy all dressed up. It's a fancy jar, and we don't have so many nice things, as Mum is fond of saying.

When Mum saw me watching her, she said: "Willie, this is our secret, now. Something for a rainy day." And I nodded because I knew sure as she did that if Dad found the money, he would drink it.

'TWAS AFTER ABOUT a week of working for Mr. Marconi that I went home to a storm. You could hear the yelling all the way from O'Brians', and what do you know but there was Mrs. O'Brian herself sticking her old grey head out her door and when she caught sight of me she gave her head a shake as if to say: sorry for what you're walking into. I may not have the schooling, but I'm not stupid. I stayed outside, pressed up against the siding by the kitchen door, listening.

"Enough with you," my mum was shouting. "You come home blind drunk, every penny I've earned this week into your glass and nothin left for food and I've traded the last of the salt cod. We've nothin in the larder and the root cellar's near empty and here 'tis, calendar's just turned December and months of winter to go." Her voice was shrill, spitting angry but cracking at the edges, too.

"Mind your mouth, now, woman," my dad said, but there was no threat to it, and no edge to the words, either, softened at the sides as they were by the drink. "I got some work for Fergus, promised me he did, carvin buoys. Can do that on me arse."

"Arse forwards, that's you, by Jayzus. Fergus won't be payin any help, that's certain. You can't put that one on me, John Harvey. And if he did ye'd drink it sure enough, and Willie needin shoes, and me needin—" and that was when I heard something break, a dinner plate sounded like, and we had few enough of those. I didn't need to be lookin in the window to know that Mum had thrown it, if not at Dad, then close enough to make it clear she meant business if t'weren't clear before. So I ran back to Cabot Hill. I didn't know where else to go.

Mr. Marconi was still there, making a click click sound with something on the table, then writing something on the paper beside him. There was almost no light from the window, late as it was, and with just the one bulb in the ceiling. He looked up when he heard me at the door, his face annoyed, and then he saw mine, I guess, the way I must've looked, and his mouth changed.

"Come in where it's warm, boy," he said, 'though it wasn't.

"My mum smashed a plate," I said, surprised myself when the words came out. I can't say why I said it, but there 'twas.

"Did she." Mr. Marconi put his hands on his knees and looked at me, waiting. But I'd said enough, I figured, with my mum's words in my ears: we keeps our business to ourselves, Willie. I stood in the doorway wondering what I'd been thinking, coming up here.

"Close the door, William," he said. "The winter is coming in."

I sat on a crate near the stove watching my pants steam. We were both quiet for a while, and then he said: "When I was a boy, I broke an entire set of dishes."

I waited, listening to the dry wood pop in the stove.

"An experiment. My mother was very angry. But it was my father who was really furious. He forbade me to do any more experiments. In fact, he insisted I put it all aside and enter the Naval Academy."

"The navy?" He didn't look to me like the seafaring type.

"I didn't pass the exams. I did very badly. Just as I had in school."

"You did?" Mr. Marconi's shoes were shiny, a thing that made no sense in St. John's. *Eyetalian* leather, by Jayzus, I'd heard Mr. Walsh say to Mrs. Kelly over the counter in Mr. Walsh's shop.

"I stopped going," I admitted.

"Well, so did I. There was nothing interesting for me there. And you?"

"I—lots of kids got to work. And I never liked it much. When I made my letters, my teacher hit my knuckles with the ruler. And the girls laughed."

"Ah."

I heard the wind pick up outside, and the sound of something blown about hitting the wall outside.

"My mother, she helped me," Mr. Marconi went on. "She gave me a room in the attic, and we kept it a secret from my father. That was how I was able to continue my experiments. Sometimes, I think secrets are necessary."

I thought about that a minute. "Where are the other fellas?" I asked.

"My engineers? In the pub, I expect. They're becoming a little impatient with me, I think. But it has to be just right. We cannot fail."

I must have looked confused. I never knew what it was he was doing, not really.

"We will receive a signal sent all the way from England, William. Do you know where that is?"

"'Course."

"Yes, of course you do." He stood up. "Do you see this?" He pointed to a small glass tube filled with what looked like metal dust. "When the electrical current comes through, the particles cling together, and the current flows through, here—" there were two pieces a little smaller than a tin can, wrapped in copper wire "—and here is the coherer, and here is the Morse receiver. When we pick up the signal from Poldhu, it will have travelled all the way across the ocean. There are those who think that the signal won't carry because of the curve of the Earth, but it will. The signal will be three taps, and they will come here," he pointed to the receiver. "Communication across the entire Atlantic Ocean."

I thought of my mum and dad, inches apart and yelling up a storm.

"Communication is the future," Mr. Marconi said. He closed up his book of lines and squiggles and pressed his fingers to his eyes like he was tired. "I must be getting to my rooming house. If only I could sleep here—"

I felt the lonely tower around us, Deadman's Pond not so far away, and shivered. There was the cot with its grey blanket, and I could see he'd slept there more than once already. You'd not get me to stay in such a place as this.

"If I gave you a few more coins," he continued, "I wonder if you know of anyone who might send up some dinner each

ows of St. John's. The mittens were stiff with the salt, the thumb and forefinger standing up solid beside the pocket for the last three fingers, and I slapped the mitts against my legs to soften them up as I walked up the hill with the dinnerpail.

The three were at it with the kite again when I came up, and they were arguing over something, so with that and the wind they didn't hear me. I ducked into the room and put the pail in the corner by the stove and then went back out for wood since the fire was near cold, and as I did I saw a figure come 'round the corner. His head was down and one hand on his hat with his thin coat hugged around him, and he was so surely from away that I wanted to laugh. He didn't see me with his head down under his hat and me behind. He was shouting to the men against the howl of the wind.

"I'm from the *Herald*!" he yelled as he climbed the hillock to where they was standing. "New York!"

They all came in, their faces red from the wind, because you couldn't be heard against the weather out there, wild it was. I came in after and stoked up the stove some, taking my time, stalling. New York was exotic, more than England, even, where the signal was supposed to come from, or Italy, which was where Mr. Marconi was from. New York was the real world.

"I understand you are setting up to communicate with a Cunard Liner," the reporter said. He dropped his pen, fingers numb I guess, and picked it up again.

Mr. Marconi cocked his head.

"The Cunard Line. If you're successful, this will be a great boon to the shipping industry, especially passenger liners, won't it?" He tapped his pen on his notebook. "And for the sealers, too, I suppose." He glanced at me, taking me for the Newfoundlander I was, sure enough. I thought of the sealer last winter got stuck between icebergs, stayed there for days until finally the two icebergs moved, snapping the boat like kindling. Nobody to hear, way out there.

It seemed a good thing if 'twere true, but Mr. Marconi crossed his arms and said: "At present, our intentions are not public."

The reporter waited there, and we all waited with him, and nobody offered him tea. When he had gone, "Spies," muttered Mr. Marconi. "William, please bring in some more wood."

Mr. Marconi sent me home early that day; I trudged down the hill in the half dark, trying not to look t'wards the pond, the sun hardly up at all with the days so short. "Thank your mother for the scarf and the mittens," Mr. Marconi said as I left. "And tomorrow, see if you can bring a little something for my tea." I knew what he meant, but I couldn't ask, liquor being a delicate subject in my house. "I won't be leaving this hill until we've reached our goal," he said, nodding towards the cot in the corner. It would be a cold night here, I thought.

As I came down the lane with the empty pail banging against my leg, I heard my mum's voice in the yard. She was bringing in the laundry from the line, piling the longjohns and shirts stiff as cardboard, to let them soften and sag by the fire. In better days we would all watch as the longjohns collapsed like old men, comical.

I heard another voice and knew it to be Mrs. Kelly next door, herself doing the same no doubt, and as I approached on the other side of the fence I could see through the gap their two kerchiefed heads, but they didn't see me.

"Such a thing it was, there in the window of Miller and Sons," Mrs. Kelly was saying. "Never seen the like. Wouldn't any of us like a new dress half as nice?"

28

"We would. Any of us would deserve it too, for all the work that we do. You knows yourself." My mum snapped one of her old housedresses flat, then folded it and bent to put it in the basket. She straightened up, and I knew without seeing all of her that she'd put her hands on her hips the way she does. "It's the lavender I've got my eye on."

I saw Mrs. Kelly lean forward, the two not a cow's length away from where I stood. "It's the blue I wants. I've got enough saved," she said, "from the butter and cheese."

"He lets you keep it?"

"Aye, he does. Made it clear from the front of things. A girl needs her pin money. My Sid, he does want to keep me happy," and she winked. "What about you? All the extras you do— I'm sorry, Maggie. I wasn't thinking. How's he getting on?"

I heard my mum's sigh. "He's getting on fine, Lil. Be right as rain in two shakes."

When I came in, I was relieved to see Dad sitting at the table, a mug of strong tea at his side. He looked at me, his face grey. His hand shook as it reached for the cup. My mum came in and took the pail from me.

"What's the pail for, b'y?" my dad asked me, but Mum gave me a look and shook her head.

"I, uh—"

"Maggie?" he said. "What's Willie got my dinnerpail for?"

"William," she said, not looking at my dad, "tell your father that you're working for Mr. Marconi, because sure enough somebody in the family needs to earn a living. If my poor dead mother could see—"

"Oh, enough about your mother, woman!"

"—where we've got to, after she suffered so, comin over on the boat when she was just a wee thing, and the hunger and the hardship growin up, and then worked so hard to raise us decent—"

"Here she goes. William, better get that dinnerpail to catch the tears, she'll be weepin 'til we all drown, sure enough."

"William, tell your father it's a crying shame when it's the son needs to feed the father. Tell your father," she said, slamming the pail on the counter, "tell your father—"

But Dad was out the door, cane banging on the step, the blast of cold air that followed him almost as cold as Mum's face as she stood with the pail in her hand and the laundry basket on her hip.

"Maybe he'd stay off the bottle if you'd quit yellin," I said into the thickness of it, surprised I had the courage to speak at all.

"Don't you talk back to me," my mother hissed, and she walked into the bedroom and slammed the door.

I sat at the table in the silent house, with the wind howling all around. I drank my father's tea and the memory came to me of when the mummers came, and the fiddles and the spoons, and my mum and dad danced. Outside, the night grew black as coal.

I WOKE BEFORE dawn, the fire out, my breath fogging the air. I got a blaze going and sat by the fire, warming myself, waiting. My father had come back in the night, now a roll of blankets on a nest of oilskins in the room where the fishing gear mouldered. It was just close enough to the stove, there, for warmth, and not so cold as the back shed, but it was clear he wasn't braving the bedroom, where I could see through the crack in the door my mum curled tight against herself.

The sun was coming up. I'd have to find Mr. Marconi some dinner on my own, then. I started by looking for a bottle, something to put in Mr. Marconi's tea. The search warmed

me some, and I ate a piece of bread as I did it, with some drippings, cold, but good for the weight of it in my stomach. It was
behind the outhouse that I saw the overturned bait box, the
broken one, and knew before I even looked beneath it, 'though
I was half surprised to find it still there. Perhaps my father
thought he'd already drunk it. There was the bottle, quarter
full, even, and I tucked it under my coat. Then I put together
some more bread and drippings and slathered the pieces
with bakeapple jam, pressing the two together. Mum had
made a jigs dinner two nights before. I found it in the cold
porch, fat congealed on the top. I put some in a jar to warm
up on the stove in the room up on the hill. Mum couldn't have
done better, I thought, and I felt proud, later, when I put the
pail by the stove, and 'specially proud when I pulled the
bottle from my coat and poured some in Mr. Marconi's tea
before he could see the grime on the bottle from where it had
lain under the bait box in back of the outhouse.

"Tomorrow," Mr. Marconi said, wrapping his mittened
hands around the cup. I wondered where the other fellas were,
and Mr. Marconi must've read my mind for he said: "I gave
them the day to rest up. It will be a long day tomorrow. We
will raise the kite—" he nodded through the wall as if we
could see it where it lay under a tarpaulin "—with an aerial
attached, and with this we will pick up the signal across the
Atlantic. Three dots. Do you know about Morse code, Willie?"

I shook my head. He drew on a piece of paper, a dot and a
line, and beside it he drew the letter A. I recognized it, having
been to class enough for that, at least. He wrote out all the
codes and their letters, explaining as he did, and then he put
down a whole lot of dashes and dots.

"What does it say?" he asked. He sipped at his tea, sighing
at the warmth of the whisky. "Wait," he said, while I stared at

31

the marks on the paper. He found a jar and poured me a cup from the pot, then picked up the bottle. "Here," he said. "To warm you."

I'd never tasted whisky. It slid down my throat and made a little fire in my stomach. I could see why my dad might like such a thing, and I set the cup down, wary, then picked it up again and sipped. It wasn't the taste, it was the warmth that held the goodness. A protection against the cold, and I thought of the icy cold in our house these past days. Which came first, I wondered, the cold or the drink? Mr. Marconi interrupted my thoughts.

"What does it say?" he asked again.

I shook my head. They made no sense.

"Look," he pointed to the first combination, a dot and two dashes. Then he pointed to the letter *W*. "Match them up."

I found the letter for each set, but I didn't recognize them all, and I didn't want to say. I could tell the *W*, because I knew it was the first letter of my name. I'd learned that in school. And I could tell the *A*, because it was the first letter of the alphabet, and the very first one we learned in class. But the others were a mystery. Even after I had pointed to the matching letter, and Mr. Marconi had written the letter under it, I couldn't tell what it said. He looked at me, waiting. I felt the shame of not knowing how to read, hot and prickly under my skin. Suddenly, it seemed important to keep it secret. And all at once, I knew.

"William," I said. "It spells William."

Mr. Marconi clapped his mittened hands, a dull thud. "Now, listen!" he said, and he tapped out my name with a clicker attached to his tabletop concoction of wires and tubes. "Tap, tap-tap," it went. "William, William," he said. "Now Guglielmo— my name. Do you know, it is William in English? But Daisy,

32

she called me Guli. That's shorter, easier to tap out." He did this, and we listened to the taps while his lips mouthed the letters.

"Who's Daisy?" I asked.

"My Irish cousin," he said. "My mother, she is Irish."

Most of St. John's was Irish, come during the great famine. My own grandmother came from Ireland. And it came to me that Mr. Marconi wasn't such a foreigner after all.

"My cousin Daisy believed in me even when my father did not. She was my friend. You have a friend, William?"

I shook my head. "Not really."

"I will be your friend," Mr. Marconi said. I looked over at the bottle, which was almost empty. "Everyone needs a friend," he said.

I WAS LATE leaving that night, but not because there was much for me to do. "Keep me company," Mr. Marconi had said, so I sat with him while he wrote in his book. I was almost at the foot of the hill, my head full of letters and symbols, when a figure approached out of the dark. In his hand was a New-foundland note, more money than I could make in a week from Mr. Marconi, and I stared at it.

"Boy, I understand you are working for Marconi," the man said. He had a muffler wrapped 'round under his nose, like everybody did in this weather, but it made his voice muffled and scary. His hat was pulled low, and anyways, it was dark. He was like the mummers, impossible to recognize, but there was no fun in this. I thought from his voice that he might have been the reporter fellow, but I couldn't say for sure.

"I'll pay you well," he was saying.

It was hard to tear my eyes from the note in his hand. "What do you want?"

"He's not communicating with ships, is he?"

"I don't know what he's doing," I said. "Honest."

"You work there every day. You must see what he writes in his logbook—." He leaned forward and pressed the note into my hand. "If you can get me proof that he's attempting to receive a wireless signal from England," he said, "there's a lot more of this for you."

I clutched the note. "How?" I asked.

"Read the logbook," he said. "Copy down the words. And the date. I'll meet you here tomorrow at this time."

I didn't have time to tell him that I couldn't read the words in Mr. Marconi's logbook.

WHEN I CAME home my dad was there, sitting in his chair by the stove, shuffling cards. He looked worse than before. "Heard those for'ners been playin cards back of Sam's," he said into the thick air. "And losin."

I looked at my mother, who was cutting potatoes like she was chopping the heads off chickens.

"Tell your father," she said to me, "he stays sober for a week, maybe he'll be able to stand straight enough to make an honest livin for five minutes."

"Tell your mother I'm tryin."

"Tell your father there's no money to be losin at the cards."

"Mr. Marconi? Bettin at Sam's?" I couldn't fathom it.

"No, t'other two," said my dad. "I'm goin tonight."

I knew he was out of liquor from the edge in his voice. When I come in the yard I'd seen the bait box overturned, the scuffs in the earth where he'd paced and searched.

My mother turned and waved the knife in the air. "With what money, then?" she demanded. "With what money are you going to play cards and lose, or play cards and drink your winnins? Same to us either ways."

"Never you mind, missus," my father said, with a mean smile because she'd spoken directly to him for the first time in two days.

"Tell your father—" she began, but Dad was in his boots and out the door again before she could finish.

THAT NIGHT I tossed on my cot by the stove, the stranger's banknote under the mattress, burning there. I kept thinking about Mr. Marconi, who had called me his friend. In the morning, the spot by the door where my dad's boots usually stood was empty.

I was crumpling up the newspaper Mr. Walsh had wrapped the bones in, stuffing it in the stove with the kindling, trying to get a good blaze going to take the chill off the kitchen. One piece of newspaper in the box had been smoothed out, and I recognized the letters, same as the sign at Miller and Sons, and I remembered my mother's conversation with Mrs. Kelly. The drawing showed three ladies posing in dresses that had a bit of lace at the top, the ladies wearing fancy hats, and if I didn't pay much attention to the things my mum wore, I knew she didn't wear such as this. My mum herself came into the kitchen, then, and I shoved the paper in my pants pocket, though why I didn't stuff it in the fire with the rest of the paper I couldn't say.

Mum looked at the space where my father's boots usually sat. "Hmmph," she said. "You'll be leavin soon, won't you? I'll get Mr. Marconi's dinner together for you, then."

Before I left with the dinnerpail, Mum asked me for the money I'd made working for Mr. Marconi, as well as the dinner money he'd sent home with me the day before. I gave it to her, feeling just a little guilty for the penny I held back. I minded what Mrs. Kelly had said about pin money, and I had a mind for something for myself, for all my work, sweet and warm from the bakery on Water Street. I was almost to the end of our own street when I heard her cry out.

I ran back through the clouds of my own breath, the dinnerpail banging against my knees. When I opened the back door into the kitchen there was my mother, standing at the doorway to the pantry, the empty English marmalade jar in her hands.

I WAS LATE getting to the room on the hill that morning. Mr. Kemp gave me a look, but they were too busy wrestling the kite against what looked to be the start of a good winter blow. The men shouted at one another against the blast of it.

"This is insane," Mr. Kemp was saying. "We need to postpone—"

"No, the order has been sent," Mr. Marconi caught sight of me. "William, stoke up the fire. We'll need to get warm."

I went around back for more wood, and as I bent down I felt a hand on my shoulder. It was the man who had given me the note, still tucked in my pocket, a secret.

"What do you have for me?" His face was right up against mine, with the muffler around, but I could see in the light of day it was the fellow from before, the one from the newspaper in New York. "Did you read his notes? Did you write them down?"

"I—"

"William?" It was Mr. Paget's voice, calling for me.

"I'll be waiting," the man said. "Write down everything you can. There's another note for you if you do." He ducked around the side of the building just as Mr. Paget rounded the other corner.

"The fire can wait," Mr. Paget said. He looked angry, and shook his head. "We'll need all hands if we're going to get this thing aloft."

We didn't. After several tries, we came in and I got the fire stoked and we warmed ourselves, the men talking, me keeping quiet, listening. The memory of the man who had given me the banknote was weighing on me so, I felt as if he were looking over my shoulder.

"How is this any different than the balloon?" Mr. Kemp asked. "We can't afford to keep losing equipment into the sea. It's ridiculous, trying to do this on this Godforsaken hill."

"Never mind that Anglo-American would shut us down. If only they knew," Mr. Paget mumbled.

My ears perked up. I had heard of the Anglo-American Telegraph Company, listening to the conversations at Mr. Walsh's shop. "A stranglehold on Newfoundland, thanks to the wisdom of a foolish few," I had heard him say to Mr. Kelly. "A fifty-year monopoly! For a cable, so some rich bugger can talk to some other rich bugger in Boston, by Jayzus. They've sold us short, sure enough. Who's getting rich, now?"

All at once, I knew who the man was who gave me the banknote, and who'd promised me more. The note felt heavy in my pocket.

"Well, they won't know," Mr. Marconi said now, his voice quiet. "And in a few hours, it won't matter."

IT WAS A morning of shouts and curses, of freezing in the icy salt wind, of thawing fingers by the fire in order to mend a broken strut, of shouts and stony silences. Just before dinnertime the kite was aloft, and stayed that way for several minutes. Mr. Marconi put a cup, attached to his contraption by a wire, to his ear and listened. None of us breathed. "It's the atmospherics," he said. "It's hard—"

It seemed like we waited a long time with nothing but the wind and our own breathing. When it came, I didn't hear it at first, and then it came again: three sharp clicks as the tapper struck the coherer, and then Mr. Marconi smiled the first real smile I'd seen on him. He handed the cup to Mr. Kemp, then. "Yes!" he said. "There it is."

That first moment was exciting, sure enough, but I began to feel fidgety in the time that followed. Nothing happened at all. Nobody breathed. But just when I was sure nothing more *would* happen, there were clicks, and everyone would sit upright again and lean forward, listening. I must have looked towards the dinnerpail more than once, because at one point Mr. Marconi waved at it and said: "Eat, William." The others seemed to have forgotten about food altogether. Finally, Mr. Marconi put down the earphone.

"Write this down, Mr. Paget," he instructed. "Signals at 12:30, 1:10, and 2:20."

When he sent me home, late in the afternoon, he tucked some paper into my hand, closing my fingers around it and holding them there. "It's been a great day, William," he said. "Thank you for your help."

THE WINTER DARK had already settled when I stepped outside, although it was still early; I'd have to wait until I reached the lamplight at the foot of the hill to see what Mr. Marconi had put in my hand, but the papers I clutched had the feel of the banknote the stranger had given me, so I knew it to be money. I was just passing the pond, and thinking about the ghosts that lie there as I always did, when a figure stepped into my path near scaring the very soul from my body.

"What do you have for me, Boy?" he said.

I opened my mouth, but nothing came out. In my mind I heard Mr. Marconi's words, telling Mr. Paget what to write down. *Signals at 12:30, 1:10, and 2:20.*

"What have you found out?" the man demanded again.

"I—" There was the money, and scarce enough it was in our house most times.

"Did you write it down?"

There was Mr. Marconi, who said he was my friend. There was my father, who'd as soon drink it as put food on the table.

The words came out of their own accord. "I can't read or write, sir."

There was a noise, angry or disgusted or both. I didn't wait to see what the stranger might say or do. I dropped the dinnerpail with a clatter and ran.

I ran down into the streets of St. John's, past our house and kept running, until my sides wheezed with the pain, and then I walked. I found myself coming up Duckworth Street, clear where I was from the presence of the stumbling, drunken men whose tabs had been cut off at the bar, or who'd lost at cards. And there I found my father, sitting on the wall below the churchyard, the stones of the dead looking down. He had managed to keep his cane, which he waved at me.

"Son. It's you," he said. "Don't s'pose you have a penny or two for your old man?"

I shook my head, the paper money still crushed in my palm. I held my hand close by my side.

"S'pose that's not a bad thing," he said, his voice terrible sad. "I am a sorry bugger." He looked at me and shook his head. "Lost it all."

I nodded, still standing there, not knowing what to say.

"Not speaking to me neither, are you? S'pose I deserve it, too."

"Dad, I—"

"You got a right to be ashamed, Willie."

"You maybe better go home," I said. "You maybe better."

I left him there, and thought I'd go down to Water Street, my stomach rumbling with the thought of a warm bun or tart from the bakery, which would surely be closing soon enough. The excitement of the day, the fear when I met the stranger, and then my father had all left me sad and tired, and sure home was not where I wanted to be just then. Truth be told, I didn't know what I wanted.

I stopped under a streetlight on the corner and looked at the notes in my hand. I turned them over, one by one. I was not so good with letters, but not so bad with the counting, and I knew this to be more money than the stranger had given me, more than I had ever had. When I looked up I saw I was right under the sign for Miller and Sons.

I FOUND DAD where I had left him, a half-block back sitting on the wall. I took the piece of newspaper I'd been carrying folded in my pocket and I smoothed it against my leg and held it out.

"What's this?"

"Mum wants it," I said.

Dad took it and looked at it, then dropped his hand, the paper resting on his knee. He sounded weary. "So what if she does, b'y?"

I set the notes on top of the drawing of the smart dress. "She's been dreamin of it. She likes the one what's lavender."

Dad's eyes grew wide as he took in the money in front of him.

"If you go back in—" I nodded towards the pub. Two men came out, laughing and stumbling, then moved off into the darkness. I shook my head. I didn't know how to say what would happen if he took the money and went back inside there. "Miller's is open a half-hour still," I said, and walked away, leaving him there.

I WAITED BY the back fence in the dark. I waited so long I thought I'd perish, my feet like blocks of ice, they were, and 'til I'd near given up altogether.

I heard him before I saw him, the click of the cane and the thump of the bad leg, but it was a steady sound, one foot in front of the other; cane, foot, foot, cane. I waited 'til he was caught in the lamplight. I could see the bundle under his arm.

I took myself back up the hill towards the tower. The night sky clear for the first time in days, the moon full, lighting the path before me and shining on the black water of Deadman's Pond, and I knew the ghosts were asleep for now. I thought I'd bide awhile there, in the room on the hill. Maybe Mr. Marconi would let me sit by the stove while he wrote in his book about the signals we'd heard coming from all that way. And when he finished I thought he might show me the marks and letters again, and maybe let me tap out a message of my own, just to say I was here.

William. W-i-l-l-i-a-m. .-- .. .-.._ _

THREE

HOME GIRL

·1913·

Olive

FROM WHERE I sit in my wheeled chair I can see, through my
bedroom window, the barn, and the manure pile out back. I
can also see the creeping clematis vines below my window,
which by midsummer will be festooned with purple flowers
like open hearts. And I can see the steaming brown flanks
of Bella, the cow, when my son-in-law Albert brings her out
after milking. When Ruth goes out to hang the washing, I
can see from where I sit the sight of my bloomers going up,
peg by peg, but not quite hear the exasperated sigh of my
daughter as she hangs them.

I didn't want to come here. I had my house in town,
which, after my second husband died, I kept and let rooms
to young women of good background who came to study at
my old friend Adelaide's school. Addie and I agreed on many
things: that young women should be taught the art of running a household, and given skills that will see them through
life, and that these skills were too often not taught in the

home as they used to be. But we didn't agree on suffrage—
Addie believed women are better able to influence the course
of things through their husbands and sons—and I suppose
that's where our falling-out occurred. To this day it seems to
me that the pain in my bones began the morning after our
final argument, in which I told her I thought women were
better served by having our own voice, and the power to
determine our own destiny.

Now that doesn't matter, because Addie is dead these
three years past, and my own destiny has become quite clear,
with any power I might have had over its course long removed.
For I am a bent old thing, folded up upon myself and completely under the power of my daughter Ruth and son-in-law
Albert. They see me the way they might see a stall that needs
to be mucked out—again—but they don't hear me, as if my
brain and my voice were as diminished as my body. Ruth
shouts when she speaks to me, although I am not deaf. Albert
doesn't speak to me at all. Instead, he looks at me from time
to time as if thinking: "What? She's still here?"

Over time I've watched as my daughter has become slowly
eroded, diminished such that she now sees each day unfold
in a series of chores and hardships. It was Ruth who wanted
a Home Child, someone to help with me, as she told Albert.
It was the first time in years I'd heard her state a firm desire
about anything, although I have sometimes seen her gazing
out the kitchen window across the roll of the landscape with
a longing that fills the room.

Winnie

THE PASSAGE WAS dreadful, with the heaving back and forth of
the boat and the smell of sickness. We were told we were
coming to the fresh air of Canada, which sounded a sight

better than the awful smell of the boat, and more hopeful than the close quarters of the Home. We were to be helpful to the kind families who had agreed to take us in, whose generosity was saving us from a life in the slums.

I'd been at the Home in London almost three years when they told me I was going to Canada. Canada! I told them I didn't know what I'd do in a place like that. I told them I wanted to see my mum first, and Miss Bexley told me she had died, and so there was no one for me anymore. She told me as if it were nothing to get excited about. It wasn't until I was in bed that night I cried, and then Emmie, in the cot next to mine, came over and spooned herself around me, although you could scarcely fit one in those beds let alone two. You'll remember me in Canada, won't you? Emmie whispered, and I promised.

One nurse was dreadfully sick on the passage, and so I ended up looking after a four-year-old boy called Martin who reminded me of my brother George. And the thought of George made me weep, and Martin cried, and so there we both were, the waif and the wee one, a puddle of tears in a tangle of blankets in steerage. I grew close to Martin in those days on board the ship; it was hard to say goodbye when we'd finally docked. He clung to me, and I had to push him away. He was going to a nice farm on the prairie, the nurse said, but he looked so frightened. It turned me right inside out, it did.

From there, several of us boarded a train, and by then I was so tired I scarcely remembered a thing. The station where we got off was grand, though, with its turrets and arches, and it reminded me of London, and that made me homesick. The sign said Hamilton, and the man who met me told me he was Mr. Brust, and that I'd be coming with him. I felt all turned around and lost, but "My name is Winnifred Blair," I said as confidently as I could, the way I'd been taught.

"Come on, then." He was already walking towards a farm wagon with a big white workhorse hitched on. I picked up my case and followed, and the metal corners banged against my legs. I was afraid I'd tear my stockings along with everything else. I studied the back of his head as I scrambled to keep up: he had thinning hair on a large head, making him look like a toadstool, especially with his short bowed legs.

The horse swung his big head around as we came up. I wanted to go up and pat its nose, but Mr. Brust nodded his head towards my case and then the back of the wagon, and so I pushed it up and over the side. It was autumn, and in the back of the wagon was a basket of apples.

"You can have one, I guess," he said. "The market wouldn't take them. Ruth'll have to make more apple sauce."

The taste was sweet and the flesh was juicy, and I felt better at once. I thought: this must be the taste of Canada.

Olive

I was at my window when Albert's wagon rounded the bend in the drive. At first I squinted to get a clearer view of the girl he had brought home, and saw it was a girl of thirteen or fourteen on the seat beside him. As he drew up I could see she was a skinny thing with lank brown hair, but pretty in the face, with large eyes. As she stepped down— no help from Albert—she looked straight at me through the window. Ruth came out to meet them, her hands wringing a towel.

"You're older than I thought you'd be," I heard Ruth say. "I hope you'll be a good girl, and be a help with Mother," and then all three faces turned to my window.

45

Winnie

THE OLD WOMAN is a crippled wee thing. When I first saw her I thought she was weak in the mind, but she's no such thing. In the morning when I get her up she opens her eyes and gives me a funny, crooked smile and calls me dear. I must dress her, help her eat, and help her to the commode.

That is after I've fed the chickens. When Mr. Brust explains things it's as if he thinks I'm daft not to know already, but we never had such things in London, or at the Home. I'm to milk the cow, when Mr. Brust teaches me how, and then I will rise even earlier. No one has said a word about school, although that's what I was told to expect. From the chicken house I can see the road, and in the morning children walk to school along that road. It's getting colder; I can see my breath when I stand there, watching, with the chickens all around.

My room is off the kitchen. It was a storage room before. There is just a small, high window. The cot is better than what we slept on in steerage, but not as good as the ones at the Home. Mr. Brust found a mirror for me in the barn, with just a small crack in the corner, and it sits on a dresser that has three drawers. I have my own brush and comb, and I've put them on top of the dresser, which I don't have to share with anyone.

Yesterday, I picked up some bright leaves from under a huge, spreading tree—they are brilliant red, and unlike anything at home—and I put them in a jar from the kitchen. Mrs. Brust smiled when she gave me the jar.

"They're maple leaves," she told me.

"Yes, ma'am," I said. "I never seen anything quite so red."

"I used to pick them all the time," she said.

"Don't you anymore?" I asked, then shut my lips together because we were told not to talk too much or make ourselves a nuisance.

You could have knocked me over with a feather when she looked at me like she was thinking hard and said: "Would you like to call me Auntie Ruth?" I'd been at the Brusts' almost a fortnight, calling her ma'am. But then a look came across her face, like the sun gone out. "But when Mr. Brust can hear, it would be better to call me Mrs. Brust," she said.

"What about—?" and I looked towards the old lady's room. Auntie Ruth—it'll be a job getting used to that—put her hand on her hip and looked at the door for so long, I thought she forgot the question. But: "Mrs. Calloway," she said at last. "You'll call her Mrs. Calloway."

At that moment Mr. Brust—or at least the sound of his boots—was heard at the door, and Auntie Ruth pulled her hand away from the leaf she was touching.

"I'll get the tea, and then you can wheel in Mu—Mrs. Calloway," she said. "Go get some butter from the cold cellar."

I don't much like Mr. Brust. When he's in the house, it's as if the house holds its breath, and when he's not there, it lets its breath out, the way you do when you drop a glass and then catch it before it hits the floor. He only speaks to me when he has to. "Those two brown hens is both broody," he'll say, not looking at me at all. "Make sure they got some water close by." But sometimes I'll catch him looking at me when I straighten up from some chore. He looks and he looks, and then he turns away.

Olive

WHEN THE GIRL, Winnie, comes into my room in the mornings, the shy smile she gives me reaches into me and pulls on something. It's as if I'm remembering some distant thing, but I can't quite bring it to the surface. She is strong for her age, and has that ruddy-cheeked complexion you see on English girls. I was curious about her past.

"Where were you living before you came here?" I asked her. She startled slightly. Perhaps she was surprised by the bluntness of my question. "I'm too old to beat around the bush," I told her. "I could die any moment."

"You wouldn't really?"

"I might, if you don't tell me something about yourself soon," I retorted, and she smiled with real humour. I could see her teeth weren't very good, but that didn't change the way her smile brightened the room.

"The Home. They taught us how to behave, and how to talk properly, not like a ragamuffin—that's what Miss Bexley called us. My best friend was Emmie," she paused. "Before that, East London," she said. I patted the bed and she sat down timidly. "I lived with my mum and two little sisters, Molly and Katie, and my brother George. We had a flat where you walked up three flights, and I would carry George, and Mum would carry Katie, and Molly would carry herself. We were waiting for my dad to get back, but he never."

"Never got back? From where?"

There was a long pause. "Don't know," she said at last. "But then Mum got a letter and she cried, and then I went to the Home."

"Just you?"

"I don't know what became of the others."

She sounded so wistful, so lonely, that I felt compelled to tell a story of my own, to share something in common.

"My first husband came from Britain," I told her.

"Really?"

48

"From Ireland, actually. A place called Waterford. Oh, he was a wonderful man. Tom. His name was Tom."

"What happened? Did he die?" Winnie asked, and then she put her hand over her mouth. "I'm sorry," she said.

"Sorry for what? I like people to be frank when they speak. And it's a reasonable question." I paused, and the image of Tom when I first met him came to me with such force and swiftness that I had to take a breath before I could continue. "He worked for my father as a gardener," I admitted. "We eloped."

Winnie was still sitting, fingers on her lips, as if she were afraid of what she might say.

"My father was a lawyer. Toronto. We were fairly well off. He would never have agreed to my marrying the gardener. Do you know—? I don't know if it was his good looks or the lovely way he spoke that did it. Or his gentle nature. He was such a kind man. But it really was love at first sight, just like they say. He'd come across on one of those coffin ships from Ireland with his family when he was about your age. His mother died on the way. I think it changed him—well, it would, wouldn't it? Oh! Now it's my turn to be sorry."

A tear had slipped down Winnie's face; no doubt she was thinking of her own mother. But, "please go on," she said. "It's nice here, with you."

I played with the coverlet with my old fingers, thinking of the hand they'd once held. "Well, it's not a happy ending. Tom caught fever and died when Ruth was just a baby. He was never well, really, after the hunger of the crossing."

I looked up. The look on Winnie's face could break your heart.

"But there—it was such a long time ago. And we had two lovely years together. I always wanted to find his brothers and sisters, but do you know, I never did. He struck out on his

49

own quite young, there was not much for them in St. John's, and it's such a very big county. He told me they had scattered across the country, like the leaves of that lovely maple in the yard." We both looked at the tree, crimson as blood. "Sometimes I think if Ruth had known her aunts and uncles and maybe even cousins, she'd have been a happier girl."

We were both quiet for a few moments, the air between us full of dust motes as the sun streamed in the window. And then she seemed to shake herself out of some place she was imagining and stood, all business. "Hadn't I better get you up?" she said. "Auntie Ruth will have your breakfast ready."

As Winnie pulled back the coverlet and helped me move my twisted legs, I reflected on that. "Auntie Ruth," I said.

"Is it all right?"

"Yes. Yes, it is. And you must call me Granny Olive."

"Even when Mr. Brust can hear?" she asked, and her question gave me pause. But then she was helping me into my chair, my bones protesting, and the ache of them took every thought from my head. By the time I was dressed and at the table I truly felt ready to go back to bed, thinking: I am not long for this world, and that's the simple truth.

There is no mention of the girl attending school. Of course, I am grateful for her help and company, and so I suppose I am selfish when I say nothing, not that it would make any difference. But I can see the loneliness in the girl. It's in the way she holds herself, as if she were feeling very small against a vast, unfriendly landscape. The way that, when I ask her about herself she behaves like a dog wanting friendship, but afraid of the boot.

So that morning at breakfast I thumped my cane on the floor for attention and then said, in my clearest voice: "It's too much to come to the table. I want to eat in my room. I want the girl to eat with me."

Albert looked up and saw me, something he rarely does. He was reading the farm news, ignoring all of us in his usual manner. Ruth, who had been gazing through the window over her half-finished plate, looked at me as if I'd landed from another country. I could see her mouth trying to formulate words while she looked at that son-in-law of mine, as if gauging which words would least offend.

My daughter. When Ruth wanted to marry Albert I had my doubts. I could see the Albert he'd become in the impatience in his voice if she was tardy getting ready, could see the future Ruth in the way she'd hurry, not to keep him waiting at the door. But I also told my girl a hundred times that her decisions were her own to make, and that I wouldn't interfere, no matter what. I wouldn't interfere the way my own parents had with me, not speaking to me—or their grandchild—until after Tom was cold in the ground. Although the truth is, it was my parents' influence in the end, along with the very real fear of life as a young widowed mother, that made me marry Richard. It took another death to make me find myself.

Regret is a terrible thing.

Now, I wonder if, in a way, Ruth married her own father— the one she remembers. Perhaps, left to ourselves and our human weaknesses, we just keep repeating the story we know best.

I summoned my strongest voice. "Besides," I said, "I will be nearer the commode."

"Are you sure, Mother," Ruth asked, her voice too loud as usual, her words spaced evenly as if she were talking to a small child.

Albert, who is mortally embarrassed by anything related to old ladies and normal bodily functions, flushed, and snapped the pages of the paper. "Suit yourself," he said, and that was that.

Winnie, standing in the doorway with a dishtowel in her hands, gave me a look I took to be grateful. Albert gave her a look that sent a small chill through me. Ruth began clearing up, eyes intent on her work. I looked back at Winnie, but she'd disappeared through the doorway.

Winnie

MR. BRUST TOLD me I had to learn to milk Bella. He tied her and put the stool under her and then he started washing Bella's udder with warm water, and he was rubbing and rubbing but when he looked up at me to make sure I was watching, he wasn't looking at my face, and I crossed my arms. Then he showed me how to pull on her teats, one from the front and one from the back, pushing up and then pulling down, and right away warm milk squirted, frothy, into the bucket.

"Now, you," he said, but when I tried nothing happened at first, and he pulled a box over beside my stool and leaned over and put his hands on top of mine to show me the way to do it. I could feel his breath at my ear, and I didn't want to look at him. Auntie Ruth called from the house, and he got up quickly, knocking over the box.

"You just keep doing that," he told me, and left in a hurry.

It took me a long time to milk that cow; Mr. Brust had told me to make sure each part was empty or Bella could get sick, and so I did my best. When I finished, my arms ached so I could barely lift them. Mr. Brust came in and took the milk, and I hurried out, because Granny Olive would be waiting for me, wondering why I had taken so long to get her up.

I got better after that at milking, but I never liked it, and I don't think Bella ever liked me. One morning she was quiet for a change—perhaps she'd gotten used to me—and I fell asleep against her warm flank; it was very early, and I'd had a bad night's sleep, unable to get warm in my bed with the weather turning colder. I would have to ask for another blanket, I remember thinking, and then there was Mr. Brust, shaking me awake.

"Wake up, girl. Cow won't get milked if you don't pull her teat," he said. He was standing above me, but he wasn't looking at my face or at the cow's udder. I hunched my shoulders around and got back to work without looking up, but before he moved away I could feel Mr. Brust's hand on my hair, as if he had some of it between his fingers for the feel of it. I kept working, and he went away. My hands shook as I pulled at Bella's udder, so that I pulled hard to steady them and she shifted her feet and whipped me with her tail.

I left the bucket for Mr. Brust to separate, hurrying to be gone before he came back. When I came into the kitchen, Auntie Ruth looked up from the stove. Mr. Brust wasn't at the table. "All finished the milking, then?" she said, and I looked down. "Was Albert working in the barn when you were there?"

I didn't answer. She sat down heavily in the chair while I stood, waiting. I knew I should be getting Granny Olive's tray ready. Auntie Ruth seemed nervous. "Are you happy here, Winnie?" she asked.

"Yes, ma'am," I told her, suddenly afraid. They told us at the Home we could be sent back. I missed my mum, but she was dead, and there was nothing but the Home for me there, and all that ocean to cross. Then Mr. Brust came in, and Auntie Ruth got up quickly and started putting his breakfast on a plate: eggs, sausages, biscuits, and jam.

"Winnie, you'd better go get Mrs. Calloway up," she said over her shoulder. I didn't look at Mr. Brust. I put together the tray for Granny Olive with a bowl of porridge for me, working alongside Auntie Ruth, who slipped a fresh biscuit onto the tray with the tea and porridge. Granny has trouble chewing, so I knew the biscuit was for me. She'd put a dollop of jam inside.

Granny Olive was awake when I came in, with her hands folded on the top of her blankets. "Do you want to sit in your chair?" I asked, but she shook her head.

"Breakfast will be cold by the time I get myself out of here and into there," she said, but she sounded chipper. "Breakfast in bed! How sinful! Here," she patted the bed, "sit beside me."

I helped her eat, leaving the biscuit until she waved at it and said, "Go on."

It was nice there with Granny Olive. The morning light slanted through the window, making squares on the floor. I stayed as long as I could that morning, hoping she would tell me more about herself, or about Auntie Ruth when she was a girl, but she never. Still, I didn't want to leave that room, and after a bit she asked me about myself, and what I hoped to be when I grew up, and I told her I'd like to find a nice man to marry, like she did. And Granny Olive didn't say anything to that but told me about how things were changing for women, and that someday women could become anything they wanted to be.

"You could be a doctor," she said.

I had never heard of a woman being a doctor. Women were nurses, and I told her so. She shook her head. "Wait and see," she said. "The world is changing."

I spent the day with housework, helping Auntie Ruth with the laundry. I didn't like wringing out Mr. Brust's long underwear, but Auntie Ruth wrung and shook things out and snapped them out onto the line and I just had to keep up with her. Then we made bread, and she was impatient with me when it was time to knead the dough because my arms were tired from the milking.

"Haven't you done this before?" she asked me.

"No, ma'am—I mean, Auntie Ruth. I learned about cleaning. I was to learn cooking, but then I was sent over. I'd have learned before, but I was sick."

"Sick?"

"The Chicken Pox. All of us in our dormitory got them. They were terrible itchy, and we had to stay in bed. And so I missed my lessons."

"Here," she said, showing me how to fold and push the bread dough. "There. You're doing better, now." She began to prepare the pans, and as she did she started talking in a chatty sort of way, not like usual. "I had Chicken Pox when I was a girl, too. I didn't mind so much, because my mother would sit on my bed and tell me stories. They were funny stories—about a big ginger cat. He would have all kinds of adventures, most of them involving playing tricks on a rich farmer." She was standing with her hands folded on the counter, not doing anything, just looking out the kitchen window. "I loved those stories," she said.

"I always wanted a cat." It was all I could think of to say. I felt like my arms would fall off if I pushed that dough one more time.

"Here. We'll let this rise again," she said, then: "Maybe in the spring we could get a cat. We'll tell Albert we need one to kill mice." She smiled at me.

Through the kitchen window we could see Mr. Brust raking hay in the field, with Snow, the big workhorse pulling the hay rake while Mr. Brust sat on the little seat. He'd hired a boy to stook it, and I could barely make him out, distant in the field.

Since Mr. Brust had hired the boy, Sam, he'd done nothing but mutter about the cost.

Auntie Ruth looked through the glass and then ran the back of her hand across her forehead, leaving a dusting of flour behind. At that moment she looked so much like my mum I thought I'd cry.

Olive

THE NOVEMBER WINDS smell like snow. It comes in through the cracks around windows, and down the chimney flu, and I feel less inclined to leave my bed and sit in my chair. Now that I'm taking meals in my room with Winnie, I see less of the house, and my view has become narrowed to what I can see from my window: Winnie, as she trudges out to the barn in the early mornings, the steam her breath creates, and the heat that escapes the barn when she pulls open the big door. Albert slipping in a few minutes behind her.

I imagine Ruth looking out through the kitchen window after him, relieved to have the house to herself (because I don't really count, after all), anxious for Winnie to hurry up and return so she can keep an eye on her. But it's not just that. I've heard their conversations, Winnie and Ruth, through these walls, and I can hear in Ruth's tone the tentative steps towards something approaching friendship with this girl. I can hear in her words her longing for her own lost child, born too early such a long time ago, now.

When did our own closeness become so far away? There was a moment when I first came here, the very first day. A moment between us as we sat together at the kitchen table.

"Mother," she said, "I—"

A confession? A warning? An admission of regret? A wish for us to be mother and daughter again, the way we once were?

"Mum, I—" she said, then: "Albert—"

Whatever it was she wanted to say, I'll never know. Albert came in, then, and the temperature dropped noticeably, and then she was up and getting him his tea and he was looking at me and saying: "So you're here, now, Mother, are you?" and all I could do was nod. Because even then it was clear where things were going. Within six months I had moved from cane to chair. Now, when Winnie helps me up, every cell of my old body wants to stay put.

At first, I used to dream I would get better. That one day I would pull the slim folder from beneath the mattress I lie on and take out the notes I have stored there, saved from the sale of my rooming house. I gave most to Albert, of course, to keep me, but not all. I kept enough to escape.

Now, here comes Winnie across the yard, her head down as she walks, shoulders hunched, her pretty eyes downcast. In a moment she will be in with my breakfast, and she will sit on my bed while I try to warm her with my words, wishing that I could draw her to me and wrap my arms around her the way I had with my Ruth, when she was small, the future large with possibility.

Winnie

I S'POSE I always knew. I s'pose I knew but I thought that surely Auntie Ruth would say something. I'd look at her, sometimes, and I'd open my mouth, the words almost there, and then she'd catch my eye and see the words there and turn away.

It was this morning, I was coming into the barn, and I could hear Bella shuffling from hoof to hoof the way she does when her udder is full. I'd overslept, and I knew that if Mr. Brust saw me starting the milk so late he'd have something to say. I had a wrap around my shoulders and I was in a hurry and it slipped and fell as I pulled the barn door closed.

When Mr. Brust appeared from the shadows my heart near jumped right out of my chest. I hadn't expected him there. He picked up my wrap and put it around my shoulders, but kept his hands there too long. I held my breath. Even Bella hardly moved, there was just Mr. Brust and me, his face so close I could see the pores in his nose, all red from the cold air, and smell his sour breath.

A bang against the barn door, and Auntie Ruth burst through in a fury, almost crashing into the two of us as Mr. Brust let go. Her eyes met his, and then she turned on me, angry.

"Winnie! Mrs. Calloway has fallen trying to get out of bed. Why didn't you check on her before you came out? What were you thinking, girl?" And she slapped me—hard—across the cheek.

The tears sprang up and Mr. Brust slipped out the side door of the barn. "I thought—" Of course, I'd thought if I was very fast with the chickens and Bella, I could get back before Granny Olive woke up, because already I was so late. But Auntie Ruth pushed me out the door, back towards the house, and all I could do was go.

Later, Mr. Brust complained he'd had to milk Bella himself, but he didn't complain very hard, and he was quiet at tea. And Granny Olive was kind, too, even though I had not been there to help her to the commode, and she fell, and now she has terrible bruises. Her skin is like paper, and there's no meat on her bones. I must have told her a dozen times I was sorry until she told me I wasn't to say it again. She said there were bigger things to be sorry for.

Olive

AFTER THE MORNING's kerfuffle I went back to sleep for an hour, so exhausted was I, but when I awoke at noon, just before dinner, I insisted I eat at the table, even though I've been taking my meals in my room with Winnie for some time. I had something I needed to say. Albert had come in from the last of the raking, and Ruth was setting chicken and potatoes and green beans in front of him. Winnie was at the counter mashing turnip, and Ruth snapped at her to hurry up.

"I want Winnie to sleep with me, in my room," I said, loud enough to be heard. "I need her, in case I should fall again."

Winnie turned and looked at me. Ruth looked at Albert. Albert looked at his chicken, his fork gripped like an axe.

"No," he said.

"What?" I was not expecting such a blunt response.

"No," he said. "She's to stay put." He nodded toward Winnie's room behind the kitchen.

"But—" I am not usually at a loss for words.

"You're enough of a burden as it is," he said.

"Albert—!" But Ruth didn't have the words, either.

Albert banged his fork down with such force, the glassware jumped. There was a moment of thick silence, and then he resumed eating, stabbing at the meat on his plate. Ruth dropped the dishcloth she was holding and rushed from the room. I'd have thought she'd have rushed to me—I was the one insulted, after all—but she ran to their bedroom and closed the door, leaving Winnie and me in the kitchen with Albert.

"Winnie," I said. "I'm going back to my room. Please bring me my meal there." I looked at Albert, and thought better of it.

Winnie would have to gather together my tray. "Never mind," I said. "I'm not hungry after all. Please just push my chair."

When the sound of the kitchen door indicated Albert had left the house, I sent her back for some food, two plates on the tray. Ruth, shut in her room, could hardly object.

Winnie

AUNTIE RUTH STAYED in her room until supper, and when she came out she made a stew from the rest of the chicken and vegetables. She made hard chopping sounds with the knife, and I tried to make myself small as I did the things she told me to. Other than that, she didn't speak to me at all.

I ate with Granny Olive and got her settled into bed, and when I said goodnight she held my hand until I squirmed in spite of myself. She let me go.

"You take care, my dear," she said, finally. "I'll see you in the morning."

When I came out Auntie Ruth had already gone to bed, and Mr. Brust was sitting in the parlor, trying to get the radio to come through on the old set, and swearing at it. He looked up as I came out of Granny Olive's room, but I slipped into my own wee room and shut the door. I took the spindle chair from beside my bed and wedged the back under the doorknob. My room with its mirror and dresser all my own looked different, now. I thought about Emmie, and wished she were here to curl around me the way she had that night in the Home. Where was Emmie now? I got undressed and slipped under the covers, shivering. I couldn't seem to get warm.

Olive

AFTER WINNIE LEFT I lay awake and fretted for a long time. If things were different—but oh, there was no wishing for things to be different. Never in my life had I had·so little influence. Never had I felt so small, or so old.

The next day it was as if nothing had changed. Winnie came in, not late this time, and got me up and got me breakfast, the two of us eating our porridge, neither of us talking. Finally, I asked if she had slept well, searching her face, and she nodded, and from her expression I was reassured. A few times I thought to speak, but the words wouldn't come. Finally, "I better get to the chickens, then," she said, and began to set the tray to rights to take it back to the kitchen. I stopped her, my hand on her wrist. My papery, wrinkled skin against that freckled youthful flesh.

"You're a good girl, Winnie," I said. It was all I could think of to say.

Winnie

AFTER I GOT Granny Olive up I hurried to the barn. I didn't see Mr. Brust anywhere, which was fine with me. The chickens made their hungry clucking noises as I hurried past, but Bella would have to come first. I wanted to get her milked while Mr. Brust was out working.

I had just settled on my stool and was washing Bella's udder, feeling her flinch against the cool water and wishing I could warm it. As I finished, she turned her big head with its soft eyes, and I thought she was looking at me in a friendly way—it had taken some time, but we'd come to like each other, Bella and I—but she had heard a noise, and there was Mr. Brust, a horse blanket in his hand. At first I thought that maybe Snow, the workhorse, had taken ill, but he made no move towards the horse's stall.

I didn't look as I heard him set the blanket down.

I didn't look, but kept my attention on Bella's teat as I pulled, the warm milk squirting into the bucket.

I didn't look, but I could feel the heat of him behind me, smell him, felt his breath at my neck.

When his hand touched my breast I jumped up, knocking aside the milking stool. His body blocked the door to the stall as he grabbed me roughly, both hands where they shouldn't have been, hurting me. I could not seem to force a breath or make a noise, but I could see the vein that twitched under his eye. Bella lurched, alarmed, and kicked out at nothing, but it was enough for me to twist my way free and run.

Olive

I SAW THE girl running from the barn. I saw Winnie, her hair come loose, her face wet with tears and her dress in disarray running towards the kitchen door, and I cursed my legs and this chair. My voice, when I tried to cry out, was a small, weak animal in the room.

Winnie

AUNTIE RUTH WAS in the kitchen, when I pushed through the door. She had just turned from the stove with the big pot of water she'd boiled for the laundry tub on the floor. When she saw me, the pot fell, the scalding water flew, and Auntie Ruth's scream filled the room.

Olive

RUTH HAS BEEN taken to the hospital in Hamilton. Albert took her in the wagon, which is as fast as an ambulance coming from the city anyway, but I'm worried for the moans I could hear as Albert carried her to the bed he'd made up in the wagon, and I can imagine her discomfort over the twenty miles they must cover.

When Albert heard Ruth's scream and discovered what
had happened, he sent Sam running for Mrs. Plaskett on the
next farm, who came quickly to bathe the burns on Ruth's
legs and chest with cider vinegar, and wrap what she could
in strips of clean sheet. Winnie pushed my chair into the
living room to be near my daughter as she whimpered under
Mrs. Plaskett's ministrations, and I imagined my own hands
applying the cool, vinegar-soaked cloths to Ruth's damaged
skin, if only they could.

Now, Albert will be back in a few hours, maybe less, and as
I fret about my daughter I look over at Winnie, who sits in the
chair beside me, clearly troubled, both of us watching through
the window of my room for Albert's return. The girl sits, and
there are no words between us. An odd silence has settled
across the house, so that we can hear the clock where it ticks in
the next room. She has made tea, but it grows cold in our cups.

"Wheel me to the bed," I tell Winnie, my voice as gentle as
I can make it.

She looks up from her hands, where they twist in her lap.
"You want to go back to bed?" Her surprise is reasonable. It
is, after all, not yet noon.

Winnie

SHE PULLED A thin leather book from under the mattress, but
when she opened it I saw it wasn't a book at all but a folder,
with pockets inside its covers. I didn't know what to say when
she took out the banknotes. She began to divide them, then
changed her mind and pushed them all into my hands.

"Go," she said. I thought she'd gone daft, but her blue eyes
were clear. I pulled my eyes away and looked down at the
notes in my hand. So much money!

63

"It's not that much," she said, as if she read my thoughts. "It's enough to get you a train ticket to Guelph, to help you make a start. It's enough for tuition. There's a school there, begun by a dear friend of mine. Go to this address."

She was holding a piece of paper. "But—".

"Go before he comes back."

She said to go now, her voice firmer than I've ever heard it. She said to pack quickly, although there isn't much to pack. She told me she would be fine alone until Mr. Brust returned, and that he would arrange for Mrs. Plaskett to come in. When I told her I'd pay her back, she waved her hand in the air.

AND NOW I am at the doors of the Ontario Normal School of Domestic Science and Art. It says so on a brass sign beside the big wooden doors. The woman who opens them has a strong face, but her eyes are kind.

"Can I help you?" she asks. I pick up my suitcase and step inside.

· F O U R

ANGEL

·1929·

MURPHY CALDWELL LIGHTS another cigarette, his right hand manoeuvering match against box with a single-handed practice that might astonish the young woman passing the bench on which he sits, should she glance his way. She doesn't; most don't look at a one-armed man, but rather avert their gaze. He's a reminder, after all, of a war more than a decade past. If you didn't look too closely, it's almost as if it never happened.

He watches as the woman greets a friend, kissing both cheeks European-style. She's dressed in the new fashion among well-dressed Montrealers of the feminine persuasion: shorter skirts, bobbed hair, and that low waist. He waits for it, and then hears her speak, that deeper voice Francophone women seem to have. Sultry.

Helen dresses like this, fashionably. She says the new fashions are freer, no constricting corsets or stays. They make life feel fun, she tells him. It's easier to put the bad economy, never mind the war, behind them. Murphy can't imagine putting the war behind him. It's there all the time, if not in his waking moments, then certainly in his sleep. Sometimes, he can't remember the dreams, only the dread. Other times, he's back there: the death, the rats, even the smell. Who knew you could smell in dreams? He'd roll over, wishing someone was there, but it's easier to imagine himself back in the war than imagine Helen beside him as his wife, much as he wishes he could. He can't bring himself to ask her, because who would want a one-armed man?

But a one-armed employed man, and that is something, at least, in his favour. It was the radio job that brought him to Helen, and it's the money he's saving from the job that will give him the nest egg that might make such a question possible, eventually. He worries that it won't come soon enough, or just won't *be* enough. The things Helen wants are bigger than he can provide.

Murphy sits, an island in the busy street. Ste Catherine feels like the centre of everything, with the to and fro of people and streetcars, the occasional, impatient honk of a horn. When Helen approaches, Murphy rises to meet her. He is always surprised by her beauty, the way you might be surprised by the blue of the sky, and then surprised at your own surprise. It's just the sky; it's just Helen. But Helen is not *just* anything. Her eyes dance as she approaches, and her colour rises. Across her mouth skips a silent tune of good humour, slightly bemused. Her expression seems older than her twenty-one years.

"Murphy!" she says, turning her cheek to accept his kiss. "You look more like a rumpled suit than ever!" This, although he's taken care to dress well today, knowing she would be meeting him after his early-morning broadcast. "You sounded wonderful this morning, though. I swear, nobody else delivers news so you really *want* to know."

"I don't think most people want to know," he tells her, feeling the warmth of her return kiss, still, on his own cheek. "Not really. But I'm glad you were listening."

They start to walk towards Parc Mont-Royal, a nice place to stroll on a late-summer morning. She's taken his arm, the one that's there, and although this puts her on the outside by the street, it's a compromise he's learned to accept. The air has a golden cast to it, Murphy thinks, as they walk. It brings out reddish highlights in Helen's hair, and plays across her nose, where he can see the slightest hint of freckles. He watches her mouth move as she talks, and it takes him a moment to catch up to her words.

". . . it's been nine years, and she's still having to put up with that kind of thing. You'd think, in this day and age . . . "

Murphy knows, even out of context, that Helen is warming to her favourite subject: her father's cousin Agnes Macphail, the only woman sitting in the House of Commons. She is furious that her beloved relative is frequently belittled on the floor, whether she's talking about women's equality or prison reform. Murphy nods. Best to just let her talk. He's a little baffled by her, a little awed. She talks like no woman he has ever met, and he is intoxicated. He met girls like Helen in Europe, city girls who seemed to know so much more than he did. But Helen isn't hard, as they had been. As they approach McGill campus she lengthens her stride, fluid as chocolate.

". . . she wants me to come to Ottawa. Daddy would disapprove, of course—even if she *is* his cousin. But I don't care. I could live with her, she says, and she could find me work, perhaps in the Parliamentary Library."

"Ottawa?"

"Yes. It's exciting, isn't it? If Daddy won't let me go to McGill, then I might as well go to Ottawa and learn *something*. I'm not going to sit around waiting to get married, to be somebody's housewife. I still can't believe Cynthia settled for that, marrying Charlie and moving way up there in Manitoba to wait out the war. Murphy, this could be a chance for me to really do something."

Murphy has never met Helen's sister, ten years her senior, but he hears about her often enough, the Strattons' disapproval of that marriage clear, but for different reasons than Helen's disapproval. Now strolling in the midst of the campus, they are surrounded by the purposeful movement of students—the majority of them male, as far as Murphy can see. An earnest student comes jogging down the library steps at a clip, and Helen watches with unconcealed envy.

"How I'd love to study law. But my father would never pay for that, of course. He'd have me married off and comfortable. For now, Ottawa is my best option."

"But if you were married," Murphy ventures. He means if *we* were married, but he can't make his lips form the word. Helen won't be anyone's housewife, not if it means giving up dreams of being more than that. He doesn't care what George Landry at the station says, about women who go for gimps: first, they want to mother you, then afterwards, walk all over you. What does George know? He certainly doesn't know Helen.

He tries again. "Marriage doesn't have to stop you, Helen. I wouldn't stop you. You could go to McGill. You could become anything you want." She smiles at him, and he continues, encouraged. "You could run for office one day."

Helen laughs, and it's like fairy bells. Murphy laughs, too, but there's a catch to the sound. "Education takes money, Murphy. No man is going to support me to study, and Daddy certainly won't. No, I have to work, and I won't just be somebody's secretary—at least, not for long. Agnes can give me a foot in the door. My father will be beside himself, but who cares?"

"Your mother?"

"My mother doesn't have opinions. She lets my father have them for her. Sometimes I can't imagine how it is that he and Agnes are even related."

They continue, the rising elevation requiring concentration, and a little more work. Soon they have crossed Avenue des Pins and are standing at the entrance to the park. Helen is backlit by the sun as it rises towards midmorning. She takes off her hat and shakes her hair, and Murphy feels a flock of birds burst from his heart in a warm wash of pins and feathers. He closes his eyes.

"Murphy, listen. What we have is . . . nice. More than nice. You treat me—you don't treat me the way most men do. You treat me like I have a brain in my head—"

"You do—"

"Shhh. Let's just enjoy the afternoon, okay? When do you have to be back at the station?" She takes his arm again, and they move over the pavement, pigeons parting before them like schools of fish.

"Four o'clock. To get ready for the five o'clock news."

"And what's in the news this evening?"

"Doom," he tells her. "Doom and gloom and more gloom."

"Oh, *Murphy.*"

IT'S THE SMELL. It's the smell of clay and blood and metal. Piss and shit. Creosol; cordite. Sweat. Fear. Guillaume's face is gaunt, blackened by the backfiring of the Ross rifle and the falling dirt from the trench walls.

"*'ay, Anglais*," he sneers, and it's Guillaume's voice, exactly as he remembers it. He's alive! He's alive after all, not dead, how could it be—

And then the face dissolves and now it's Helen. She's smiling, her mouth is opening, she's saying something. "Sniper?" He knows it's her, but the voice is still Guillaume's. He holds out a cigarette; it's all he can think of to do, but then he sees it's lit, and knows with sudden horror that the glow will be seen by the sniper. He's on guard duty; how could he have forgotten? And with the rising panic he tries to put out the giveaway glow with his bare hand just as the bullet strikes the face that is Guillaume and Helen, both, a face that breaks like glass. Glass, falling in shards to the muddy floor, and he's searching for them frantically, two hands feeling in the dark, as if he could put everything back together if only he could find the pieces.

He awakes, his hand scrabbling at the sheet. He can sense in the air of the dark bedroom the fading sound of his own cry. Sure enough, there's a pounding from the floor above, three raps. *Tais-toi.* Shut up, they say. He gets up, feels his legs shake beneath him, but by the time he's standing at the toilet he's calmer. Standing in the dark, he hears the stream hit the water in the bowl. Through the cracked window he can smell the dry autumn air and wonders at the passage of time; he hadn't noticed summer's end.

His hand pauses at the light switch, then lets it drop. He doesn't want to see his face, to see how old he's become, although in years he's not far past thirty. He still has a full head of hair, and when he smiles, he knows he looks younger. He tries to smile when he's with Helen, as often as he can remember to. Now, in the stark bathroom light, he knows what he would see were he to turn it on: lines and shadows. Too many lines and shadows.

In the kitchen he pours himself a glass of rye whisky from the bottle he keeps in the cupboard for this sort of thing. He doesn't need to turn on the light; he knows exactly where it sits on the shelf. He sits in the dark on a kitchen chair and puts the bottle between his knees to unscrew the cap, then pours a juice glass full, enjoying the amber colour in the streetlight that seeps in through his landlady's gauze curtains. He lights a cigarette, puts one foot up on the warm radiator and leans back, feels the hot liquid slide down his throat.

THE RATTLE OF the streetcar has a calming effect, and Murphy is glad for that. He's had little sleep, and now he's heading for Westmount, where he'll meet Helen's parents, who have decided, finally, that if this fellow of Helen's is still going to be in the picture after three months, it must be serious enough to warrant Saturday dinner. At least he didn't have to work today. He's dressed as well as he can be, in a relatively good suit with the empty sleeve nicely pinned, thanks to Mme Langille, who got a fair bit of mileage out of teasing him as she did.

"Ah, you *Anglais!* So busy you are, not saying what you feel. Say what you feel! *La vie est trop courte*—too short, you have to—*quelle est l'expression?*—take the bull by his horns. You meet the parents, then one-two-three you get married, *non?*"

He'd smiled and watched her able fingers smooth his sleeve, met the humour in her eyes. She made him feel like a teenager off on his first date. He felt as nervous as one; he was ashamed to find himself hoping that he wouldn't have to admit to the Westmount Strattons that he lives in the east end.

He watches the people in the streetcar, imagining lives for them. This one has five children at home and a wife

71

round as a pudding; that one's having an affair with her boss. Across from him is a priest, dressed in a suit with vest and clerical collar. The man is sleeping, nodding forward, soft folds of flesh hang over his collar and Murphy wants to reach over, push him back to the safety of the backrest. He can imagine the priest toppling forward, Murphy unable to catch him with his one good arm. The priest awakens with a snort and adjusts his posture, blinking as he looks out the window at passing buildings, and all at once Murphy knows he must get off, away from the close air filled with people, their thoughts and problems. It's not the first time, this sudden claustrophobia. He disembarks with perhaps a mile of walking still ahead of him.

Helen is standing on the front porch of the house when he arrives. As he starts up the long walk he thinks he can see, even from that distance, the sharp inhale and the flick of ash that tells him she's impatient, just this side of angry. He's surprised; she's told him before that her father doesn't approve of women smoking, that it's low class. Clearly, she's angry enough not to care.

"Where *were* you?"

"Sorry." He leans to kiss her cheek but she moves her head away and stubs the cigarette in the ashtray sitting on the filigree iron porch table.

"It's just Daddy. It's important to be punctual. *Especially* the first time you meet them." Her look softens. "Never mind." She pauses, appraising him, and he feels his empty sleeve like a sail billowing in the wind. "You look good," she says.

They enter, and her mother meets them in the hallway. A wispy woman, she extends a thin hand in greeting. Murphy's hat is in his hand, and so when she extends hers there is a double awkwardness: not only is it the wrong hand for him to shake, it's occupied in holding his hat. Helen's father comes to the rescue.

"I'm Maurice Stratton. My wife, Sybil. Here, let me take that." He pauses. "And your coat," he says, clearly unsure of whether Murphy would need help with the latter. He doesn't. His hat taken care of, he shirks off his coat with a practised motion and hands it to Mr. Stratton, then extends his hand to Mrs. Stratton, who takes it in her right, gives it a little squeeze as if in sympathy, and lets it go. Mr. Stratton just opts for a friendly pat on the shoulder.

Dinner is not as awkward as it might have been, and Helen appears to have forgiven him. Murphy keeps up his end of the conversation, mostly answering questions about himself: his name? Murphy's an old family name, on his mother's side. Yes, Irish. Murphy wonders if there's some problem with that—could anti-Irish sentiment still exist, after all this time?—but he pushes on, trying to appear comfortable.

His father is a small business owner, selling home electronics. Radios, in fact. Yes, it was an old friend of his father's who had worked for Marconi in the first days of xwa who had introduced him to the station manager. (There was an unspoken effort to employ the vets, and in any case Mr. Galsworth, who himself had not served for reasons of myopia or flat-footedness or some such excuse, was able to, in hiring Murphy, assuage some guilt he felt—but Murphy doesn't offer this latter information.) It's been a great opportunity, he agrees. Salary? Yes, a decent salary, he replies vaguely. Room for advancement? Perhaps.

After dinner, in Mr. Stratton's den, the two men smoke and conversation turns to the economy, and eventually to the stock market.

"Things are taking a turn for the better," Mr. Stratton tells Murphy, tapping ash into the heavy glass ashtray by way of punctuation. "*Much* better. My own investments have more than doubled this past year. You can't get much better than that. It's been a bad decade, Murphy, but if you can, now's the time to invest. Build a nice nest egg." He raises eyebrows like twin caterpillars. "Helen seems quite taken with you."

"Your daughter is lovely." Murphy hopes he's struck the right tone. He's not sure how much he should say. "I don't know if she told you, I met her when her Glee Club came to the station to perform. It was a live broadcast. For Dominion Day."

"Is that so? Well, the Glee Club does her no harm and keeps her out of trouble, I suppose." He pauses, and Murphy smiles inwardly; he knows that half the Glee Club meetings are actually political meetings for Quebec women's suffrage. "She's headstrong, my youngest daughter. What I think she needs is a strong hand—" Murphy can almost feel Mr. Stratton's effort not to look at his own missing one "—and someone in a good position to look after her. Settle her down."

"Uh. Right," Murphy nods.

Later, saying his goodbyes at the door, Murphy thanks them both for their hospitality and says he hopes to see them again. He catches the glance between them, knows it to be cautious approval. He still has much to prove, and they are the least of his worries.

Helen steps onto the porch with him, after her parents have closed the door. She smiles, and her kiss is warm. "They seemed to like you. Did he give you the third degree, Murphy dear?" she asks. "He talked to you about the stock market, didn't he?"

"He wants you to settle down."

74

"Murphy, they have to win. Honestly, I can't believe it's even a court case! It's ridiculous. So much is happening, finally! And here I am, wasting away in Montreal. Can't work, can't get an education, financially dependent on Daddy and his antiquated ideas. There's a world of change going on out there, and here I am."

Murphy lets that one slide. He knows it's not a slight against his company. He just wishes she would take his arm, the good one with the hand tucked into his coat pocket between them. Helen always walks on his good side; he's never even had to ask. She just knows. It's one of the many things he loves about her. To Helen he is himself, no less for his handicap. But does she love him?

"I can't believe I'm still living in the only province that hasn't given women the vote. All the more reason to go to Ottawa," she tells him. "I can't live in Montreal anymore." She shows him a new letter from her cousin, pulling it from her bag and waving it at him. "Look. Agnes is the first woman delegate to the League of Nations. She's going to Geneva! And she wants me in the Ottawa office. Not the library. Her office."

There it was. He'd do anything for her, but he can't afford to marry her, or even follow her to Ottawa. And supporting Helen to attend McGill, or any other university, is out of the question—at least, not right now. Not yet.

"Listen," he tells her. "Let's plan a dinner. A nice dinner, in a nice restaurant. Right after the court date, what is it, the eighteenth? We can celebrate—the victory of the Alberta Five. And maybe some other news. Some good news."

She looks at him quizzically, then: "You do think they'll win, don't you?" she asks, ignoring his enigmatic comment.

"Yes," he tells her, finally taking her hand in his. "We're all due for some good news."

"He wants to intimidate you. He's testing, trying to find out how much money you have." The words are washed in derision. "And anyway, they don't want a repeat of Cynthia," she adds.

"Was it so bad?"

"Charlie didn't have a lot of prospects even before the war. After—he wasn't the same."

Murphy recalls his own nightmares. None of us is the same, he thinks. "I—"

But Helen tosses a look towards the door, and beyond it, her father's den, cutting Murphy off. "I haven't told them about Ottawa." She leans against the pillar and crosses her arms. She turns back to face the street, but it looks to Murphy as if she's seeing something quite a bit more distant.

"That's not your only option," he says.

"I don't see another one right now."

"I've been thinking—"

"Murphy." All at once the tension in her shoulders subsides, and when she turns her gaze is one of affection. She puts a finger to his lips, then lets it fall. Her eyes dance in the glow of the streetlight across the road. "You have to trust. Things fall into place the way they're supposed to. Don't you believe that?"

Around them loom wealthy Westmount houses, their wide verandahs, glowing lights, long front walks.

"No," says Murphy.

IT'S SEVERAL DAYS before Murphy manages to have a conversation with George Landry. Something George had said to him, compounded with his conversation with Helen's father, has got Murphy thinking. George and Murphy work opposite shifts: George works the afternoon shift, coming to work in time for the midday stock reports, and staying to help set up the studio for evening programming, when it isn't bumped by another station. There's talk of technological changes so that several stations won't share frequencies, but Murphy sees no evidence of things changing any time soon. Meanwhile, CFCF has a morning news slot, and early mornings suit him, since he sleeps badly anyway. Often, it's a relief to wake up early.

He's stayed around after morning news shift rather than going home as he sometimes does, so he's sitting on the bench outside the building when George walks up, looking dapper. Murphy blows on his hands as he watches George approach; he can see his breath even though the bench is bathed in a last gasp of October sunlight. Murphy has never really liked George. He's too quick to boast about his service record, about how his special assignments saved thousands of poor buggers like Murphy from the trenches.

George struts towards the front doors, two arms swinging. "Murphy, old chum," he says when he catches sight of Murphy on the bench. "Been thinking about you."

"Have you."

"Yep. What got me thinking," he sits down beside Murphy and looks at his pocket watch. "Ten minutes. What got me thinking was my last statement. Murph, you really need to get in while it's good."

"That's why I'm here. I wanted to talk to you. You said something about—"

"About borrowing on margin."

"I just—I was brought up to not go into debt, that's all. Never buy on time, always stay in the black. But if I want to—"

"If you want to get ahead, chum, you want to take a risk. You *need* to take a risk. The market's all *about* risk. But it's calculated risk, see? And right now it's working for people,

really working. I should know, I read the stock reports every day. I've invested every cent I got, and bought on margin, too. Double the luck. You know what I'm doing in two weeks?"

"What are you doing in two weeks?"

"Taking a vacation. In *New York*. Joan and I are going to do all the shows, all the best restaurants. It's our fifth anniversary, and now we can afford to do something extra special. She deserves it."

"I'm sure she does," Murphy says. "Congratulations, George."

"Could be you, Murphy."

Murphy thinks about celebrating a wedding anniversary with Helen. First, there would have to be a wedding.

"Maybe," he says.

And then, for the next few days, it seems that everyone is talking stocks. Murphy remembers how, as a child, he'd hear a word he'd never heard before and then suddenly it was everywhere, this word that until recently didn't exist for him. Now, the words are Block Trade, Blue Chip, Dividend, Equity, Market Order. It seems everyone is buying on margin to get in: borrowing half the cost of the shares in question, matching whatever savings they have. In no time the loan's repaid and they're earning big returns. It's gold, just waiting for a shovel.

THE NEXT TIME he sees Helen it's for a stroll in Parc Lafontaine. The evening descends quickly now that 1929 is waning, and so they walk briskly in the chill air, the click of Helen's shoes sharp on the cobbled walkway. It's a fitting aural backdrop to the intensity of her mood, sharp words falling from her lips as she describes the looming Supreme Court case set in motion by the Alberta Five—a group of women challenging the *British North America Act* that does not recognize women as "persons."

THAT NIGHT, THE nightmare is worse than usual. He's in the trench again, but this time his fellow soldiers are all scrambling up the sides. He tries to grab at their ankles, but they slide from his grip; they are ethereal, and he can find no purchase. As each ascends there is a flash of light and they are gone, and he knows he can't follow. He will be in this trench forever, and as the black mud sucks him down he has never felt such despair. He awakens, sweating and sobbing.

When the shadows recede he pads again to the kitchen, pours a glass of whisky, and imagines Helen's cool hand on his sweating forehead. He knows, all at once and with absolute conviction, that if Helen was here, the nightmares would stop. He's certain that his survival depends on this.

For the next few days Murphy is preoccupied, his nights sleepless or dream-filled, his days fretful. On Monday, he does what he knows he must do. He waits on the bench for George, who is happy to write him personal introductions to his bank manager and his broker.

"You won't be sorry, Murphy," George tells him. "This is your lucky day."

FOR A WHILE, there's a period of calm. Helen's cousin Agnes is away, and Helen is content to wait it out, seeing Murphy on weekends and attending Glee Club and political meetings, helping her mother, and patronizing her father. In the weeks that pass Murphy's impatience subsides, replaced with a sure hopefulness. George winks when he sees Murphy in the station lobby; it seems every time Murphy sees George, George is wearing a new suit. Even Mme Langille remarks on Murphy's good humour, but "a little quieter with the whistling, *s'il te plait*," she says.

On October 18th the morning paper's headlines could not have been clearer: WOMEN DECLARED PERSONS. Murphy buys a copy and reads the story right there, with the morning flow of city workers all around him. Emily Murphy, Henrietta Muir Edwards, Louise McKinney, Irene Parlby, and Nellie McClung were successful in their challenge, even if the words of the British Lord Chancellor were less than memorable: ". . . to those who ask why the word 'persons' should include females, the obvious answer is why should it not?"

He can imagine laughing over the quote with Helen later, but now, he'll be late reading that very news if he doesn't hurry. Walking at a clip, he remembers the promised dinner date. If George is as good as his word, there will be two things to celebrate.

"Looking good today, Murphy!" calls the technical operator when Murphy enters the studio. "Something different about you . . . what is it? New suit?"

"Just that the world is full of possibilities, Bob, that's all." Murphy hangs up his coat, the newspaper rolled in the pocket. He sets his hat on the stand, then sits at his desk to review the teletype sheets and reading list prepared by the story secretary.

"Congratulations, Eloise," he says when she puts a late item on his desk. He waves at the teletype announcing the Supreme Court ruling.

"Think it'll get me a raise?" Eloise quips. "Otherwise, I don't half care."

Bob leans over the board, "Your girlfriend won't be taking no guff after this," he teases. "Isn't she some kind of suffragette? You marry her, Murphy, it won't be you wearing the pants."

"Oh, I think there's enough pants to go around." Murphy smiles into his sheaf of papers. A happy Helen is a Helen who might just say yes.

"Three minutes," warns Bob.

Murphy nods. "George in today?" Maybe he'll wait around. His first investment statement hasn't arrived, and it was supposed to be in his mailbox on the fifteenth.

"Don't know. He's been out all week. Fred Bennett's replacing him."

ON FRIDAY, MURPHY places a call to the broker, the one George set him up with. The secretary tells Murphy that "Mr. Richardson is busy. He isn't taking calls." Murphy can't keep the frustration from his voice as he insists, and in any case there's nothing to be done. "Call back tomorrow," she tells him.

Murphy wants to make the dinner date with Helen, but he wants to be sure of his news. If the numbers on paper are indeed what George had promised they would be, he'll be able to show them to Helen—and then present the ring. He's put away rent money for that, what with the first investment payout scheduled just before month's end. It's waiting for him at Birks, half down already. Today is payday; he has the rest in his pocket.

But with nothing concrete, he doesn't want to call Helen—not yet. In any case, she's in Ottawa for the weekend visiting her cousin Agnes, "just to see." Still, he can't shake the feeling of hopefulness. It puts a jaunt in his step; it makes heads turn. He touches his hand to his hat at a matronly woman who smiles—not the smile of sympathy he's used to when people see his missing arm, but the smile of infectious recognition that comes spontaneously when one spots a fellow creature who's on top of the world.

As he heads for his apartment it occurs to Murphy that he hasn't had a nightmare for weeks.

When Murphy sees Helen on Friday, she's fresh from her trip to Ottawa and full of admiration for her cousin Agnes. The late October air is cold, and they stop in an almost-empty diner, sliding into a booth where they blow steam across their coffee cups.

"We talked about everything Murphy. We talked about marriage—" there's a pause in which Murphy holds his breath "—and do you know what she said to me? She said: 'I don't want to be the angel of any home. I want for myself what I want for every woman—absolute equality. Once we have that, men and women can take turns at being angels.' I told her she should use it in a speech."

"Helen—"

"She's just so inspiring, Murphy. There's an opening in her office in a few weeks. I can have it if I want it."

"Helen—"

Helen turns to face him. "Yes?"

He places his hand on her shoulder, keenly wishing the other was there, fearing—ridiculously—that without two hands to anchor her she might spin away from him.

"It's not an angel I want. It's you. However you want that to be."

She kisses him briefly, a butterfly touch. He has no idea what it means.

IT'S HELEN'S MOTHER'S fiftieth birthday, and so Helen is obliged to be at home during the weekend to help entertain family members from Smith's Falls, Kingston, and Cornwall. Even Cynthia has come from Dauphin, Manitoba, bringing her son, Stephen, but leaving her husband behind. Murphy isn't invited. But on Saturday, he finds he needs to hear her voice. He calls her on the telephone from the station, apologizing to the security man as he lets himself in with his key and ascends to the third-floor studio. Not many families have their own telephones, but Westmount homes do as a matter of principle; he's seen the set in their big front hallway. He waits while the operator connects them, imagining Helen picking up the phone, delighted to hear his voice.

But, "Murphy? Why are you calling?" she asks. In the background he can hear voices and laughter. He must have called right in the middle of her mother's party.

"I just—I've been thinking about that dinner. Remember? We said we'd go out to celebrate."

"Celebrate?" There's a burst of laughter behind her, on the heels of a punchline to some joke.

He allows himself to chuckle. "Your newfound person-hood. And I'll have some news."

"Sure. Sure, Murphy. That would be really nice. But after everyone leaves on Sunday." Another crescendo of sound in the background. "I have to go now, all right?"

"Sure. Monday?"

"I'm sorry—there's a Glee Club rehearsal Monday night. I can't miss another one."

"Is it really a Glee Club rehearsal?"

"Yes. I don't lie to you, Murphy." Her tone is offended.

Murphy presses on. "Tuesday?"

"Tuesday. Yes, all right. Tuesday would be wonderful."

"Helen—"

"I'll see you then, Murphy. Pick me up at seven?"

"Yes. Helen—?"

"What?"

"I may have figured something out. This is—it's important. To me. For us."

"The cake's coming out, Murphy. Don't worry—" Helen lowers her voice. "I love you."

Murphy stands smiling in the dark, empty office.

ON MONDAY MURPHY asks again about George. He asks Hal, because he knows Hal was also talking to George about getting into "the investment racket" as Hal called it—laughing, but you could tell he was really interested.

"I don't know what's up with George, Murph. Don't know anyone who's seen him. What do you want him for?"

They're standing in the lobby of CFCF. Murphy takes a few steps out of the flow of business so they can talk in a corner, away from reception and near a large potted fern. He feels ridiculous, and yet he doesn't want someone walking by to hear his words, although he couldn't have explained his reasons if he'd had to. Murphy keeps his voice low.

"Hal, you invested with George's broker. Have you received a statement?"

"Nah, I never invested. Just didn't sit right, plus I knew if anything happened to our savings the wife would never let me forget it. Thing is, I hear it's a good thing I didn't listen to George."

For Murphy, the floor beneath them sinks slightly, a small but ominous shift. "How so?"

"Heard he was getting a commission for every joker he sent over. Know what else? You know Cy Thibodeau, works in accounts? He also does accounts for the Veteran's Commission. Says Landry never even served! Got himself excused for medical reasons. All that talk of his? Hot air."

ON TUESDAY, MURPHY rises far too early from a troubled sleep, the slightest glow staining the still-dark sky. The dreams of the night stay submerged, a murky underpinning to his morning as he moves about the kitchen. It's October 29th. Three days until the rent is due. Fourteen days since he should have heard from the broker. Still, he's picked up the ring, a leap of faith. He has played out their conversation over dinner, honing his words, imagining her response.

There must be good cause for the delay, he's reasoned again and again; the broker is a busy man. He'll call today, as soon as office hours begin. He'll get verbal assurance, at the very least, as to his growing wealth, and put his fears at rest. When he thinks about it, he knows it's preposterous to imagine anything could have gone awry. He'd seen the office, seen the framed certificates on the wall. Witnessed the efficient professionalism of Richardson's secretary, her desk positioned as guardian to opulent inner office. Heck, he'll go right over there after work. He can't think why he hasn't just done this before.

Everything is fine, Murphy thinks; the market is growing by leaps and bounds, so it stands to reason that a small-time investor like himself might not merit a quick return on his calls. And as for George, well, it's not *about* George, is it?

He has the ring. He can imagine telling her: you can do whatever you want to—study anything, *be* anything, travel to Timbuktu if that's what you want—

I'll make sure of it. We'll take turns being angels.

He'll ask her tonight.

As he boils an egg on the gas element, Murphy considers how to fill the time afforded by his early waking. He's too alert to return to bed. He'll go in to work early, he decides. Arriving on time as he usually does, he misses the early-morning office banter, and suddenly that water cooler camaraderie is exactly what he wants. Dressed and presentable, he's out the door and at the streetcar stop before the news agent even opens. There are few travellers on the early car, so he watches the sun as it illuminates the tops of the buildings along Rue Ste Catherine. It's a beautiful day. And tonight, dinner with Helen. The ring is a hot weight in his pocket.

Bob Claridge is just coming out of the lobby washroom as Murphy heads in before going upstairs.

"You hear the news?" he asks.

"What news?" Murphy doesn't want to chat in the door of the men's washroom, but something in Bob's voice stops him. "Shouldn't you be setting up already?"

"In a sec. It's early. Anyways everyone's talking, even though nobody's supposed to know."

"Know what?"

"George Landry shot himself."

MURPHY CALDWELL STANDS in the studio looking at the darkened On Air light that, in a few minutes, will be red. The day has taken on a surreal quality; there's a dull roaring all around him, as if he was entirely surrounded by ocean. He has today's news in his hands, but he hasn't yet reviewed it. On the other side of the glass he can see Bob, Eloise, and Cy from accounting gathered around the teletype, reading the words as they appear, letter by letter, on the curling paper. There is some excitement, but he can't hear anything from where he stands in the soundproof room. He peers over the disc of the microphone as Eloise hurries towards him, paper in hand. "Top story," she whispers as the red light goes on.

86

STOCK MARKET CRASHES are the first three words.

Murphy can't imagine getting through the morning's newscast, and yet he does. The feeling in his chest is not so far removed from the sinking dread of his nightmares. His lips move; words emerge. Page after page, from the top story on down, he utters word after meaningless word until the red light goes dark and he looks up to see Helen on the other side of the glass. She has the morning paper in her hands. A sudden memory of Helen's father, talking investments in the den after dinner, swims before him. An earthquake levels everything equally.

There is a wall of glass between them, and a thousand miles of space. He can't look at her; he has no idea what she's even doing here. What can he possibly say to her?

But when he meets her eyes, all at once Murphy sees what Helen sees: a whole man. An equal partner. Her face is wet, and she presses her palm to the glass. There is no thought involved: his own hand is there to meet it, palm to palm.

FIVE

FLYING
WITH AMELIA

·1934·

September 23, 1934
Dear Mr. Penner,

I am writing in response to your advertisement in the *Yarmouth Herald* for a pen pal. You requested a woman, and I guess I fit the bill.

I started this letter four times, trying to find just the right tone, and no matter what I do it comes out awful, formal. This was my best try so far. So I think I will just keep it at that, but this time I'll go on in what I hope will be a friendlier tone. If we are to be pen pals, then it seems important that we strike the right tone, and that it be an honest one. And so I will pledge, Mr. Penner, to be as honest and forthright as I can be if you will promise the same. Honesty is the least we can give one another in these times, generally speaking, and quite often it is probably the most. Although things are for sure a little better here than they are for you there, where I hear the farms are dust if they're not grasshoppers. I've seen the newsreels at the movies, and I'll tell you, I won't complain about the weather. Can't buy a new pair of shoes, but at least there's always a fish in the pot.

But see, I'm nattering on, which is what my friend Sally says is my very worst trait. Sally works at the desk right next to mine at the *Herald*, which is how I saw your notice, right away before it was even printed, because I have become right good at reading backwards and in reverse. In fact, at our last Christmas party at the newspaper we had a contest to see who could read our publisher's editorial for the next edition (which of course, was still set in its lead type, and so reversed) the fastest, and without stumbling, which I can tell you was hilarious, especially with some of the men who just might have consumed a little too much eggnog. I won, which tells you I have one talent, at least.

So now you know two things about me: that I live in Yarmouth (but you knew that, didn't you, or did you place your advertisement in all of the Nova Scotia papers?) and that I work at a newspaper, and I'll tell you now that I'm not doing anything glamorous but simply typing letters to the editor (outrage at the state of things, mainly) that have come hand-written so that the typesetters can read them to set them (this is harder than you'd imagine. Or maybe not, since my mother tells me my own penmanship leaves something to be desired) as well as letters to advertisers who have not paid their bills (and I do hope that you are not among them. Wouldn't that be funny?) and other dull things right short of any kind of interest or creativity.

And what else do you know about me? Well, if you've skipped to the bottom of this page (and I suppose you might have. I would have) you know my name is Peggy McGrath. And you know that I read the papers and watch the newsreels and that I have a good idea what's going on in the world, not like some. I hope you do, too, Mr. Penner, because correspondence can be such a lot of fun when you really get to discuss things.

Now, I think I've said enough. If you really want to correspond, you will have to tell me enough about yourself for me to be convinced that you will be honest and forthright. And you will need to be very clear about your position (by this I mean whether or not you are married, because if you were I would not continue writing), your age and occupation, your intentions as far as this correspondence goes, as well as your thoughts and dreams.

I await, with anticipation, your reply.

Sincerely, Peggy A. McGrath

Yarmouth, Nova Scotia

October 1, 1934

Dear Miss McGrath,

I can't begin to tell you how delighted I was to get your letter, and to get to know so much about you all at once! I will tell you right off that my intentions are honourable, friendship through correspondence my only goal.

You sound like a very charming and very intelligent young lady. Of course, you didn't give me your age, although I noticed you asked mine, and since I am responding to your letter I suppose you could take that as agreement to your plea for forthrightness, and so I will tell you that I'm 27 years old, and unmarried. And in keeping with that promise, I will also tell you that I am unfortunately unemployed, my position as a schoolteacher here in Ernfold having ended when they shut down the school, because so many families have now moved into the city or just left Saskatchewan altogether. You can't be a farmer if you can't farm. I taught just four children for the month of September, all of them the Moresland children, and when they left . . . well, it was a sad day, watching the backs of them as they left the schoolhouse to walk down the lane, the smallest, Maisie, without even shoes on her feet, all of them holding hands in order of age and height with Sarah at the left, Maisie at the right, and the twins, Perry and Paul, in the middle. Their father has relatives in Regina and the promise of a job at a machine shop. I walked past their place last week after they had left. They didn't even take the time to board it up, just walked away, a dishtowel still hanging on the line. And now I am writing this in my landlady's house, the Ministry of Education having paid my room and board three months in advance and so in my spare time I am teaching my landlady, Mrs. Wolyniak, to read while I apply for teaching positions elsewhere, when I know there are none. So you see that your letters will offer me some distraction from life's mundanities.

I suppose I should tell you why I decided to send my advertisement to a Nova Scotia newspaper, because I'm sure you are wondering. Of course it was because of the shipment of potatoes, turnips, carrots, and salted fish that came by rail, a monumental kindness from your province to mine, and that left not one dry eye in the community hall where the bounty was distributed. Oh, and apples! An apple never tasted so good, I can assure you.

Can you tell me, how does one cook salt cod? Mrs. Wolyniak tried soaking it in water and even a bit of milk, but we can't be cooking it right because it remains dry and salty and not very palatable, even to the very hungry.

How happy I am that you're interested in current affairs. I'm anxious to find out what you think of Mr. Bennett's chances for re-election. With this man Hitler becoming altogether too powerful (although some say he's all bluster, no bite), it seems to me that a strong leader is very important, but more than that, it seems to me he has only a year to get us out of this mess or suffer the consequences.

I wonder what it's like where you live. I've never been east of Regina (where my sister lives). Actually, that's not quite true: I crossed the Atlantic when I was just six, in a boatful of orphans destined for new lives with Canadian families. They say we block out the memories we don't wish to remember, and I suppose that must be the case; I'm sure I was terrified! But I don't mean to cry a sad tale. My parents were kind people who raised me like their own. I'm afraid I was never much of a farmer, though.

And now here I am, my parents gone, the farms all gone to dust, and few prospects, if any. I suppose I could join the navy, and then I'd have no excuse, would I? And then I could dock at Yarmouth and take you for dinner, and, if you'd permit, perhaps even dancing! Just as a friend, of course. I know there is a large harbour at Yarmouth (I looked it up in the encyclopaedia set in the schoolroom; I still have the key, for the moment) but I don't know if there is a place for dancing. Is there? Do you like Swing music? I love Tommy Dorsey, and Benny Goodman, and when Mrs. Wolyniak goes to bed I will sometimes stay up late and catch the radio stations as they drift in and out from the States.

Cordially yours,

Martin Charles Penner

October 24, 1934

Dear Mr. Penner,

Today Sally brought in a copy of *Life Magazine* with a feature on the Quints, and then there we were, all of us (well, the girls, anyway) cooing over the images of those five little girls, now toddling in their matching dresses and bows, until our boss came out and blew right up at us, threatening to fire the lot of us if we didn't get right back to work. But I think we need the good news stories to counter the news of relief camps and children starving in their own homes on the prairie and frightening things going on in Europe that we read every day as part of life in a newsroom. But my Uncle Allan, who served in the Great War, says there won't ever be another, and I suppose I want to believe him.

Don't you?

I can see that you've known hard times before now, even if you don't remember. I think these experiences make a person stronger, don't you? Or more empathetic, at least. You seem like a person with empathy, the way you talk about the Moresland children, and about teaching your landlady to read. I think empathy is a very important quality to have.

My boss is not an empathetic person, so for now, no more Quint-watching on work time for me. I'll be clack-clack-clacking away with my eyes on the keys from now on, because I can't afford to lose this job.

You asked my age. I am 22 years old. I live in a rooming house with my own room, and all the tenants are girls working in offices: one keeps the books for the plant, another takes dictation from our local member of the legislature when he is here and not in Halifax, and Sally, who I mentioned works with me, lives on the main floor at the back. Last year I lived in an old house on Main Street, and there everyone but me worked in the fish plant, the smell absolutely everywhere, right in the plaster on the walls, and some rank, let me tell you. Speaking of which, you asked about the salt fish, and so I will write two recipes on the back of this letter. Fish'n Brewis is a Newfoundland recipe that's been in my family just about forever, since my grandfather came from there. As for the Finnan Haddie, it's better with smoked fish, but you can use salted, too. The important thing to remember is that you will need to soak it more than once to get the salt out.

Sometimes when I get up and go to work I think: maybe today something new will happen. All day we can hear the blast of ships' horns and they are all going somewhere. But I am sick of the smell of salt water and the fog that curls my hair every which way and I long to go somewhere where the January wind doesn't blow right through you and out the other side. I am some tired of Yarmouth, and that's the truth. I wonder, do you long for the bite of the sea air, out there in all that dust? Can you even imagine what it's like? It seems as if we are never content where we are, but always wanting to be somewhere else.

If I could be anyone I would be Amelia Earhart. What courage, to fly across the Atlantic, from Newfoundland all the way to Ireland! And then she doesn't stop there, but conquers the Pacific as well. My word. Next she's planning to fly around the whole world and where will I be? In Yarmouth Nova Scotia, reading the news in reverse.

You didn't tell me about your hopes for life, and I did ask you. Is it too soon to ask such questions?

Yours very sincerely,
Peggy McGrath

FINNAN HADDIE
½ lb salt fish (smoked is better)
2 cups milk
¼ cup butter

¼ cup flour
2 eggs, slightly beaten
2 cups cubed cooked potatoes

In a shallow baking dish cover salt fish with milk. Let Stand 1 hour.

Bake 30 minutes. Drain, save milk, and separate fish into flakes. In a saucepan melt butter. Blend in flour until smooth. Gradually stir in leftover milk. Cook, stirring constantly, until thick. Blend in eggs. Add fish and potatoes.

FISH'N BREWIS
5 pieces hard tack
1 lb. salt fish
8 strips of bacon
2 large onions
1 tbsp butter

Soak bread in cold water for 24 hours. Fry bacon and drain fat, remove from pan and cut bacon in small pieces. Chop 2 large onions and put in bacon pan. Cover pan and steam on slow heat until tender. Put the soaked dry bread with the water in a saucepan and boil for 1 minute. Drain well. Cook fish until tender. Remove bones and add to the drained hard bread. Add cooked onions and bacon. Add butter and stir.

November 7
Dear Miss McGrath,

I wonder if you would call me Martin? It would be a lot easier to tell you about such personal things as hopes and dreams if we were on a first name basis.

Thank you very much for the recipes, which I have shared with Mrs. Wolyniak, the two of us spelling them out together in the evening. I believe she is not too sure about the Brewis dish, but thinks the Finnan Haddie looks like it might be good. I'm looking forward to it, especially since they are recipes you suggested.

Miss Earhart is certainly an inspiration, but I'm not sure I would want to go up in the air. The truth is, if the school hadn't closed I'd have been content there for a very long time, boring as that may sound. On the prairie I will walk for miles, happy under all that sky with no desire to be up in it. When the wind blows through the fields I imagine it's like the sea, the waves coming into the shore, and it's the sunset that turns them gold. They really do look as if you could swim in them. Of course, it is dusty, and little grows, and there are so many abandoned farmsteads that it feels as if some catastrophe, like war or plague, has driven people away, and I suppose that in a way both are true. Even homes with people in them have an empty look.

We have lost the war with drought and our poverty is a plague. There are hobo camps along the sidings, men heading west, hoping for work. I hear the work camps are full; there is nothing for them. And I think: there but for the grace of God . . .

I have been writing to various school boards, inquiring about positions. I am not by nature a farmer nor a labourer, much as my parents might have wished, and if you saw me you would see this immediately. I am told I'm a nice-looking man, with a full head of dark hair and blue eyes, but slight in stature, and I do wear glasses. Bookish, I guess. I hope that doesn't put you off. I guess I've given myself away: I've been hoping maybe someday we could meet. You write such a nice letter. Is that silly?

Could you tell me what you look like? I'd like to be able to picture you when I read your letters.

Yours,
Martin

November 17
Dear Martin,

It seems fine to me that if we're going to keep up this correspondence we should be on a first name basis. As you can see by the typewriting I'm writing this at work, although I'm prepared to whip the paper out if Mr. Swain comes out of his office, but he's been in there all day talking with some man about I don't know what, and as there are no near-illegible letters-to-the-editor and no letters to type to delinquent advertisers, there is not much to do. And I've read both today's paper, and tomorrow's in letterpress, so there: I've read the news backwards and forwards!

You wanted to know what I look like, so I'll tell you. I am five feet, five inches, and I have blonde hair and a very nice smile, I am told. I have freckles from my mother's side and my father's nose, which thankfully is a fairly nice one. I didn't tell you about my parents before. They live in Shelburne, where I grew up. Dad makes dories. Those are boats, in case you don't know. That's about it. It was my Granny who paid for the secretarial course at Yarmouth, and here I am ever since. I have five little sisters who are still at home. My favourite, Binnie, is the smallest.

I don't really go to the dances much at all. But if we meet, I would like to go out dancing with you. Swing music is swell, but I don't get to hear as much popular music as I'd like. I can't listen to the radio at the rooming house because of the thin walls and the thick landlady.

I have been thinking about you a lot and wondering what will happen at the end of the month. Will you stay on with Mrs. Wolyniak? (And I wonder, did she ever make the Finnan Haddie?) Have you had any responses to your job applications?

Write soon,

Peggy

December 3

Dear Peggy,

As you can see by my return address, I'm still here. Mrs. W. couldn't find another lodger for December, and so she's offered to keep me on so long as I pay for my own food and keep her in firewood, which, although I'm not terribly swift with the axe, I can certainly do—and happily. If I was any good with a gun, I suppose I'd be out hunting rabbits, but I'm not very handy that way. I'm still teaching Mrs. W. to read, which isn't much good at filling the belly but which has been a very rewarding experience for both of us in its own way. I haven't ever taught an adult before, and she is so keen! She can already read the grade one primer, and is delighted when she comes to the end of a sentence like: Bobby saw the cat cross the road.

I have a few savings left, enough to keep me from starving, but there are no jobs. I have looked for work in town, right down to grocery delivery boy, but there is nothing, and everybody is looking. Maybe I should head West, as everybody else seems to be doing, and see what I can find in British Columbia, leaving Mrs. Wolyniak to her culinary experimentations (she is a genius at cooking something from nothing) and her read-ing. We did eat up the salt cod, and while I'm not sure if a Ukrainian interpretation of a Nova Scotian recipe left us with exactly the same dish, whatever was lost in translation didn't matter in the end as we ate every scrap.

Yours fondly,
Martin

December 15
Dear Martin,

We will stop work on December 23 and I will take the bus to Shelburne and spend the holidays with my family. I'm so looking forward to it. Binnie especially (she is the sister of my heart) but all the others too, and Mum and Dad, who will pamper me. It's so much better going home after you've been away. You stop being one more mouth and become the one who's made good. Although Mum will ask me why I'm not married, and that's always embarrassing. And then church, of course, where everyone will want to know about my life in Yarmouth and I suppose I'll have to make up a thing or two to keep them satisfied. What do you think Amelia Earhart tells her family when she goes home to visit? You can bet she doesn't have to make anything up.

It's been bitterly cold and the bit of water I can see from the office window is the shade of grey that tells you it is just this side of ice and would freeze solid if it could. When I go home at night I have to dress in three sweaters in order to stay warm in my room.

As you can see, I've been knitting. It makes me feel warmer surrounded by wool, and makes my heart warm to think of you all wrapped up in this scarf. I hope you like the colour. I thought of the wheat fields you mentioned, and so I chose a golden colour that I hoped would suit you, and at the ends, blue for your eyes.

Yesterday's paper reported that King George appears to be failing. I'm not at all sure about Edward. Do people in the prairies follow the Royals? We all do, probably because it's such a different life.

Well, I hope you have a fine Christmas, Martin. I don't suppose you are travelling all the way to Regina to visit your sister. Do you have any other siblings? Did you all come over together? Does Mrs. Wolyniak have children?

As for my Christmas, all I want is another letter from you, and so I'll be watching my mailbox.

Very fondly yours,
Peggy

January 1, 1935
Dear Peggy,

Happy New Year!

Thank you so much for the beautiful scarf, which is keeping my neck warm as I write here in my room (which is now on the main floor behind the kitchen, as my upstairs room has become quite frigid in this cold snap we are having. Forty-two below!) Mrs. W. has moved into the parlour, and so the only place to sit is the kitchen, which is where we do our reading every evening, beside the stove. She can now read the Eaton's catalogue, and we play a game in which we open it at random and point with our eyes closed, and that is the item we will buy when the economy turns around. Mrs. W. opened her eyes to find she'd be buying a complete Santa suit (only $3.98). We had a good time laughing over that. For my part, I have promised to buy a taffeta-trimmed crepe dress, apparently the latest style. I suspect it will look better on you than it would on me.

It's hard to be optimistic in the cold, except for the package sent by Mrs. Wolyniak's son in Winnipeg, which was full of lovely things to eat and made us quite cheerful. I've not heard from my sister, which is unusual.

You asked about my family. I'm afraid that Marjorie is all I have, as my parents are both dead. In fact, Marjorie is not really my sister; we both came over at different times. I can't imagine growing up with all of the siblings you have! Your Christmases must have been very different from ours, which were always very quiet affairs. In my house, nobody ever raised his voice, in joy or in anger. Anyway, Marjorie married an accountant for the city offices and we don't correspond except at Christmas. And I have settled here and seem unable or unwilling to move except that you can't stay in one place forever, can you, especially if you have to find somewhere to make a living, if only to buy that new set of trousers in the Eaton's catalogue so that when we finally meet, I'll cut a more dashing figure than I do now.

Mrs. W. and I rang in the New Year last night with Guy Lombardo and his Royal Canadians on the radio. At midnight we toasted one another with a glass of elderberry wine (the one thing that still seems to be growing heartily around here), which was beautiful in colour but made my cheeks pucker.

I'll leave you with that mental picture of me.

With abiding affection,

Martin

January 30, 1935
Dear Martin,

I'm so sorry for the delay in writing. I had to move to a new rooming house and somehow I misplaced your address in the process. You must have wondered what happened to me! I have been cut back to three days a week at the paper, because now the paper has a new partner, Mr. Brougham, and he is insisting on "efficiencies." And now I wish I'd never complained about the cold or the thin walls or even fat old Mrs. Doane because I've had to move right downtown over-top Connaught's Jewellery, and instead of sharing a bathroom with working girls my own age I have to share with whoever is in the room across the hall, and that seems to change weekly. And I can hear the blast on the foghorn like it's right in the room with me, and so I am getting little sleep and I have to watch my pennies very carefully. In fact, I will have to borrow a few pennies for a stamp from Sally, who seems to have charmed Mr. Brougham, and as a result kept her hours at the *Herald* (and her room at Mrs. Doane's!).

Christmas was exactly as it always is, a steady stream of family and friends and relatives, the kitchen full of people every waking minute and a great sharing of food and laughter. I thought of you many times, and wondered how you'd like all our noise and confusion. At one point there were so many pairs of boots beside the back door you could hardly get in! We had a big lobster boil, turkey being too dear, although of course we'd all have preferred that. I'd rather eat something that walks on two legs or four any day.

I'm so glad you liked your scarf. I don't suppose you could have a photograph taken and send it to me? I would surely send you mine. I feel as if I've known you forever, so it seems strange that I don't really know what you look like. In fact, I will take the first step and go down to Archer's first thing and get one taken. I hope you won't be disappointed.

Very fondly,

Peggy

February 24

Dear Martin,

I haven't heard from you. Was it silly of me to include my photograph? Have you decided you'd rather not continue writing? I wait for your letters. The day one comes is a red-letter day, and everything looks brighter while I'm going about my day at the *Herald*, knowing it is waiting on my bureau in my room for me to come back and read it again. Knowing there is a new letter keeps me closer to you. That may be something I shouldn't admit, but I promised at the beginning to be forthright and honest and so I will be, whatever the cost.

Yours,

Peggy

March 15

Dear Peggy,

I am so sorry! First off, I have to tell you how happy I was to get your photograph, and how beautiful you look—even more than I had imagined. And I'll be truthful too I feel the same way about our correspondence. Circumstances are such that I did not receive your letter for some time, as I've been in transit, but I can't tell you how glad I was when the postmaster forwarded it to me. And then I was unable to write to you as I lacked even the price of a stamp! A great deal has happened. You can see from the postmark that I'm now in British Columbia. I'll try to explain.

Mrs. Wolyniak's widowed brother took a stroke and she went to Estevan to care for him. I think in truth the winter took a lot out of her, and when she received the bank foreclosure notice that was the last straw, and so in a way she welcomed the chance to care for someone else and left with hardly a look of regret for what she was leaving behind. Of course, I had to leave as well and with no prospects and very little money I did what other men in my position are doing and caught the train, albeit with a ticket rather than hopping a boxcar as so many men are forced to do.

The last of my money was stolen while I was staying at the YMCA. I had my wallet tucked into my shoes and was sleeping on the bottom bunk with my hands resting on the laces, unwilling to sleep with my shoes on as I was advised to do. In my exhaustion I didn't feel the slip of leather beneath my fingers. Imagine the surprise of the thief when, along with a good pair of shoes, he found all of my savings, paltry though it was! And so there I was without shoes or money or a bed for the night. This circumstance eventually led me to the Salvation Army and another pair of shoes (that don't fit so well) and then to a relief camp, where we are preparing ground for a road. The days are long and the pay is poor: twenty cents a day! We work six and a half days a week and live in shacks. But we are fed, more or less, and if I can save enough for a suit of clothes I may be presentable enough to apply for teaching positions. As it is, stamps and even paper are a luxury, let alone a new suit.

I know it sounds like I'm crying a sad tale, and certainly I'm not physically suited to hard labour but I'm getting stronger, and I suppose that's a good thing, the silver lining as it were. But there are sadder tales than mine. The fellow in the next bunk lost everything in the stock market crash, including his wife and children who left him for someone who hadn't been so unlucky. I can see that to fall so hard and so very far has been hard on him. He has a bewildered look, and he's far worse on the crew than I am, earning him derision from those for whom this is just one more hardship in a progression of hardships. But at least the other fellows send money back to a family they hope someday to see again when the economy improves, and as for me, I suppose I have you.

Your letters mean more to me than ever, Peggy, and I hope you don't find me so down and out as to lose interest in writing. You can write to me now at the address on the back of the envelope, care of the Sally Ann. I'm sorry I'm not able to include a photograph. I'd have taken a new one if I could, or at least sent you the old one I carried of Marjorie and I before our parents died, but that was lost with my wallet and my shoes. And Marjorie? Regina was where I went first, but she and her husband had moved, no forwarding address. As I think I mentioned, we never talked much after our parents passed away, as they did within just a few months of one another as it so often goes. And so West I went, and here I am.

Do please write, Peggy dear, and I will respond as best I can and with all optimism that we will someday meet, and that all of these hard times will be behind us.

Yours always,

Martin

April 10

Oh, poor, dear Martin—

What troubles you've had! Your letter was a very long time finding me, for one thing because you must have forgotten my new address and sent it to my old (Sally rescued it from the clutches of Mrs. Doane, who would have marked it Return to Sender, the old cow) and since the postmark was well after the date on the letter, I imagine you had some trouble getting it mailed. But it's here now, and that's what's important. Whatever happens, I promise to be there for you.

I don't mind in the least that you're down and out (I mean, I don't mind as far as my feelings for you are concerned. I do mind that things are not going well for you). I have come to know the man you are, as I'd hoped I would, and so your circumstances are a trial, not a measure of worth. As for a photograph, looks are not so important as the heart, no matter what Sally says (she did suggest you might have one eye and a club foot. She's like that, placing great importance on looks and money both, and has wiled Mr. Finding Efficiencies so that she is now his personal secretary. But she did bring me your letter, so I won't be too catty except to say that she can be a right minx when she puts her mind to it).

Here is my advice for when times are tough (at least, it's what I do): think of Amelia. She found her dream and pursued it, no matter what, achieving what others only dream of. If she can fly around the world, as she plans to, then surely you and I can overcome these obstacles and find our dreams.

And now that I have received your letter I will admit (in all forthrightness and truth) that my dream (besides flying around the world, which will take some doing as I have not quite the resources of Miss Earhart) is that we will meet in person. If we keep this firmly in mind, I believe we can achieve it.

With great affection,

Peggy

April 13

Dearest Peg,

We have called a general strike! We are now, and have been for some time, all part of the Relief Camp Worker's Union, every last one of us here. There has been unrest and outright agitation building, and while I have never in my life been a political person (content, rather, to read about current events rather than partake in them) I am of the mind that enough is enough. If Bennett spent one day in our camp he would see the desperation of the men and he would take concrete action, rather than debating solutions in Parliament that have nothing to do with the plight of the unemployed or their families.

Two days ago Morris, the fellow I mentioned had lost fortune and family in the crash of '29, was found hanging from a rafter. I don't think he could face a strike, and hadn't the strength to march as we will have to do. I hope he found peace. For the rest of us, no one slept, as it brought it home to all of us just how close the fate of Morris is to our own futures. Good men can only take so much.

Tomorrow we will congregate in the streets of Vancouver, in the manner of many such demonstrations that occurred before I arrived. Public support is high for our cause. We'll win, I feel sure of it.

You can see I am now writing around the margins of the page as it's my last piece of paper for now. It's the thought of you that keeps me going most days. I have saved almost five dollars, and have hidden it away in a place no one will find it. I am planning my escape, into the wild blue, just like your Amelia, and I promise I will come to you, one way or another.

With love, my Peg,

Martin

May 19

Dear Martin,

I am so glad you are keeping a vision of a brighter future close to your heart. Think of me, too, waiting to make a future with you, if that's what's in store for us, and I hope that it is. For my part, optimism hasn't been easy, since I have now lost my job with the *Herald*, which has been sold lock, stock, and barrel to Mr. Profit-at-Any-Price, or Mr. Cradle-Snatcher, however you want to call him (Sally is not twenty, and he is fifty if he's a day). I am very much at loose ends and applying for work wherever I can, and it's looking like a waitress at the Tasty Delight may be the best I can muster. It's that or move home, and that option is about as far away as I can get from flying around the world on an airplane, so I will hold out as long as I can.

Some days it feels just like reading the paper as the type is being set: everything is going in reverse, it seems. I can't help feeling that if you could just hold it up to a mirror, you could see clearly what's spelled out there and know how to make it right. It's obvious that somebody, somewhere, is doing things backwards.

I think about the way we met, and the railcars of food, that generosity from the East to the West. I wonder if in the future Canada will remember this, how generous the generally poor Maritimers were in a time of need. I think it must always be the poor who best understand the poorer.

I am in my room by the week, now. Write as soon as you can.

All my love,
Peg

May 28
Dearest Peg,

We are just days from leaving, and I am excited with the power of the thing. Two hundred of us are on to Ottawa by rail to bring our plight face to face with the decision-makers in Parliament. To talk to that scoundrel Bennett in person! We hope to gather numbers as we go, so that when we arrive we will be thousands, all bringing the message that action must be taken now.

It is a terrible thing for men to ask for relief for their families. Having to cash in food or clothing vouchers is almost as bad as not having food. For some, going away to work in the camps spares them that humiliation. Everyone with his hand out must bear the burden of poverty along with humiliation, and is too often made to feel less than human by relief officers. These are the things we've been talking about every night by lamplight, listing our grievances, choosing our spokesmen. We want forty cents an hour, and a five day work week. We want the right to vote in provincial and federal elections. How many Canadians even know that relief camp workers cannot? It feels good to be taking action, to be doing something. It's like an animal thing, the feeling in the camp tonight. Crouching. Waiting.

It will take us some time to get to Ottawa, but dearest Peg, I will write whenever I can. We have scheduled stops to rest and to eat, and in one of those I'll beg a stamp and send you a letter. When this is all over I hope to find enough work, perhaps in Ottawa, to come the last leg and see you. You are the light at the end of the tunnel for me, as I hope I will be for you. If I could, I'd give you everything. I'd give you an airplane, so you could fly as high as you wanted, and I'd be there when you landed, with a big bouquet of roses and the biggest kiss you ever had.

Love always,
Martin

June 6
Martin, my dear,

I am coming to Ottawa. There is nothing for me in Yarmouth. I have sold the little bit of jewellery I had to Sally, who bought it out of sympathy, but I don't care. I have enough money for the train fare. You must write me as soon as you can and tell me the date you expect to arrive in Ottawa. I'll be waiting anxiously for your letter! I will meet you at Parliament Hill, which I hear is not too far from the train station and in any case, easy enough to spot.

I'll get work with the *Ottawa Citizen*; Mr. Brougham gave me a letter of introduction, although I feel sure it was Sally's good word that got it for me. You'll be able to tutor the sons of ambassadors to foreign countries, and the daughters of politicians. We'll make a good life.

Until then, love,

Peg

June 14

Dear Peg,

I received your letter the day before we left, and I can't begin to tell you how happy I was. But first, I'll catch you up. It's been quite a trip so far. In Kamloops there wasn't nearly enough food for the lot of us, but the citizens were generous and before long we had mustered food enough for all. I was weary of being with so many men, and so after we had eaten I walked down a street and rested under a tree—and a little girl of about four years of age brought me flowers! In Golden, there was even a reception for us. It made me feel proud of what we were doing, knowing that ordinary people sympathized, were proud of us, even.

Later, two fellows turned up drunk and were told they could not continue on with us, and then even later we found out that one was an agent of the police, planted there to discredit us. But it has been a heartening experience crossing the county so far: our numbers have risen by a thousand,

and at every siding those who can't join us cheer. One woman met us with a bathtub full of beef stew! We are, for the most part, in good spirits, the act of doing something so much better than the dull resignation of before.

So it is all very exciting, although when the train went through Connaught Tunnel en route to Calgary (seven miles!) I have never felt so closed in, and wasn't at all sure I wouldn't faint with the choking stench of smoke and dust and when we came out of it, I leaned so far out the doorway, filling my lungs with mountain air, that I had to be pulled back or lose my balance and fall under the wheels.

We are now in Regina, and the train has been stopped, but we don't yet know why. Most think the Mounties are here as an escort, and that we will be on our way soon. I don't know if this will reach you, but I will make a pledge: whatever happens, I'll meet you at Parliament Hill on Dominion Day, for I will surely have arrived by then. If you aren't there, I will come every single day and look for you. I can't wait to see your sweet face in person. From here on, I believe in my heart that everything will be different.

Love forever,
Martin

PEGGY ANN MCGRATH sits on her suitcase beside the big iron gates at the entrance to Parliament Hill. She watches a bus go down Wellington Street and marvels at all the people packed inside. Everything here is larger, faster, louder. As she watches the long shadows stretch across the lawn, the Peace Tower chimes six o'clock, beginning with a singsong sixteen notes, and then six to mark the hour. Her train chugged in at 3:17; she last ate at noon. She's hungry, but she's unwilling to move, afraid she may have missed him, that perhaps he waited for her and gave up, afraid that as soon as she leaves, he'll come. It is, after all, July 3; she has arrived two full days later than she'd intended, the train having been held up twice, and for hours, by a freight car derailment farther down the track. She decides to wait until the sun dips below the buildings, and then she will walk to the address Sally has given her, some distant aunt who had suggested where a room might be available in a good house for a single young woman. At least the summer sun is still high. She sets her mouth; she will wait as long as she can.

There is no sign of the On to Ottawa men, no sign of demonstrations of any kind. She's not sure what she was expecting, but it wasn't this: the city going about its business as usual, full of its self-importance, as if nothing was going on anywhere in the world that required attention. She thinks of the lady with the bathtub full of stew, meeting the hungry men as the train ground to a halt. She thinks of the letters to the editor she typed at the *Herald*, letters of outrage at this or that, but action, some sort of action. It's important to take some sort of action. She wants to shake the people on the street, shouting: do you know what's happening? Don't you read the papers?

The air smells of automobiles and sulphur. She remembers the matchbox on the mantle at home, from the E.B. Eddy Company in Hull. Just across the river from Ottawa, her mother would say, laughing. The devil's never far away from the politicians, that's for sure.

She found a newspaper on the train and snatched it up, hoping for news, but the front page was missing. Instead, she read ads for shoes and wigs and men's suits, thinking of Martin and their new life together. If she can't get on at the

Citizen she'll get a job straight off as a waitress or a cleaner. It doesn't matter what. And she'll buy him a suit with her first earnings, something with swagger, so he can get himself a good job. But first they'll go out for a big meal, roast beef or turkey. She's heard you can get a full dinner with all the trimmings at a place on Clarence Street for twenty-five cents.

What if he doesn't recognize her? What if he sees her sitting there and walks right by, unable to recognize her from her photograph in which, after all, she had tilted her head for the photographer so as to hide her double chin, and in which the softer light removed the hard angle of her nose and cast shadows below her eyebrows making it look as if her eyelashes were long and thick instead of barely noticeable. In the photograph, her close-mouthed smile is winsome, worldly; in real life, she covers her mouth with her hand when she laughs, a reflex after years of teasing for her overlapping teeth. She crosses and uncrosses her legs in their threadbare stockings. They are nice legs, anyway. She longs to take off her stockings in the Ottawa summer heat, which shows no signs of abating with day's end. She thinks of the afternoon breeze you could always count on, drifting up Water Street from the harbour.

If there had been a demonstration, wouldn't there be some sign, still? What if they weren't yet here? Should she come back every day? For how long? Isn't it possible that she and Martin could continually miss one another for days on end? She doesn't even know what he looks like. Could she pass him again and again, and not recognize him? She feels the rise of panic, the sting of tears.

The man who approaches is tall, bearlike really, and she knows at once it's not Martin. She tucks her legs up against the suitcase and crosses her arms, looking up at him, waiting for him to speak. He has his hat in his hands and she watches it, a dun-coloured oval turning around and around.

"Miss McGrath?" he asks.

It's not Martin. It couldn't be. Could it? She stands up.

"I'm Peggy McGrath."

"Arthur Stouffer. A friend of Martin's. He asked me to come."

There is a rush of wind all around her, and then she realizes it's inside her head, her heart. A roaring. Something is wrong. "He did?"

"There was a riot. In Regina. More than a hundred arrested. There was tear gas. The police were firing into the crowd. A lot of injured."

"Martin was injured?"

He looks down, his large fingers turning his hat, moving, she thinks, like small animals. "He was killed. They'll tell you he wasn't. They'll tell you there was a policeman killed, and that's all, nobody else. They'll tell you we started it, that we were shooting, that we had to be put in our place. But it's not true. We didn't start it. And someone else *was* killed. I was there." He pauses. "I stayed with him at the curb, in all that chaos, until he died. I don't know where they took his body."

When she crumples, he's there to catch her, and then he apologizes awkwardly while she collects herself and sits back down on her suitcase. In her hands is a scarf, gold-coloured wool, blue on the ends. She didn't notice when he pressed it into her arms, and now he's handing something else to her. An envelope.

"He'd saved a little. He wanted me to give this to you. These two things."

Overhead a small plane catches the light from the descending sun, glowing. She watches it for a minute, the scarf pressed tight to her chest like a bandage to a wound.

"Can I help you find a place to go?" he asks at last. He looks back over his shoulder, and she recognizes the gesture as awkward, embarrassed. Clearly he is as lost as she is.

"No. No, thank you. I just need to sit for a moment, catch my breath. Then I'll be on my way. Please," she says, looking at him, seeing the fear in his eyes. He'd rather be anywhere but here right now. "Go."

"What will you do?" he asks, and she answers, absurdly: "I suppose I'll start writing letters." As soon as she says it, she knows it's true. There are things that must be said.

He nods. "That's good," he says.

She watches as he steps onto Wellington Street and into the throng of day's-end workers, watches while he places his hat back on his head and adjusts the peak. He doesn't look back as he breaks into a long stride heading eastward. He would run if he thought he could, she thinks. If he knew I wasn't watching. She closes her eyes for a moment, as if giving him permission. Sometimes, it's good to run.

She turns her head to look west, blue descending into gold, and as she does her eyes catch the final flash of light on wing-tip as the plane slips behind the skyline and out of sight.

SIX

ALL OF
THE COLOURS

·1944·

WHEN ARMSTRONG FIRST SAW Hirsch he was struck by how much the prisoner looked like his son, Stephen, who was overseas fighting the very Krauts Armstrong was paid to guard. At the time, Hirsch had just stepped from the mess hall and was chatting in low tones to another POW. Armstrong released the breath he had not realized he had been holding and watched for a moment. It was something in the tilt of Hirsch's head, and in the flush that spread like a peony bloom from jawline to cheek. There was that blond, blue-eyed, downy look that for Armstrong recalled Stephen as a toddler, an adolescent, and later, a soldier. Stephen had seemed impossibly young when Armstrong had seen him off at the station two years ago, so that the father had had to turn away to hide his tears from the son. And now, there was Stephen's easy smile in the strong face of this German, who himself seemed far too young to ever have been at war.

There was a short burst of laughter and the other man strolled off toward Bunkhouse 4, leaving Hirsch standing alone in the fading April light.

"Did you cut much wood today?" Armstrong asked as he approached; he assumed Hirsch would have been out with one of the crews. He spoke slowly and clearly and then waited, unsure if he was understood. Most had some English, but not all.

Hirsch was just lighting a half cigarette, and he blew out the match as he turned on one heel, in what was almost a parody of military precision, to address Armstrong. "Today? Not so much as was expected, I think. But it is hard, *ya*? Saws are dull. And we are not cutters of wood by trade." He waved the short cigarette vaguely. "Not so many cigarettes left before Red Cross comes," he said by way of explanation, in flawless if accented English. "And our mail is again held up."

Despite the accent, the timbre was so like Stephen's that Armstrong's hand shook perceptibly as he lit his own cigarette. They stood side by side smoking, watching the rosy light fade over Whitewater Lake and the Manitoba forest beyond. Around them, men drifted back to the bunkhouses, talking quietly in small groups.

Hirsch took a final pull on his stub of cigarette and squinted at the last rays of sun before turning toward Armstrong. "Do you come out on the work crews? I have seen you out there, *ya*?"

"Sometimes. Not your crew, I don't think. It's good being out of camp, out at the work site."

Hirsch laughed. "If you are not working, it's good. If you are cutting wood, not so much. But we have not the bugs yet. And that is very good."

117

Armstrong had been at Whitewater POW camp since Christmas, having volunteered to serve with the veteran guard the summer previous. He was fifty-five years old, he had run out of options, and when it became clear that the tide of prisoners being sent to Canada by the British would not abate any time soon, it was an opportunity. He was relieved, initially, to be stationed at Neys instead of the really big camps such as Medicine Hat or Lethbridge, where there had been so much trouble. But things had not gone well at Neys. Armstrong's nervous nature had put fellow guards on edge; his behaviour courted danger within a prison populace who already regarded their captors with unconcealed contempt. Consumption of contraband liquor helped when he could get it, and this as much as anything hastened his transfer. He'd been dry since then.

Whitewater, with only a few hundred prisoners, came as a welcome reassignment. Perhaps it was the recreational atmosphere, for in fact this was a National Park, now seconded for double-duty in this time of war.

In an absurd way Armstrong was grateful for this war, because if he had to say what he'd done since the last he'd have been hard-pressed to come up with much: odd jobs, short-term positions. Cynthia had left, eventually, her mother's decline in Montreal a welcome excuse, and then found reasons not to return until Armstrong had stopped asking. The wealthy Strattons had never really approved of the marriage anyway.

It's hard to come home from war, he thought, not for the first time, and he felt freshly sorry for the boys in the camp, even if they were the enemy. You couldn't ever come out of it the same as when you went in. Armstrong glanced at Hirsch again and wondered where, at this precise moment, Stephen might be.

"You are not on duty?" Hirsch asked after a bit.

"No. I'm off today, actually. They do let us off once in a while."

"And you are still here? You do not go home to your family?"

"My wife passed away a few years ago, and my son's overseas," Armstrong told him, surprising himself to be revealing so much to a POW, but surprised more at the loneliness that crept into his voice. "There's a card game later," he added, masking it.

Footsteps from behind, and then Block's voice, sharp. "Hirsch! Don't you have something to do? Write a letter to your *Führer* or something?"

Armstrong turned to catch the disapproving look on Block's face. Must've been a formidable force at Ypres, Armstrong thought. Block had seen serious action in the Great War and lived to brag about it; others, such as McGrath, joining them now, were of gentler stock; McGrath himself had been a POW in the Great War, and although he didn't like to talk about it, his feelings were evident in his empathy for the prisoners. Armstrong, whose first scuffle in the European Theatre had led to the injury that put him behind a desk for the remainder, kept quiet when talk arose. Now, Block waited impatiently as Hirsch took a final drag, smiled laconically at Armstrong, and ambled towards Bunkhouse 5.

Block snorted, then tossed a look at Armstrong. "Bloody Krauts. Act like they run the place."

McGrath grunted. "Three more didn't show up for roll call this morning. Col. Trevaine was close to calling a search."

"But they came back," said Armstrong, a statement. He didn't know, but it was a good guess; they always did.

"About ten hundred hours. They just hiked in and went straight to work crew. Came back with the boys for lunch."

Block ground his cigarette under his heel. "Trevaine's too lax. It's a joke."

"Aw, c'mon, Sid," McGrath said. "Where are they going to go? And what are we really going to do to keep 'em here, with no fence and no tower?"

"There's a war on, for Chrissakes." He looked pointedly at Armstrong and nodded in the direction Hirsch had gone. "Who's he, one of your new bosom buddies? You gonna play cards with your new friends, or with us?"

"I'll see you later," Armstrong addressed McGrath. He headed for his quarters through the gathering dusk, left leg just a little slower than the right.

THAT'S WHERE IT began. After a while, Hirsch didn't really look like Stephen anymore—clearly he was older, his face a little rounder—but by then the friendship had taken on an easy camaraderie, despite the almost thirty years between them, never mind the war itself, and despite the fact that when his shift was over Armstrong could go home if he wanted to, and Hirsch could not. Block didn't like Hirsch, and made no secret of it. Armstrong could not be sure why Hirsch, exactly, except that Hirsch was everything Block was not: charming, intelligent. It became worse when Hirsch was elected Camp Spokesman from within the prisoner ranks.

"Arrogant bastard," Block said one evening as he dealt a fresh hand to the table. Armstrong sat to his right, with Carruthers and McGrath across.

"You wait: they'll be wanting their own copy of the Geneva Convention—in *German. And* more privileges. It's already a bloody holiday camp."

And so it was, in a way. The food was decent, the work not particularly hard, and as the war went on crews cutting firewood were often left to police themselves, a few trusted officers responsible for a crew working their paced way through a stand of fire-damaged poplar. The YMCA and the Red Cross ensured that educational and cultural opportunities were present, and the recruitment of volunteers for the work camp from the big camp at Medicine Hat included cooks, clerks, tradesmen, doctor and dentist, and in this way almost all needs were satisfied, save a notable lack of women.

For the most part, the camp was a welcome alternative to combat, and nobody wanted to risk jail time for a failed escape. In any case it would be hard to get very far with a big red circle on your back, and not just stitched onto the shirt, either; the cloth was cut out and the patch inserted, so if you didn't have a two-foot bull's-eye between your shoulder blades, a hole in your shirt the size of a dartboard would surely attract attention. But mainly, there was just nowhere to go. In the summer, blackflies and mosquitoes; in the winter, cold. And miles and miles of nothing. There were times when every resident of Whitewater felt something of a prisoner, regardless of the uniform he wore.

Now, McGrath spread his hand out and whistled under his breath. "There's a bunch haven't got mail for ages. Dunno if it's the censors or what," he offered.

"Gah," said Block. "You guys ready to roll here or what?"

"Who's on lookout tonight?" Carruthers asked, laying down a ten of hearts.

"Peabody," McGrath offered, laying down the jack. "Horgan. Carter."

Block played a king. "Good thing there's nowhere to go, then."

"Nowhere to go," Armstrong agreed, setting down the six of hearts, the highest card in his hand.

"My trick," said Block.

Armstrong put his cards down and pushed his chair back. "You know what?" he said. "I'm knackered. Next time, okay?"

"Sore loser," Armstrong heard Block mutter as he closed the door.

IN HIS BUNK, Armstrong picked up the letter he'd been crafting to Stephen for the past week. Mail pickup was Tuesday; he really needed to get something down, and yet his days seemed identical. But perhaps to Stephen, some mention of the day-to-day would be a comfort, wherever he was. He took the pages out from inside his leather writing folder and scanned what he had written.

> Son,
>
> I hope this finds you safe and out of the line of fire. It's been some weeks since I've received a letter from you, and of course that is always cause for concern. In your last letter, you were waiting for your orders, and relatively comfortable. That dance sounded like great fun. I'm sure your observations of young women being a little "freer" during wartime are not so far from the truth, although I am sure in your conduct you remained the gentleman that your mother raised you to be, God rest her soul.
>
> I am grateful to be a member of the Veteran's Guard, and yet I feel almost unpatriotic when I say that a little excitement would not be such a bad thing. The days are relentlessly the same for the Guard, and I daresay the prisoners have found more innovative ways to amuse themselves. Sometimes there is a soccer game, or ping-pong, and cards, of course. Last winter the hockey became quite skilled despite the fact that there are only 19 pairs of skates for a

population of more than 400. Now with spring, I hear base-ball will start, inmates against staff.

There's a blacksmith shop, where some of the men are learning the craft and turning out decorative things such as hooks and fire pokers and the like. Many are excellent craftsmen, carving some of the animals they see when they are out cutting wood, and they seem endlessly fascinated with our wildlife. Not so fascinated with the pigs we are rais-ing, and yet there are a few who tend to them as if they were children, much to the amusement of others. Perhaps they miss their own.

And we have music, with a hodgepodge of instruments from the YMCA, and a rather good baritone choir. Sometimes the prisoners put on a play, with men playing women's roles, of course. Which is the other thing these young men must very much miss.

As for me, I miss you, Stephen, and I miss your mother still.

This was as far as Armstrong had got, and as he read his words, he felt the weighty impossibility of continuing, every cheerful word sure to be exposed for the lie it was. He had reached the bottom of the page with the words *I miss your mother still*; starkly honest, it was clear he could not leave his letter there.

For me, he continued, *the day is structured around roll calls and meals, and if it is my duty to accompany the men to the work site, and it is a fine day and not raining, the forest lifts everyone's spirits. On patrol we walk the perimeter of our camp, and on inspection there is sometimes the thrill of dis-covery when we find some wire beneath a mattress, a radio receiver in the works, foiled by us.*

Armstrong stopped there. Much of this would not get past the censors. It wouldn't do for word to get out about how relaxed things were at Whitewater, and anyone reading it would have no concept of the futility of barbed wire and hard rules in a place such as this. Instead, he got a fresh sheet and wrote:

> *Of course, it is no holiday camp, as these prisoners well know. Last year, they cut more than 33,000 cords of firewood for destinations from Dauphin to Winnipeg—not as much as was hoped, but something to improve upon. With better discipline, we hope to see 50,000 cords this summer. Three-quarters of a cord per man per day is what Wartime Housing wants; we're not there yet, but these men are relatively new to the job.*

Armstrong imagined the censor reading this last paragraph and felt reasonably confident it would make it to Stephen unscathed. He closed the letter with an expression of hope that the next mail delivery would include a missive from Stephen, and that his son was keeping as safe and well as could be expected.

IT WAS A sunny Sunday in May when Armstrong agreed to accompany a group of men who wanted to hike up the mountain. Maybe it was the grin Hirsch gave him, the easy hand on his shoulder. Col. Trevaine had approved it, hoping to keep morale up, the better to encourage increased firewood production, the need for firewood pressing with so many men overseas. It was unusual for the veteran guard to accompany the prisoners on such an outing, the job more often left to civilian guards. Armstrong wondered what magic Hirsch had worked on the camp commandant to get approval for what was clearly the guard of his choice, and Armstrong felt complimented.

"You need the exercise, no?" Hirsch laughed, nodding towards Armstrong's waistline, and Armstrong found himself grinning back. Hirsch leaned in, still smiling. "Unless you think it would be too hard for you, my friend. Your leg?"

"It won't slow me down," Armstrong told him.

"No," Hirsch said. "You are still a young man. We'll go then. When?"

Armstrong found himself nodding, distracted. It hadn't occurred to him he might be seen as old. "After mail call," he said.

Armstrong was waiting in the mess hall with a week-old newspaper when Weiler approached with a letter. Around him, cookhouse staff were cleaning up; the midday meal was over. Weiler, originally at the camp as a conscientious objector due to his Mennonite background, had been part of the work detail to build the camp, and when the German Afrika Korps arrived he'd slipped into cookhouse duty, a reasonable way, he said, to pass a war. He held the letter out, the others to be delivered tucked into the crook of his arm.

Armstrong looked up into Weiler's affable face, long and narrow like the horses he often spoke of from his Manitoba homestead. Unable to manage it with the sons gone and no men to work, Weiler's parents had drifted into melancholy before fire took what was left, including their tenuous lives. Weiler had told Armstrong this on night duty, Armstrong trying to stay awake and Weiler unable to sleep. Now he held onto the letter with both hands, unwilling to tear it open in another's presence, but Weiler had moved on into the kitchen. When he came back ten minutes later, Armstrong was still there, the pages in front of him curling like onion skin.

Armstrong picked up a page and set it down again. "It took a month to get here. Bloody censors," he said. "He could be anywhere by now." He waved the paper. It looked like ticker tape.

Weiler sat down across from him, folding his long legs under the chair legs and resting his elbows on the table, hands folded down between them like a praying mantis. "I'm sorry, Charlie," he said. "Must be tough."

All at once, anger seized him. "What would *you* know about it?" Armstrong snarled.

Weiler recoiled, surprised. "I—"

The anger left Armstrong as quickly as it had come. "I'm sorry," he said. There was no point, and there was nothing to dislike about Weiler beyond the fact that he wasn't overseas, as Stephen was.

"We're all sorry," said Weiler.

LATER, HALFWAY UP the steep slope, Armstrong felt the familiar ache begin in his left leg. Hirsch was striding ahead at the front of the column of eight men who had been introduced in turn when the group had rendezvoused at the cookhouse. Only two were familiar to Armstrong, those being, a short, square man named Koertig and another fairly young officer, Roehm. Armstrong remembered Roehm for his rendition of St. Nicholas at the prisoner's pageant the previous Christmas, and it occurred to him then, as he struggled to keep up, that Hirsch had also been in the play, dressed as a fox. The play recalled the German children's story of animals receiving the gift of speech at Christmastime.

Hirsch called a halt, and Armstrong joined the group as they reached a rocky clearing. Under the shade of the pines, snow patches could still be seen, but here the sun shone warm with the promise of summer. The prisoners found spots on which to sit, setting aside the walking sticks they'd cut at the outset like eager alpinists on a holiday outing. Armstrong wished he had done the same for his leg's sake, but in any case he had a regulation rifle to carry. He stretched the offending leg out in front of him, wincing. Hirsch came over and as he plunked himself down in an agile, youthful manner, Armstrong recalled the pageant again.

"You were a convincing fox at Christmas," he told Hirsch, who laughed.

"If only I could find one to join my zoo."

"Your what?"

"You haven't seen? *Ya*, you have not been here so long, and I don't think you have been assigned to the inspections. A few of us, we keep some pets. To pass the time. Small things: I have a mouse and a squirrel—the tree kind, and also the ground kind. What do you call them?"

"Gophers," said Armstrong, tucking his leg back under him. "Keep them in what?"

Hirsch tilted his head back to catch the full force of the spring sunshine. Around them was birdsong, and the smell of earth and growing things. He spoke with his eyes closed. "Yes. Since we began just two months past it has been your colleague, Sergeant McGrath, *ya*? who is doing the inspections. He brought us an animal called a—" Hirsch searched for the word, "—packrat." He brought his head down and scratched his short hair with both hands, then looked at Armstrong. "In cages," he said, finally. "We keep our pets in cages that we make in the shop. There is a word for that. In German, we say *ironisch*."

127

It wasn't a stretch to guess. "Ironic? Yes, I guess it is," Armstrong offered, surprised he hadn't heard about Hirsch's zoo. It wasn't that big a camp, after all. "No harm in it, though."

"It is permitted. And for us, it is interesting. There are some different animals here than in Germany. Here, it is wilderness! Out there," he spread his arms to indicate the forest around them, "they get eaten, maybe." There was a pause. "Like us. No one is happy to be locked up, but nobody is unhappy not to be fighting. It is not freedom, *ya*? But it is perhaps better than the alternative."

Armstrong thought about the miles of forest around them, imagined it full of soldiers, of noise, of the stink and sounds of battle. The misery.

"I would like to find a little dog. Wild dog. I forget the name," Hirsch was saying.

"Coyote?"

"Yes."

Hirsch stood up. "Shall we continue?" He looked at Armstrong, who would have preferred a longer rest for his leg. Armstrong rose as well, but it was awkward, far from Hirsch's fluid movements.

"If you like, I will run the men to the lookout point and then meet back here for you to accompany us back," Hirsch said. "It must be boring for you, if you have climbed this mountain before. You are from here, *ya*?"

"*Ya*—I mean, yes, I am. I grew up here, and after the war I brought my wife back. We raised our son here."

"Your son is also a soldier. You told me when we met first time, at the mess hall."

"Yes, a soldier. A private."

Overhead, the kew of a hawk hunting some small prey. Around them men were standing, screwing the lids back on canteens, picking up walking sticks, preparing to continue. Armstrong thought of the terrain, an hour of solid, rocky, uphill trail. "I got a letter at mail call." He patted his breast pocket. "I think I'll just sit here and read it again."

Hirsch nodded. Armstrong watched as the men found the path again and began the ascent. He did not take the letter from his pocket. There was nothing in it to read. Instead, Armstrong napped in the warm sunshine in the clearing, and after he awoke passed the time by entertaining thoughts of returning to camp alone, his charges vanished into the woods. He rehearsed explanations, imagining a situation in which he would crack himself over the head with something to make it look as if he'd been overpowered, perhaps lose his rifle in the underbrush. Although he hadn't really expected an escape, he was nonetheless relieved when he heard a cheerful whistling and saw Hirsch emerge from the trees. It struck Armstrong as odd that Hirsch had come from a different direction than the path he had ascended some two hours earlier, and that Hirsch was out of breath and sweating, as if he hadn't been descending the mountain, but rather climbing it. A shortcut? A moment later the remainder of the men appeared above them on the trail, and Armstrong, looking at his watch, managed an impatient tone and told them to get a move on.

Hirsch leaned in. "*Ach.* You're worried about that Jew? Block?"

Armstrong looked sharply at Hirsch, but his face betrayed no venom. "Block? He's not Jewish," he said, affronted, then felt his affront oddly misplaced, and then, muddled and unsure of what to say next, found himself stuttering: "and anyway, it's getting late."

"*Ya*, his name perhaps not—" Hirsch didn't finish his sentence. Instead, he turned to the men who had been talking among themselves. "*Schnell*!" he said, grinning. "Dinner is waiting."

IT WAS A week later that Hirsch didn't turn up for morning roll call. Armstrong was positioned at the rear of the assembled men while the names were called in bunkhouse order. Roehm, standing ahead and to the right of Armstrong, startled when the guard touched his arm, but fell out.

"I know. He is usually back by now," Roehm told Armstrong when asked about Hirsch.

"Back? Back from where?"

Roehm leaned forward. "He has a girl," he whispered.

Armstrong didn't have time to ask more. Roll call had begun. When Hirsch's name was called, Roehm called "here!" and Armstrong said nothing.

When Armstrong thought about it, it wasn't such a stretch. Several of the more trusted prisoners had access to trucks for deliveries and pickups in town. And last fall, local farmers had picked up some hundred men to assist with the harvest. With so many men away fighting, the help was certainly needed—in fact, the camp itself would buy many of the potatoes and squash. Some farm families virtually adopted the prisoners, treating them as family, and in return the men worked hard. Had Hirsch been among them? Armstrong could imagine a farmer's daughter smitten with Hirsch's blond good looks. Armstrong resolved to ask Hirsch about it the next time he had an opportunity, the way he'd ask Stephen about a love interest—ribbing him a little—had times been different. As for saying something to Col. Trevaine, he saw no point; the commandant would simply wait 'til evening roll call, and by then Hirsch would be back. Block certainly didn't need to know.

Later that evening Armstrong, coming off patrol, decided to drop in for an unscheduled visit to Bunkhouse 5.

"Ho ho!" Hirsch said, looking up from his bunk where he had been sitting, a deck of cards in his hand and a spread of solitaire before him. Had there been a surreptitious movement? Armstrong couldn't be sure. "Have you come to see our small zoo? Or maybe you have come to see our fine handicrafts," he waved his hand to indicate a ledge above a row of coathooks on which sat the handiwork of his bunkmates: animal carvings, several ships in bottles, an elaborate whirligig. Most guards traded cigarettes and the spoils of packages from home for some of these prizes. "Rudi, here, is the best at putting the boats in the bottles." He nodded towards Koertig, who was reading a well-creased letter. "Wilhelm prefers the real boats. It is he who makes the dugout canoes. You have seen them, down at the water?"

"It smells like hooch," Armstrong said. He hadn't meant to say it; it was what he'd been thinking, and what he'd blurted.

The men, who had been engaged in various pastimes— cards, wood-carving, letter-writing—looked up as one. There was silence, save for the small rustling movements coming from one of the makeshift cages in the corner. Armstrong could smell sweat, and wood shavings, a stench of something he recognized as packrat—he looked again towards the cages, at least a half-dozen, and—there it was again. Alcohol. He looked at Hirsch.

"Ah, you miss nothing, my friend. We just poured from a new batch. You like?"

After a beat, "Why don't you show me your zoo," Armstrong said.

IF THE FRIENDSHIP was not cemented before, it was cemented that evening, when Hirsch, leaving the bunkhouse a few minutes behind Armstrong, found the guard sitting by the lake on the end of one of the overturned dugout canoes. There was still a bit of colour to the sky, and the air smelled of water and pine and the distant smell of skunk. Hirsch approached with enough noise so Armstrong would know he was coming.

"Now, that is not an animal I would like to have," Hirsch said, sniffing the air as he settled himself on the canoe beside Armstrong's. He had a jar and two tin cups, and he handed one to Armstrong who took it and held it against his knee. Hirsch filled it.

"No," Armstrong said. "I'd stay away from porkies, too."

"Porkies?"

"Porcupines."

"Ah! Yes. One fellow did try to get one. It was before you came. He saw it in a tree and climbed up with a sack. Came down looking like the—what is it called again? Porcupine. Doktor Schroeder spent most of the day getting out the sticks."

"Quills."

"Yes."

Armstrong was laughing quietly. The alcohol tasted strong, and a little sweet. He couldn't tell its true colour in the waning light, but it tasted—brown. "What's in this?"

"Raisins. Some other things, but raisins, mostly. We tried potatoes, but raisins are better. Sugar, when we can get it."

They sat for a while, the darkness drawing around them. Armstrong slapped a hand gently against the canoe. "I was looking at this, before. Nice craftsmanship."

"Yes! Like the Indians. In Germany we are—*fasziniert*—fascinted?"

132

"Fascinated."

"Fascinated by the wilderness of Canada, by the wild animals—and the wild Indians! This is why, partly, many of us volunteered to come and work here. We take the canoes out to fish—it's good to have fish to cook—and we take the canoes over to that island, and there we pretend for a time we have no camp, no wood to cut. No war."

"Is that why?"

Hirsch looked at Armstrong quizzically.

"Why you volunteered to come here? You came from Lethbridge?" Armstrong drained his cup, and Hirsch refilled it from the jar.

"Medicine Hat. Things there were—" Hirsch took a drink and coughed. "How is your leg these days?" he asked.

"I heard there are Gestapo at Medicine Hat," Armstrong offered. "Organizing within the camp."

"Ah, these things are often exaggerated." Hirsch waved his hand dismissively. "But I asked you about your leg."

Armstrong realized he could not entirely feel his leg. And on the heels of that realization, he saw clearly the degree to which he had been compromised. The alcohol in his stomach turned acid. Who was this German, really? What were his motives?

"What about you? Where did you fit in the camp—at Medicine Hat?" he asked Hirsch abruptly. He went to stand, but whether it was the loose beach pebbles or his war injury, he found he could not quite get his legs under him. His head swam. He turned to find Hirsch's eyes on him, their whites glinting in the light from the waxing moon just rising over the trees.

"It is not good to ask about politics in these times," said Hirsch finally, firmly. "Only I will say that we will win the war. It is what we all know, in Medicine Hat, or here, it is the same."

Armstrong's thoughts whirled against the fog of his lost sobriety, and he struggled to focus.

"How long have you been here?" Hirsch asked.

"What?"

"Your father, your father before him, and so on. How long?"

"I can trace one side of my family to Ireland. The Murphy side emigrated in the 1840s. The other side, English, a little bit later."

"A hundred years! Pppht. Nothing." Hirsch leaned in, and Armstrong saw with alarm a new intensity in Hirsch's eyes. "My people have been in Germany five hundred years. More. You are just children here. This is one reason we will win."

As Armstrong tried to grasp Hirsch's meaning, around them rose, like a sudden tide, the unearthly yipping of coyotes. Hirsch laughed, breaking the tension. "Do you hear? They are singing. *That* is the sound of wilderness."

Armstrong, listening to the eerie, undulating sound, felt like crying rather than laughing. He saw his cup had been refilled, and he took a drink from it and coughed. The moment, whatever it was, had passed.

"And you?" Hirsch asked. "Why did you volunteer to be here?"

Over the next hour, any misgivings drowned beneath a warm and fuzzy lake of contraband liquor, Armstrong told him: about his war, the relentless noise and fear, about surviving with a shrapnel wound while his buddy died in pieces, about returning to Cynthia a changed man. About the nightmares, the suffocating melancholy. The hopes that a child would change things, and how it did, for a while. But every job ended badly. There was always the day when he could not bring himself to perform the simplest task, as if opening his mouth to speak was equivalent to lifting a building one-handed. Sometimes, he could not even leave his house.

"There were times I would go as much as a year without any problem," he told Hirsch. "And then something would happen, and it would start. Once, it was the sight of ketchup spilled across a white tablecloth." He put his hands over his face and drew them downwards, feeling the numbness from the alcohol. "I volunteered because I thought that the duties would be straightforward. In the forces, you just follow orders. And because Stephen was overseas, and I had to do something. But they sent me to Neys, first. Where the Black Nazis get sent. I—it was too much."

"Black Nazis? I don't understand."

Armstrong looked at Hirsch, and saw Stephen, and was momentarily confused. And then he was back. It didn't matter. He knew, of course, that Hirsch was the enemy, but he didn't care: it felt good to talk.

"There are three levels that have been identified: black, grey, and white. Neys is a real camp for Black Nazis: towers, barbed wire, Bren guns." Armstrong paused and brought the cup to his lips. "I had some problems, there. But it was when my nightmares came back that I was transferred. They said it was bad for morale. So they sent me here."

Hirsch looked sympathetic, his face washed in moonlight. "You are better now?"

"Yes." He laughed. "For the most part. If I can stand, that is."

They walked together back to camp through the scrubby brush, falling into one another a little, trying not to laugh. Miraculously, they were unseen. As they approached the back of Bunkhouse 5, Hirsch reached for the cup that Armstrong still held, forgotten.

"There is more than black and white and grey," Hirsch said. "There are many colours. And of all the colours, you, my friend, I think you are green."

And with that, Armstrong turned towards a wild rose bush and threw up.

AS SUMMER TURNED to fall, Armstrong saw Hirsch on several other occasions. Once he found Hirsch, reassigned to the barn as penalty for a missed roll call, mucking out stalls, and this led to talk and a discovery of a shared love for horses. There were more hikes; sometimes Hirsch slipped away, sometimes not. Once, when Armstrong's leg became particularly painful, Hirsch piggybacked him down the last half-mile while behind him Roehm carried Armstrong's loaded rifle. Just before camp, Armstrong regained his legs and his rifle, complicit grins all around. He trusted these men, he realized.

It was the next evening, at roll call, that everything changed. Block was in charge. The men assembled in rows in the yard, Block at the front with a civilian guard alongside. It had been a warm day for late September, and the men who had been out cutting were tired in a happy, relaxed way, jostling and joking with one another. Armstrong was stationed at the west side of the group. Probably he thought, they'll be happy to get roll call over with and go relax; they've earned it. The cut that day had averaged to just over a half-cord each, the best so far. Armstrong reflected that as a young man working one summer for the railway he'd felt the same after a good, productive day of physical exertion: pleasantly tired, reasonably fed, at ease.

At the front, Block paced. "Atten*tion!*" His voice was knife-edged. Walking up and down the rows, Block stood in front of each man in turn until the prisoner assumed the rigid stance expected. No prisoner was found acceptable; it was agonizingly slow. On top of that, it was beginning to rain, a fine, cold drizzle. Armstrong could feel the tension thicken like ice on the lake.

Block got to Hirsch. "Straighten up, prisoner!" he barked. Around them there was no movement, not an intake of breath nor an exhalation.

"I am straight," Hirsch told him, stiff-backed, hands at sides, eyes forward. "But you, sir, are crooked."

Everyone in the front row looked at Block. There were a few suppressed snorts, and then laughter erupted. The men in the further rows strained to see. By the time Armstrong realized that Block had, in fact, mis-buttoned his uniform, the hilarity was universal.

"Take over, Carter," Block hissed to the civilian guard beside him, who was, himself, trying not to laugh. Block glared at Hirsch. "I'll deal with you later," he muttered.

As Carter called roll, getting through the names as quickly as possible so as to release the men before pandemonium ensued, Armstrong caught Roehm's eye from his position at the west edge of the assembly. Roehm winked. They both knew that the incident would not be reported.

TWO WEEKS LATER Armstrong encountered Hirsch in the infirmary. With eight fresh stitches from a slipped axe, Hirsch was delighted to be off work for a few days and allowed to rest up for the rest of the afternoon, and said as much. Armstrong had had another bad night, and as a result, was suffering the vice-grip of a headache and came in looking for aspirin. Finding the doctor away and Hirsch alone on a cot with a book of German verse, he stayed, stretching out on the next cot and closing his eyes. The pillow was cool against the back of Armstrong's skull, and he gratefully fell into the ease of conversation to which they had become accustomed. Soon, talk turned to Hirsch's girl.

"She is very sweet," Hirsch told Armstrong. "Very loving. I think that after the war is over I will ask her to come home with me." Hirsch lay in his underwear, fresh bandage around his calf, smoking. The flat afternoon light was filtered through windows that had likely not been cleaned since the camp was erected. The doctor, Armstrong heard, was over at the far cut block where a man had been struck by a falling tree. There had been too many accidents, lately.

"How did you ever meet her?"

"At a dance. A few of us go to a dairy farm just at the park's border, where we dug potatoes last fall, ya? He's a good man, this farmer, his name is Bourek—a Yugoslav. He plays the violin—you call it fiddle. He plays for dances. He takes us in his truck."

"Aren't you recognized?"

"No, no, he gives us clothes."

Armstrong considered this. "Why?"

"There are not so many men, I think, for the girls to dance with. Sometimes we bring rations, things we get in our packages from home and even from the stores here." Armstrong raised his eyebrows but let it go; Hirsch continued. "And besides, we are friends. Like you and I are friends."

Armstrong felt a welling in his heart. There are not so many friends, he thought, for a lonely ex-soldier to talk to. "What's her name?" he asked.

"Josephine." Hirsch smiled and rolled his eyes skyward, sighing. "We are too many men in one place," he said. "We think about girls, we talk about girls, we dream about girls. You? What do you think about?"

Armstrong wished that girls were what he dreamt about. The nightmares were back; he'd been waking in sweats but, so far as he knew, had not called out. He'd lie there in the dark, heart pounding, surrounded by the snores of his fellow guards.

"I think about my wife sometimes," he said. "I'm not a young man. These things change. And," he turned his head to the afternoon light, now waning, "I think about my son. His name is Stephen."

"That is me."

"Pardon?"

"Stefan. My name is Stefan."

Armstrong had never asked.

FALL ADVANCED, THE mornings chilly. It was hard to get the prisoners going; production had fallen to a quarter-cord per man per day. The civilian guard didn't seem to care, and there had been reports of prisoners and guards alike socializing over cards together in town, or at dances. If a prisoner missed roll call, the excuse was invariably that he had gone for a walk and become disoriented, lost; he'd have a story about a night spent in a barn or haystack, heading back at first light like a good prisoner.

Block, apparently with Col. Trevaine's blessing, responded one evening with a raid on neighbouring farms an hour after evening roll call was over, giving prisoners and their keepers time to get the evening's social event underway. As a result, four prisoners spent twenty-one days in detention, and the guards were docked pay. Hirsch was not among them, but

Koertig was. Hirsch was furious, and he was not alone. There was a three-day strike, and when the men finally agreed to return to work, production had clearly dropped. Then, privileges were reduced; the entertainment room adjacent to the dining hall was closed except for Saturday afternoons. Even meals appeared smaller.

"Things are changing around here," Block told Armstrong and McGrath while they waited for Carruthers at the card table a few days after the raid. "There'll be no more of this bullshit. Heads are gonna roll. We're at war, goddamn it."

The prisoners responded with work to rule, the guards with increased inspections. Block appeared gleeful with every confiscation of equipment or contraband, and Armstrong worried for his own supply. There was no clear solution in sight, the tension palpable. Guards doubled up for perimeter duty; prisoners fell silent when camp personnel approached. In the midst of this Armstrong felt himself falling, as if at the crumbling edge of something high, above an abyss he couldn't fathom.

One evening Hirsch saw in the shake in Armstrong's hands the hard edge of a sleepless night and offered to fill his canteen.

"It is a bad time, *ya*?" he said. They were behind the barn, the smell of pigs and manure mingling with the smell of dry leaves and dust. "It becomes harder to know who your friends are."

Armstrong took a long drink and felt the relief of it flood his body. "What do you mean?"

"Not everything is black and white." Hirsch slipped the bottle back into his jacket and walked away.

ONE EVENING, AFTER a bad night and a rough day, Armstrong caught Hirsch's eye following a long and particularly onerous, somewhat humiliating roll call and afterwards caught up with Hirsch behind the commissary store.

"We are without supplies," Hirsch told Armstrong without preamble.

"Pardon?"

"You think there's just a tap we turn on? It comes out, whoosh, straight from the pipes and into your cup?"

Armstrong was taken aback at the tone. "What do you need?"

"You get us some sugar. One pound. No, two pounds."

"That's a lot of sugar! Have you noticed there's a war on?"

"Yes. I have noticed." Hirsch leaned closer, his face inches from Armstrong's, and Armstrong could see the twitch in Hirsch's jaw. He looked nothing like Stephen, and Armstrong wondered how he had ever imagined any similarity between this prisoner and his son.

"Yes, there is a war on," Hirsch hissed. "And when we win the war, we will have all the sugar we want." He stepped back and crossed his arms. "Meanwhile, this is what you must do." The affable, smooth-talker was gone. "Because you want the liquor, *ya*? And you keep your friend Block away from me."

"He's not my friend."

"Just keep him away. I meet you here tomorrow night."

IT WAS MCGRATH who told Armstrong that Block had been harassing Hirsch relentlessly. They were lingering in the mess hall after supper, neither on duty for another hour. Armstrong, sleepwalking through the day after a night of terrors, most often drunk these days when not on duty, hadn't noticed, but didn't say so.

"He's on him all the time, watching," McGrath said, "wearing him down." He tilted backward in his metal chair and shook his head. The cook staff was in the kitchen; they were alone in the big hall, but McGrath kept his voice down none-theless. "Today, Block even told him he can't keep his animals. His gophers and such."

"What? Col. Trevaine allowed it. Said it's good for morale. He hasn't changed the rules about that."

"I know. But Hirsch doesn't." He paused. "You know how he sneaks out of camp pretty regular. I don't think he's been able to for a couple of weeks—more, maybe. You haven't noticed? He hasn't said anything? I know you two are friends."

"You do?" Armstrong's mind was scrambling. He *hadn't* seen Hirsch lately. It had been Koertig who made deliveries the last two times.

"Everyone does, Charlie. Block does. I'd watch my back if I were you."

"What could Block have on me?"

McGrath made a motion, cup to lips, and raised his eye-brows. "Everyone does it," he said. "Mostly, nobody cares. But Block's got something against Hirsch, and he knows you two are chummy. So by extension—"

"What's he got against Hirsch? I mean, besides that inci-dent with the buttons. It can't be just that he sneaks out every so often; half the camp does. And in any case, what's he got against me?"

"You're friends with a Black Kraut. That's enough."

"He's *not*."

"Yes. Yes, he is."

It was Block who had dug up Hirsch's past, McGrath explained, thanks to a friend in the right place in Ottawa. He'd found more than he'd even hoped for. Hirsch was as black a Nazi as they came, working swiftly up the ranks in the Afrika Korps and heading for promotion to Hitler's elite

before his capture and imprisonment at El Alamien. He had
been sent by the Medicine Hat Gestapo. Befriending guards
was one part of a larger strategy.

"Strategy for what?" Armstrong was genuinely perplexed.
McGrath didn't answer directly.

"When he played a fox in the Christmas production?"
McGrath leaned forward. "It was a reference to Desert Fox.
Rommel. That whole play was a metaphor—and a message."

Armstrong recalled the lighthearted production, remembered the warmth he felt sure was shared by prisoners and
guards alike that first Christmas he had been at the camp, so
relieved to have Camp Neys behind him. It had felt almost
like family. For a full hour—more—he had thought of neither Cynthia nor Stephen.

"I don't believe it," he said. He wished he had a drink.

"Block has evidence. He's ready to take Hirsch out."

Weiler came into the hall and began clearing a few stray
dishes. Armstrong rose to leave, but McGrath placed a hand
on his arm and leaned in.

"One more thing. Hirsch's girl? The father called Trevaine.
Peabody was in there waiting to ask for leave, and he heard.
I guess she's got a German bun in the oven."

DEAR STEPHEN, ARMSTRONG wrote that evening. He was in his
upper bunk in the quarters he shared with McGrath, Carruthers,
and Horgan, the squat black stove in the middle of the room
holding back the chill of the fall night. The letters were spi-
dery on the page, and he gripped the pencil hard to keep
steady. He could not have managed a pen. *Do you remember
the camping trip we took when you were ten? I taught you
how to gut a fish. I remember how proud I was at how quickly
you learned. What a feast we had that first night, and then*

143

later you had a bellyache. We lay on the beach and looked at
the stars and I showed you Cassiopeia and Orion. Later, there
were coyotes, and I told you not to be afraid. They were just
talking to each other, like you and me.

Sometimes I think that when you were ten was the last
time I knew anything. I am fifty-five years old, and I don't
even know where you are.

Abruptly, Armstrong crumpled the letter and fed it to the
fire. McGrath looked up briefly, but he was lost in his own
letter. It was after ten o'clock. Armstrong rolled a cigarette
and stepped out into the night air.

There were no lights on in the mess hall. It took only a
moment to slip in using the spare key he'd borrowed from
Weiler earlier that day, on pretext of need, to make himself
some warm milk on sleepless nights. Weiler was always a
sympathetic ear. It took a moment more to locate, in the
dark with just the compound lights shining dimly through
the window, the store of dry goods in the large cupboard at
the back, and the sugar. Civilians under wartime rationing
would be rightfully outraged to see what the camps sometimes had. If he was caught there would be no hiding two
pounds of sugar. Armstrong was thankful that there was no
moon, making it easier to keep to the shadows where buildings blocked the lights.

Approaching the store, he would not have noticed the
silhouette that was Hirsch had he not been looking for it.
Hirsch took the sugar without comment, and Armstrong let
it go. We are all sliding, he thought. This war has gone on
too long. He wished, again, for a drink.

As if sensing Armstrong's need, Hirsch, softening, put a
hand on his shoulder. "We will have a batch ready soon. We
were not able to finish today. We are being watched; there is

nothing to be done. Perhaps tomorrow. Perhaps next day."
He shrugged. "It is not a good time."

Armstrong tried to see Hirsch's face, but the darkness
obscured his expression. A thought occurred to him. "You
wouldn't—"

Hirsch shrugged again. "It will all be over soon. We will
win, and I will go home."

"I wouldn't be so sure," Armstrong told him. "Your
Rommel—"

"Lies." He shifted the bag to his left arm. "There is always
more to the story. And we will ultimately win."

Armstrong, unsure of what to say, watched as Hirsch
slipped around the building's side, the bag of sugar tucked
neatly under his arm.

THAT NIGHT, AND the next day, were bad for Armstrong. He had
little sleep, and sleep, when it came, was coloured by his own
private war. Two more letters he began to Stephen were abandoned. When the mail arrived and there was still nothing,
Armstrong knew he would have settled happily for all of two
words in his son's handwriting to have made it past the censor.

He saw Hirsch twice during the day, at supper and again
as the men came back from the woodlot, but Hirsch gave him
no sign, and Armstrong felt a rising desperation. After roll
call, Armstrong mustered his courage and strode between the
bunkhouses as if on a mission of some assigned purpose,
keeping an eye out for Block, and when he was alongside
Bunkhouse 5, slipped quickly inside, surprising Roehm.

"He is not here," Roehm told him. "He has gone to see his
Josephine."

He would not be back that night.

"We have nothing," Roehm said. "Nothing has been possible."

Armstrong's hands began to shake involuntarily, and he stilled them in his pockets as he walked back to the staff house, head swimming.

AT MORNING ROLL call, Hirsch was not there. Neither was Block.

"Block's really been stirring things up, and now Ottawa's taking notice," McGrath told Armstrong. "Trevaine's in a corner. He sent out a search party early this morning. RCMP, too. It's a manhunt."

Armstrong looked across the camp in the direction of Dauphin. Of course, Hirsch could be anywhere. He thought of Josephine.

"They went to that girl's farm first," McGrath said, as if reading Armstrong's mind. "Seems she's gone to visit an aunt somewhere."

Armstrong closed his eyes. Unbidden came the memory of the afternoon in the sick bay, the pale light, the easy companionship.

"Oh, and the still?" McGrath continued. "Block found it. It's gone now, destroyed. What they haven't figured out is how the prisoners managed to steal all that sugar."

As Armstrong turned away, not trusting his expression, McGrath fired a final shot, speaking softly and not unkindly. "They set all the animals free. They destroyed the cages."

How *ironisch*, thought Armstrong. He felt his own walls closing in.

THE EDGINESS IN the camp was pervasive, and it took some time to assemble the day's work crew. When the camp was finally empty, save for those working in the shop or barn or kitchen, Armstrong walked towards the lake. Both canoes were still there; he had hoped to find one gone. Better still, hoped to see Hirsch paddling towards him, having spent a quiet night listening to coyotes. Instead, the surface of Whitewater Lake stretched before him, still. He sat for a long time, until the hard underside of the canoe had left his seat numb and his leg cramped. At least with a leg like his, he thought, he was never a contender for this morning's manhunt. As Armstrong stood to leave he caught something in the periphery of his vision, a movement. An animal, doglike. His imagination? He could not be sure.

He returned to a quiet camp and found Weiler in the mess hall, sweeping. There was an air of waiting, as if the camp held its breath.

"Anything?" Armstrong asked.

"Nope. But I almost killed a packrat, trying to get it out of the kitchen. It was near tame, that thing. You okay? You look terrible."

"I need some sleep," Armstrong said. "My shift starts at noon. I'm going to see if McGrath will take it."

Weiler leaned the broom against the wall. "Mail came. Col. Trevaine ordered all the mail held 'til the prisoner is found, but I'm sure he didn't mean staff mail. Here."

"Damn. I almost had one ready to go." Armstrong reached for the letter. The handwriting on the envelope was not Stephen's, and he turned away so Weiler wouldn't see his eyes.

"Next time," said Weiler, already returned to his duties, broom in hand.

WHEN THE SEARCH party returned, Armstrong had been lying on his bunk for almost two hours, his eyes on the ceiling, but he wasn't really seeing it. He was remembering Stephen, as a newborn, a toddler, a boy learning to gut a fish. Learning to drive a car. Learning to like girls.

Learning to fire a rifle.

Now a young man, missing in action.

Horgan came in and flopped onto the bunk below. "Got him," he said.

Armstrong said nothing.

"I dunno what he was thinking. He'd gone to see some girl, but then he just kept going. He was walking down the tracks, about three miles past the Dauphin station, like he was heading West to seek his fortune. Big red bull's-eye on his back, broad daylight, it's a wonder nobody stopped him. He said he was just tired, that's all. You listening?"

Armstrong said nothing.

"Block was ready to shoot him, and I think he would've if we hadn't been there. That would've caused a stink, wouldn't it? Never mind we'd've had a revolt on our hands. Anyways, he's gone. They sent him to Neys. Turns out he was as black a Nazi as they come. Dunno if he was here to stir things up or just have a bit of a holiday. Well, he'll be with his own kind, there, anyways."

Armstrong said nothing.

"Funny, you wouldn't have thought so. I mean, he seemed like a nice guy. As nice as any of 'em are. I mean, do you ever think? You know, that they're just like us? For every one we've got here, one of ours is over there." He poked the bottom of the upper bunk with his foot. "Hell, you'd know, Charlie, wouldn't you?"

Horgan sighed and shifted in his bunk, and was quiet for several moments.

"I mean, you gotta think, sometimes, what's the point?"

IT WAS PAST midnight when Armstrong made his way back to the shore. He hadn't eaten, and as a result was light-headed, but the shaking had stopped. In the night sky were a million points of light, the effect dizzying. Walking slowly, left leg just a little slower than the right, Armstrong moved past the dugout canoes, his fingers tracing the gouges left by prisoners' chisels. He lowered himself to the ground with some difficulty, stretching the offending leg out slowly beside its mate, absurdly grateful for the cold ground beneath him. He lay back and, putting his hands behind his head, regarded the brilliant firmament above.

There's Cassiopeia, he said in his mind to the boy who wasn't there. *There's Orion.*

From somewhere in the forest rose a chorus of canine voices, in all of their colours, their song a strange and glorious comfort.

SEVEN

TO BE LIKE YOU

·1957·

IT WAS A beautiful evening as I walked back from work, with the scent of dry leaves and just the slightest hint of snow in the air. Behind me, the dark buildings of the dormitory for the Doukhobor children receded; they would be sitting down by now, at the long tables for the evening meal, while I considered what I might make for our own. There was a chilly sunset that turned the sky and the surface of the lake a rosy pink, even though you couldn't actually see the sun for the mountains. Mrs. Sato's tiny house looked like something from a fairy tale as I approached, with its dark shingles and its windows glowing yellow in the dusk.

When the door opened I was struck first with the smell of some sort of food cooking, something Japanese. Something sour, and salty. Then I was struck with Audrey, who threw her three-year-old body full tilt into my legs, almost knocking me over. Mrs. Sato came up and put her dark hand on Audrey's white-blonde head, and Audrey looked up at her with a smile that made me just a bit jealous. Audrey loved Mrs. Sato.

"You look tired." Mrs. Sato made ushering motions with her hands, and I stepped inside and shut the door. It wasn't hard; I *was* tired. "You and Audrey stay," she said. "I made some nice food. Come. Sit down."

Mrs. Sato's voice reminded me of a bird. She was very slight; around her I felt large and awkward, and yet I was no bigger than I was before Audrey was born—and I felt young, my twenty-three years to her years, whatever they were. Forty? Fifty? I couldn't tell. I am five foot six to Mrs. Sato's five foot nothing, and yet she filled her small kitchen as she bustled about between the stove and the wooden table with its two chairs, while I sat gratefully with Audrey on my lap. My feet throbbed.

"Thank you, Mrs. Sato," I said, and I meant it for more than just the bowls of rice and vegetables and pork she put in front of us. "You're so kind to us. And I don't pay you enough."

It was always this way for me: the push and pull of gratitude and jealousy. I wanted Audrey all day, every day. This separation wasn't fair. Mrs. Sato smiled and sat across from me, picking up chopsticks. For Audrey and me, she keeps two forks in her drawer.

"Ah, no. You pay me fine. And Audrey is a very good girl. It is good to have a child in my home. I will call you Bernice? And you must call me by my other name, now. I have been looking after Audrey for how long now? Two months? Call me Natsumi."

"It's a pretty name."

"It means 'summer beauty.' It was my mother's name. If I had had a girl, it would have been her name." She looked at Audrey. "Maybe you could call me Obaasan," she said to her. "It means grandmother."

Audrey didn't like her fork, and was pointing at Natsumi's chopsticks. "No, you'll make a mess," I told her.

Natsumi rose and retrieved a pair from the drawer. "Show your mother what you learned today," she said.

When Audrey fitted the small sticks in her three-year-old hand and brought a piece of pork to her lips, then looked at me proudly, I had to swallow to keep back the tears. "Finish up, Audrey," I told her. "Mrs. Sato needs her house back, and we need to go home."

WHEN NATSUMI TALKS about her sons, I think: that's what I want for Audrey and me. Natsumi's boys are living away, now, one in Vancouver and one in Salmon Arm, but they come home as often as they can, Natsumi tells me, her voice warm whenever she speaks of them. I want that kind of warmth, that kind of family. I want Audrey to have exactly what I *didn't* have growing up in Kamloops.

When I was leaving my final foster placement at George and Norma's, Norma sat me down and said: "Bernice Murphy, it stops with you. Whatever bad things happened for your mum and for you when you were small, and I don't know, maybe your granny before that—that's all behind you. It has to stop somewhere."

Of course, one thing I didn't have in Kamloops is the thing I can't give to Audrey either, and that's a father. One of my earliest memories is seeing a man lying down under a tree in the park near our house. I was sure he must be my dad, because the other kids all had one. Who knows where ideas come from in the mind of a little kid? I picked a big bunch of flowers from somebody's garden and brought them to him. We sat and talked—I can't remember what we talked about— and I thought my father was a very nice man after all, so I didn't understand when I was spanked, later, for talking to a stranger and for stealing flowers.

I never did find my dad, and Harvey won't find us. Joyce at the store says the right man could come along for me and Audrey any day now. But I have a job, we have a house, and we have Natsumi and Joyce, and I suppose we'll be all right anyway.

I would pick up Audrey from Natsumi's each day as soon as I got off shift at the Dormitory. I was off at five, having got through lunch preparation and cleanup. There are fewer of us now, and I was lucky to get the job at all. Principal Neilson has told me more than once we are on a shoestring budget. We have the kids doing a lot of the work, which doesn't seem right to me. Kids should be kids, I figure, no matter what their parents did. I think about how much I miss Audrey over the course of a workday, and I can only imagine how much the Doukhobor parents must miss their children. They come every other Sunday, visiting through the chain-link fence. Breaks my heart. But then I think: this must be better for these children. It has to stop somewhere.

But how would I feel if it was Audrey?

I was thinking about Audrey, as usual, as I was opening cupboards in the Dormitory kitchen. Wondering if I could ever convince Mr. Neilson to let me bring her to work with me, where she might colour pictures quietly in a corner, but I knew the answer already. As I pulled out a sack of potatoes for peeling, I wondered what was keeping my helper, Anna, a sullen girl of twelve or so. It was Saturday: some of the kids were raking leaves, and those assigned duties later in the day were playing ball or hanging around in small groups. The Matron, Mrs. Doerksen, was somewhere else, which was fine with me. Pale light came through the big windows in the kitchen, and

I could hear childish voices outside, now and then a Russian word, although speaking Russian was forbidden here.

I didn't hear the girl so much as feel her behind me in the doorway. A younger girl than Anna, perhaps nine, but small for her age, with wide-set, pale eyes and fine, light hair. For a moment she made me think of Audrey, the way Audrey might look a few years from now. She didn't smile, but stayed there, staring.

"Where's Anna?" I asked her.

"She went home."

"Home?" Nobody went home.

"Her father died. She was allowed to go to the funeral."

She said this without emotion, as if it was an everyday occurrence. I wondered, not for the first time, what went on in the heads of these children, but then, I had only been here since September; as Mrs. Doerksen said, perhaps it takes more than a few years to undo the damage done at home. "You'll get used to it," she told me. "They're not like Canadian children." And yet when I looked at this girl I thought: she can't be so different.

"What's your name, then?" I asked.

"Vera."

"Well then, Vera, if you are to be my helper today, let's get started."

It was the quietest potato-peeling session I've ever experienced. I found myself looking down at that blonde head, those fingers working the peeler, as my attempts at conversation fell flat until I gave up and let her work in silence.

IN KAMLOOPS, THE Indian kids spent the school year all together in a residential school, a big brick building with small windows. I never thought about them much until I graduated from high school, and for a short time before I met Harvey and got pregnant and married and abandoned all in the space of a year, I worked at the Woolworth's lunch counter with an Indian girl called Leona.

It was a town favourite, that lunch counter. You could get a ham and cheese toasted three-decker sandwich for fifty cents, and top it off with the Deluxe Tulip Sundae for two bits. Sometimes staff were allowed to eat whatever was getting old, and once Leona and I, at the end of our shift, sat down and between us polished off an apple pie. And we talked.

I hadn't talked much to Leona before, as she kept to herself for the most part. Once when we were counting tips she looked at my pile of silver and abruptly swept her smaller pile into her hand and into her pocket without counting. "Goes with the territory," she said, then pulled her long, shiny black hair out of its ponytail and pushed through the glass doors to meet a boy with black hair like hers, who was waiting in a rusted pickup truck.

Anyway, it might have been the lazy summer evening sun coming through the windows that evening, our full stomachs and the clean counters, or just that nobody was waiting for either of us and there didn't seem to be any hurry to go anywhere, but Leona got talking. She told me about the day the RCMP came to take her and her little brother. About the look on her parents' faces the day they left. About how she and her brother were separated, and how afraid she knew he felt, and she couldn't do anything about it. She told me about getting the strap for speaking Shuswap, and she said that wasn't the worst of it. She spoke in slow, measured tones as she twirled her fork in her long, slender fingers.

"Why?" I asked her when she had finished speaking.

"Why what?"

"Why did they make you go?"

A fly buzzed in the window. We had locked the door and flipped the sign closed, but someone rattled the door anyway, then moved on.

"Because they wanted us to be like you."

We had been talking companionably, but she spat these last words. I had no words to return, my mind a turmoil of feelings I couldn't quite identify: offended; hurt; something else, something like shame. We put our sweaters on and she pushed through the door ahead, leaving me to lock up. I had the keys anyway; Mr. Ferguson had given them to me, even though Leona had worked there longer.

THERE WERE A lot of potatoes, but Vera didn't complain. When she was finished, on impulse I told her to wait, and she stood, hands at her sides, by a bowl of peeled potatoes almost as big as she was. In the staff cupboard were all sorts of things to keep a boring job at bay: bags of nuts, cookies. At the back, a bottle of rye whisky. There were packages I suspected came from the parents for the children, and although I hadn't asked, Mrs. Doerksen had volunteered the information that it was better to take the food and give it to the children a bit at a time, or there would be fights. Still, I never saw the children receiving anything from the cupboard. I took an orange from a bag, and then, on impulse, took a second.

"Thank you, Vera," I said. "You've been a help today. Maybe there's a friend you'd like to share with."

It was the first time she smiled, and it lit the room. Later, as I left through the big front gates, I felt that stare again. I turned, and Vera waved at me through the fence. I waved back, and hurried home to my own girl. There was an odd

feeling in my chest, and I picked up my pace, my heels click-
ing on the road, and pulled my coat closer around me.

Mrs. Sato—Natsumi—did not ask us for supper that evening, which was fine as I would have had to say no. Audrey
was happy to see me but gave Natsumi a long hug around
her knees before we left. As we walked the short distance to
our own small house I held Audrey's hand perhaps a little
tighter than I might have.

The house was what brought me to New Denver in the
first place. It was left to me by George and Norma. Sorry as
I was about their car accident, the house—it had belonged
to George's family, I guess—couldn't have come at a better
time, with Audrey not quite three and Harvey clearly not
coming back.

Our house, when I pushed open the door, was cold, and no
smell of cooking greeted us. But I got things warmed up and
Audrey into her pajamas, and we read *The Little Engine That
Could* in the big armchair. I tucked my little girl into bed with
her stuffed cat. Her breathing was soft, her mouth relaxed,
while just above the edge of the covers the wide-spaced button
eyes of the cat stared at me. I knew it was silly, but I pulled the
covers up a little higher, until I could no longer see them.

I GOT MONDAYS off because of working Saturday at the Dormitory, and so it was one Monday a few weeks later that I
gathered up my change, dressed Audrey in the blue sailor
dress I'd bought from the Simpsons-Sears catalogue, and
walked to the grocery store. Joyce, who had become something of a friend, waved me to sit on the opposite side of the
counter and stay for coffee, as I'd hoped she would. I was
lonely, I guess, for adult company. There was nobody in the

store, and Audrey began jumping from square to square on the tiled floor and singing "Teddy Bears' Picnic": *If you go down to the woods today—*

We talked about this and that, and then: "It's nice that you've got Natsumi to look after Audrey," Joyce said, leaning on the counter and watching as Audrey came to the last twin squares of her imagined hopscotch at the same point as she got to the word *surprise*!, then jumped on her chubby legs to face towards us and, head down, continue: *For every bear that ever there was—*

"Audrey likes her," I nodded. Joyce had poured us both a cup of coffee and I had pulled the tall stool up to the counter. She felt like a real friend at that moment, which might explain why I said: "She's teaching her stuff I don't know I like very much."

"Like what?"

"Japanese stuff. Maybe I should find someone else to look after her. A Canadian."

Joyce put her cup down. "You won't find anyone kinder than Natsumi," she told me. Her voice was firm, and made me feel the twenty years between us. "And anyway, she *is* Canadian."

"She is?"

"Sure. She was born in Vancouver. She came with her husband and her boys at the start of the war. The boys would have been in their early teens, I guess."

"Why did they come here?"

"They didn't have any choice."

Audrey had become bored with her game and came over to tug on my hand. "Let's go, Mummy," she said.

"Just a minute, honey." I put my hand on her head; sometimes it seemed as if my hand and her head were meant for one another. I looked at Joyce. "Go on."

"Let's *go*, Mummy," whined Audrey, pulling.

Joyce waved us off. "Just ask her sometime," she said, and we left with the door banging behind us and a dozen brown eggs tucked under my arm. I didn't realize until later I'd forgotten to pay for them.

VERA BECAME MY regular Saturday helper. As time passed, we learned to work in companionable silence most of the time. I wasn't even sure how good Vera's English was. I wondered about her parents. How would it be for them to see Vera so seldom? She had told me that she had no brothers or sisters. And as I worked with Vera beside me, our hands, as usual, in a bowl of potatoes and peels, I wondered at the stories I'd heard.

Since we arrived in New Denver in August, things had been quiet, but memories lingered: dynamited power poles near Nelson, houses in Krestova, Perry Siding, Shoreacres, and Glade destroyed by fire, and a CP Rail substation bombed. It was baffling to consider the motive behind the burning of Sons of Freedom Doukhobor homes by the Freedomites themselves, despite Joyce's attempts to explain to the extent that she, herself understood. Her son-in-law was an "Independent Doukhobor," she explained.

"The Sons of Freedom have a more zealous interpretation of their religion," she had said on one of our Monday morning visits at the store, which had become regular events. "They don't think it's good to have too much stuff, and so setting things on fire is a way to clean out, I guess."

"Seems a little extreme," I offered.

"That's not the half of it. It's been quieter since most of the parents are in Oakalla prison. A few years back it was really bad. There was something in the newspaper every week, it seemed like. And then there were the nude marches." She shook her head, and I found myself shaking my own head. It was hard to fathom. "Walter doesn't like to talk about it. It's hard on the other Doukhobors."

I had seen the newspaper photographs of men and women, undressed in front of the Nelson courthouse. "Why do you think they go nude?"

"Walter says it's because it's the way God made them. And it makes a statement, I guess." She leaned across the counter. "I think it's to get attention. As if the bombs didn't. Still, those kids. I feel sorry for those kids. Snatched before dawn by the RCMP. Walter's cousin's kid was eventually taken that way, but it was weeks before they caught him. He'd run and hide in the woods. Walter says that some kids hide in the hay barns, and then the RCMP go through with pitchforks."

"That's awful!"

"They know the mothers will stop them when they get close," Joyce said. "But it *is* awful."

"It must be the best thing for the children, though," I said. "They can't stay with their parents, doing what they're doing. And they won't send them to school. That's against the law."

"I know," Joyce said. She pulled a licorice whip out of the box on the counter and dangled it at Audrey, whose face lit up. "I know. Walter says we can't understand if we're not Doukhobor. I just feel sorry for those kids, that's all."

AS I WORKED beside Vera I wondered if she, too, had hid in the woods, or in the back of a cupboard. It was early December by this time, and so in my mind's eye she was shivering, cold, in some hiding place listening to the boots of police officers as they searched for her, although I had no idea how it was she had come to be here, or at what time of year. What would that have been like for her? I wasn't sure how to ask. Instead, I made small talk.

"I guess you're looking forward to seeing your parents tomorrow?" I said.

She didn't look up. "I don't think my mother will come." Her English *was* very good, I noticed, but then, she'd been here, she had told me earlier, since she was six.

"Why not?" Nothing, I thought, would keep me from seeing Audrey.

"We live in Gilpin. It takes a long time to get here. Visiting hour used to be in the afternoon, but Mr. Neilson changed it to morning. So my mother would have to leave in the dark and drive a long way to be here for just one hour to see me through the fence."

I swallowed. "But they can come in. They get passes."

Vera looked up, then shrugged and went back to her work. "They don't like it that they have to get a pass from the government to come to see me. Because the government is bad. The government wants us to be like everyone else, so we're not Doukhobor anymore. So, they won't take the pass. Besides, once they came and some of us had got in trouble, so they cancelled visiting hours. It was just a note on the fence to tell them."

"What were you being punished for?"

"Some kids went to the store and stole some food." She put down the potato she had finished and picked up another. "We get tired of potatoes."

At that moment the peeler slipped and Vera went to catch it before it fell. She yelped, and the peeler clattered to the floor. We both watched for the moment before the blood reached the surface of the slice across her palm. The cut didn't look bad, but I was afraid of infection. "Let's take you to Matron," I said.

"No!" Vera put her hand behind her back. When I reached for it, to take another look, she shook her head and ran from the kitchen.

I TOLD NATSUMI about it when I picked up Audrey that evening. She poured tea and we sat at her kitchen table. Audrey was seldom in a hurry to leave Natsumi's house, and Natsumi seemed happy for my company, too.

"The first winter we were here, I don't think we would have survived if it wasn't for the Doukhobors," she told me. "Maybe they were not the same ones as the people who are always in the news right now. I don't know. They came with carts full of vegetables. Apples, cabbage. They were good people. It didn't matter to them that Canada was at war with Japan."

And that was it. It was as if a dam had opened and Natsumi let the words pour through. She described her husband's dental office above a store on Hastings Street; Natsumi scheduled appointments and kept the books. Her sons were happy, obedient boys. Her husband, who had emigrated from Japan, was so proud to be Canadian. Then, she told me, when the war came they were told to get ready to leave, and that they could have one suitcase each. Her husband made the best of it; it would not be for long. He carefully closed up the office so it would be easy to reopen when they got back.

"Of course, right away everything was taken out and sold," Natsumi said. "They did not mean to give anything back. My husband, Tadao, was very bitter."

"What about your boys?"

"They were old enough to know what had been taken from them," she said. "We have a phrase: *shikata ga nai*. It means 'it can't be helped.' The older people, especially, would say this.

They had been through so much: this was just one more thing. And Canada was our country: so we were angry, and we were worried. We were worried that Japan would win, and we were worried that Japan would lose. But the older kids didn't care so much about Japan. They were just angry. Once my father, who was with us, said to my older boy Tom, when Tom was frustrated—I remember he was chipping ice off the water that was frozen in our bucket—*shikata ga nai*, and Tom said—" she looked at Audrey, who by now was almost asleep on my lap, my chin resting on her fine hair, "—'to *heck* with your *shikata ga nai*.' Well, he said worse than that. Oh, he got in trouble for speaking back to his grandfather! But you know, it was hard, but we weren't angry at the people of New Denver. They could have felt overrun with all of us: they were only a few hundred when we came, and we were more than a thousand. Many people were kind to us. That's one of the reasons I have stayed here."

I shifted Audrey a little; she'd become a dead weight. Natsumi looked at her and smiled. "They are lovely when they are asleep, aren't they?" I nodded, thinking I should go, too, comfortable and warm to move. Our house would be cold, and the walk between our homes across the crusty snow colder. Besides, Natsumi seemed content to continue her story.

"After the war, we were given a choice: move to the prairies or to Ontario, or go home. By home, they meant Japan, but to many of us it meant nothing, because we'd never been there. My father was very frail by then, and had developed a bad cough. Tadao seemed to have developed one, too. So we stayed and moved into the building you work in now. It was a sanatorium before."

"Really?"

"Yes. And so life was really not much different than it had been, but there we were. And then my father died, and then Tadao. And I stayed."

It was said so quietly, in such a matter of fact way, that I couldn't say why I suddenly felt my eyes pool with tears. Natsumi was up and clearing our teacups.

"What about your boys?"

"Tom found work at the mill at Salmon Arm. Terry is studying dentistry in Vancouver. His father would be very proud." She had gathered Audrey's winter things from beside the door and brought them into the kitchen where she pulled her chair across from ours to help push Audrey's sleepy, bendable feet into her boots while I held her on my lap. "It is keeping family close that is so hard," Natsumi told me. "And I think it is the most important thing of all."

WE WERE APPROACHING the shortest day of the year. I walked to work in the dark and came home in the dark. The clouds sat low on the mountains, which appeared black and brooding. Even Joyce seemed out of sorts, angry because someone had thrown a stone through her window, retaliation, she was sure, for her complaints to the Dormitory after she had found two boys "up to no good," behind the building. Visiting privileges had been cancelled for those boys, and extra work duties assigned. It felt as if the air was full of bad feelings fluttering like so many bats through the cold Dormitory rooms. And the rooms *were* cold. Broken windows weren't replaced but just covered up. Two more people were let go as more funding was cut: Sally, another one of the cook's helpers, and Agnes, who cleaned. Mrs. Doerksen was in a perpetually foul mood. I waited to hear that I had been let go, too, but for now, I seemed to have a job. I had no idea what I would do if I lost it.

I saw more of Vera, then, who came to help me mornings before class with the breakfast cleanup. One morning as she pushed a cart full of dirty dishes into the kitchen, I could see something was wrong.

"Are you all right, Vera?" I asked.

"I don't feel well," she said. "My ear hurts."

I looked at her ear, and it did seem a little red. "You'd better go and see Matron," I told her. "They'll keep you home today." The word *home* sounded odd when I said it, but she didn't seem to notice.

"No they won't. They don't like us to stay behind." She began to stack the dishes from the cart beside the sink, her movements slow, like molasses on a cold day.

"Really, Vera," I said. "I'll talk to her."

"No. Please." She looked at me, and I thought of what a pretty girl she was. I imagined her on a summer day, playing outside her family's home.

"Okay," I told her. "You should go and get ready for school, then. Go now, and you'll have more time. And dress warm!" I said to her departing back.

Later, as I was getting ready to go home, the maintenance man, Jerry, stopped in to look at the stove, which had been giving us some trouble.

"Your helper's in the infirmary," he told me as he rooted through his toolbox.

Although I was anxious to pick up Audrey, I hurried over to the infirmary, my hard soles slipping on the ice in the yard. I found Vera looking very small under several blankets on a narrow cot. She had a hot compress against the side of her head. There was nobody else around.

"I fell down," she told me. "I guess I lost my balance. Mrs. Sellinger told me it was because of my ear."

"Who's Mrs. Sellinger?"

"My teacher. She said it was terrible that they sent me to school." Vera smiled a little and shifted the hot compress. There was a glass of water beside her bed, but nothing else.

I sat on the chair beside her bed. "Is there something I can get for you? Some books?" I felt helpless, there, and torn, needing to go home—Audrey would miss me. "Wait," I told Vera. "I just need to do something."

I walked over to the administration office; Mr. Neilson was there behind stacks of paper on his desk. "So many reports," he said. "That's all they seem to want, all the time."

He just waved towards the telephone when I asked to use it. I felt awkward calling while he was working, but he got up abruptly and walked down the hall to the washroom, whistling under his breath. I dialed the five numbers I knew were the number for the store, and asked Joyce if she could send someone to ask Natsumi to keep Audrey for supper. Neither Natsumi nor I had telephones. Joyce was sure it would be all right, but promised to get the message to her. Then she mentioned that Natsumi and Audrey had been in the store just that afternoon.

"Audrey showed me a Japanese clapping game Natsumi taught her," Joyce said. "She's a happy little thing, isn't she?"

I met Mrs. Doerksen in the hallway carrying a tray of soup and bread. I assured her she should take a break, and that I'd sit with Vera for a while, although it was evident that nobody had been sitting with Vera for some time. Tucked under my arm was a pad of lined paper and some pencils.

Vera didn't want the soup, I suppose because her sore ear made her stomach sick, too, with the dizziness that would have come with an ear infection. But I convinced her to eat some, and she finished about half of it before she put her spoon down and I took away the tray.

I showed her the paper and pencils. I had thought we could draw pictures together; it's what Audrey liked to do best, and although Vera was older, I thought she might like it, too. But what Vera wanted to do was talk, something she hadn't done so very much of in the kitchen. I asked her how she came to live at the Dormitory.

"It was scary, when the police came. We were told to hide, and in some houses people had made places under the floor. But I was afraid of the dark and I didn't want to go under the boards, so my mother told me that if the policeman came I should hide under the bed." Vera looked out the window as she spoke, the pictures clearly in her head, still. "They came in the early morning, when we were just getting up. I was still in my nightgown, and my mother looked out the window and saw the car, and said: 'Hurry, under the bed with you!' I crawled under as fast as I could and made myself small behind a trunk. I could hear my mother at the door, saying 'No, no children here,' and I could hear the boots of the policemen as they came in anyway. My father was trying to tell them they had no right, but he said it in Russian. My mother and father don't speak English very well.

"I had my eyes shut very tightly. I was only six, and I think maybe I thought that if I couldn't see them they couldn't see me." Vera gave me a little smile. "When I opened my eyes I saw a big upside-down face looking at me, and I almost screamed, but then it was gone, and I could just see big black boots. I heard two men talking in English, but I don't know what they said because I didn't have many words in English then, either. But then I heard my mother say 'See, no children,' and I was surprised because it meant that the policeman must have pretended he didn't see me. Then I heard the other policeman say something, and I could feel the bed being moved away from the wall, and then there was the other policeman looking down at me. I was picked up in his big hands and my coat put on me, and my mother was putting my dress right over my nightgown and my feet in my boots and she was crying and she had her hands on both sides of my face, kneeling on the floor in front of me, when the policeman picked me right up off the floor from between my mother's hands and took me to the car. Petya, a boy I knew, was already in the car, and I could see his mother running down the road towards it. I looked out the back window as we drove away and there were our two mothers, Petya's and mine, holding onto each other in the middle of the road."

Vera was crying, now, and so was I. It was more than I'd heard her say if I'd put all of her words together that I'd heard these last few months.

I was still hoping to put things in a positive light, even after all that. "But now you are in school. Now you're learning things."

"I *was* in school then. But my mother took me out; she said we all needed to be the same to protest the government. I liked school. But I don't like it now." She looked down at her hands, young fingers knotted together. "Now, my father has gone away. It's just my mother. It's hard for her to come."

"Do you write to her?"

"At first, I didn't because I was angry. Because if I'd stayed in school, maybe I wouldn't be here. Now I don't because I don't know what to say. When my mother does come, she just cries. She feels bad."

There were footsteps in the hallway, sharp heels like the hooves of horses, and we both wiped our eyes.

"I'll take over now, Bernice," Mrs. Doerksen said. "Vera should sleep if she's going to get better and get back to school." She reached over to pick up the tray.

"No, I'll take it back," I said. "I was just saying goodnight."
I reached for the hot compress. "Vera said this was helping,"
I said, although she hadn't. "Maybe it could be warmed up?"

After she left, I put the pad of paper and pencils on the
nightstand. "Maybe you could write a letter to your mother
now. I'll bet she'd like to hear from you."

Vera said nothing, just shimmied down in the bed. I pulled
the covers up and laid my hand on her shoulder for a moment,
thinking I might say something more, but her eyes were closed.

I hurried home through the dark streets.

IN APRIL DYNAMITE was found on a rail line near Brilliant. I read
it first in the *Nelson Daily News*, a copy Mr. Neilson had left
for staff to read. He'd warned us that things might be starting up again, and to keep a firm hand on the children. Less
than a month later a power pole near Glade was dynamited.

"They're crazy," I said to Joyce. We'd moved our visits to
the bench outside the store, where we could watch the world
go by on the main street while Audrey played in the sun.

"They're dangerous," Joyce agreed. "How are things at the
Dorm?"

"Not so good. At least classes will end soon. They'll have
fun swimming in the lake. There'll be more time to play. It
will be like summer camp to them, compared to this past
winter." The children would not go home in the summer, but
would stay at the Dormitory until they were of age to leave
school, or until their parents agreed to send them. I wished
their parents *would* agree to send them. I remembered what
Leona had said, back at the Woolworth's lunch counter:
They wanted us to be like you. Was that so bad?

Joyce caught Audrey up as she ran by and tickled her under
the arms until she squirmed. She put her down, and Audrey

continued running up to the corner, knowing she was not allowed past the stop sign. Joyce sighed. "Summer camps let you go home after," she said. "I just don't know what the answer is. But this can't go on. It has to stop somewhere."

ALTHOUGH I HAD not been working Sundays I was asked to work a few extra shifts because more of the staff had been let go. It was hard to leave Audrey, even in Natsumi's good hands, but the extra money would be welcome.

After breakfast cleanup I had a break before starting lunch, and so I wandered outside into the warm July sunshine. It really was lovely here, with its sparkling lake and rolling mountains. So much greener than around Kamloops. I breathed in the scent of pines and fresh-cut grass; Jerry was mowing the east side of the grounds, and the sound of that must have drowned out the sound of voices from the front of the Dormitory where I saw, as I came around the side of the building, a group of men and kerchiefed women— clearly the parents of the children—clustered against the fence. Some were singing in Russian; a small table had been set up with a loaf of bread, a dish of salt, and a pitcher of water. The children stood in a group on the other side, singing or standing quietly. I looked for Vera, but didn't see her. I stayed in the shadow of the building, watching, a heaviness in my chest. I couldn't understand the words, but the sound was beautiful, and sad.

After a while the singing stopped and the parents began to pass packages through the gaps between the fence and the gate, and, in the case of larger packages, toss them over to be caught by waiting hands. As the children approached to kiss their parents through the chain links of the fence, I saw Vera standing apart. Beyond her stood Mr. Neilson and Mrs. Doerksen, who chatted under the shade of the tall cluster of trees in the corner of the yard. I wanted to approach Vera, but for some reason I didn't want to do it when they could see me, so I waited. Before long the parents began to move away, and there was the sound of car engines starting, doors closing. It must have been the saddest sound in the world for those children.

The kids drifted back across the yard, and the matron and principal collected the packages and then moved on towards the administration office. When I touched Vera gently on the shoulder, she didn't move.

"She didn't come?" I asked her, keeping my voice soft.

"No."

"Did you write to her, Vera?"

Vera looked down and mumbled something. I squatted down, then, in front of her so that I could see her face. "I didn't hear what you said," I told her.

"My mama can't read," she said, her voice small.

"Oh, honey." I took her into my arms, that slight little body, and held her while she cried. After a while she wiped her face and straightened up.

"I have to go," she said.

I held her hand for a moment longer, and then a thought occurred to me. "Write to her anyway," I said. "It will make you feel better to write to her. There will be someone who can read your letter to your mother. And she'll know you're thinking of her. That's the most important thing."

I KNEW I'D get a week's holiday at the end of August, one year since I began my job at the Dormitory, and I couldn't wait. I had plans to spend every day with Audrey at the beach, and with some of the extra money I'd been making I thought we might even take the bus to Nelson and buy some fall clothes

171

for her, and something for me, as well. But that was still a month away. Today was just another working day.

It had never occurred to me that there might be a day when Natsumi would not be able to look after Audrey. She came to the door with eyes red-rimmed and feverish, her robe wrapped around her. I told her I'd just go and tell them I couldn't work, and then I'd be back. I could make her dinner for a change. But Natsumi assured me she had plenty of food, and insisted I stay away.

"I don't want you or Audrey to get sick," she said.

I thanked Natsumi and told her I hoped she'd feel better soon, then turned to lead Audrey down the walk, rehearsing in my head my speech to Mr. Neilson in which I would introduce my well-behaved daughter and make a case to keep her with me for the day; if I missed even a day's pay, our trip to Nelson for new clothes wasn't going to be possible. But Audrey had other ideas. I felt her hand wrench itself from mine and looked down to see the face of my lovely daughter transformed in an ugly contortion of rage.

"I. Want. Obaasan!" she screamed, and stomped her foot on the walk. I looked over my shoulder; Natsumi had closed the door and probably gone back to bed.

"Honey, Mrs. Sato is sick. She can't look after you today. Would you like to come with Mummy to work?"

"I want OBAASAN." And with that she sat on the walk with her arms crossed and wouldn't move. When I tried to pick her up, she went limp. I tried to lift her by her armpits, but I couldn't get any purchase. I was going to be late for work. I grabbed her wrist, my hand tight around it, and pulled her roughly to her feet.

My daughter was screaming. I was afraid Natsumi would come back out with the noise, or someone would hear my badly behaved child. It was very early. I was sure she was waking up the neighbourhood, and what would they think of me? I was afraid I'd lose my job, but more than that, I was afraid I'd lose my child, should someone report that, as a single mother, I was an unfit one.

"Audrey. Please," I said through gritted teeth. I leaned down. "Be quiet and come."

"No!" she yelled, and struck out, her small fist hitting the tender part of my breast. I hauled her up by her wrist, wrenching it, and with my other hand whacked her hard across her bottom, something I had never done, but that had certainly been done to me often enough as a child. There was a moment of silence during which she sucked in her breath, and I waited for the scream I knew was coming, angry and ashamed all at once. But I wasn't expecting what came next.

"I *hate* you, Mummy!"

What are the worst words a mother can hear? It must surely be these. She's only a child, I know that, but still it was a knife to the heart. Somehow I managed to calm myself, and Audrey as well, and we made our way to the Dormitory, but her words remained a dark weight in my chest. She was sulky beside me, but held my hand as I told her what fun it would be to come to work with Mummy, not at all sure that Mr. Neilson would allow it.

As it turned out, Mr. Neilson said that Audrey could stay through breakfast, and by then he'd have called in one of the other girls to replace me. By now Audrey appeared to have forgotten about her tantrum, and was content to sit at one of the prep tables in the kitchen with a big bowl, a couple of measuring cups and spoons, and some flour and split peas, "cooking." When she started humming "Teddy Bears' Picnic" I knew she'd be fine, and I set to work quickly, aware I'd lost three-quarters of an hour from my morning. There was a noise at the door, and I looked up to see Vera in the doorway. She took a step inside.

"I came earlier, but you weren't here," she said. I hadn't seen her since visiting day. "I wrote the letter," she told me proudly.

"Good," I said, but I didn't have time to talk with her; there was far too much to do. "Come, help me with the oatmeal. I need you to stir while I get things together."

Vera didn't move. "Who's that?" she asked, pointing.

"That's my daughter, Audrey. Audrey, this is Vera."

Audrey looked up from her measuring cups briefly but went back to her play. Then, "Mummy, I'm hungry," she said. "Obaasan always gives me an orange."

I didn't think. I just went to the cupboard, got out an orange, peeled it, and gave it to her. Anything to keep her busy. I could smell the oatmeal burning, and I rushed to the stove. "Vera, what are you doing standing there? Come on, now, I need your help," I said without looking up, exasperated. When I finally did look up, Vera was still in the doorway, her eyes narrowed.

"I'm not supposed to be working here today. I just came to find you," she said in a flat voice. Then she left.

I made it through the morning, and in spite of everything had breakfast on the table when the children came in. I had two helpers for cleanup; perhaps there had been a mixup. In any case, neither helper was Vera, and I thought to look for her but I could see that Audrey was at the end of her ability to be quiet and civil. We needed to go home. I felt as if I'd lived a week in that morning.

On the way out the gate with my daughter by the hand, Mr. Neilson stopped me. "Bernice, you've been a fine employee," he began. Then he stopped, and put an envelope in my hand.

"It's because of the cutbacks," he said. "I'll be happy to write you a reference."

NATSUMI GOT MUCH sicker before she began to get better. I found another woman to look after Audrey on Joyce's recommendation, but Audrey didn't like her: she didn't play clapping games, Audrey said, and she only ever ate with a fork. It didn't matter; I had only a few shifts left, and I promised Audrey that if she would go to Mrs. Barton's until the end of the week, we'd have a picnic on the beach, and we'd bring Natsumi, chopsticks and all.

It was the morning of my first day of unemployment when Audrey and I walked to the store to buy things for our picnic. I didn't know what I would do about all the questions in my head about our future, but this much I could do. Audrey skipped ahead of me, delighted to have me for the whole day, and a picnic with Natsumi besides. It was a sunny August morning in that delicious time before the summer heat takes over, when you can still feel the breeze off the lake while the sun warms your skin. For the moment, I put aside worries of the future to just enjoy what I had.

When we came into the store, the bell on the door jingling, Joyce looked up from the newspaper she was reading from the top of the stack that had just been delivered. She tapped her fingernail on an article on the front page.

"This one of yours?" she asked.

Doukhobor Mother Suicides At Gilpin, the headline read. I took the paper and sat down on the stool, feeling my heart thud in my chest.

A 32-year-old Freedomite widow whose nine-year-old daughter is held at the provincial government's special "school" at New Denver hanged herself in her home in Gilpin on Wednesday.

A letter from her daughter was found near the body of Mrs. Florence Potapoff. The letter, say authorities, described the girl's loneliness and desire for a visit. Gilpin is one of the farthest Freedomite communities from the school, making travel difficult. Mrs. Potapoff lived alone.

I looked up from the paper. I could feel the tears coursing down my cheeks.

I CALLED THE Dormitory from the phone in Joyce's store, but Vera had already been picked up by an uncle and brought home for her mother's funeral. "The community will be there for her," Joyce told me. "That's what Walter says. They're very close-knit." I hoped so. It made me so angry, and so sad, all at once. Nothing about any of it made sense to me.

That evening Natsumi and I sat on the beach as the sky turned pink, then fiery orange, before settling into a soft dusk that glowed across the water's surface. I glanced at Natsumi, who was gazing out across the lake. She looked beautiful. Like her name, I thought. What a lot she has seen.

Around us were the voices of children and families as they began to pack up their things, a summer's carefree day almost over. Audrey crouched at the water's edge looking for small things in the sand.

"She's a happy girl," said Natsumi. "You are very lucky."

"Yes, she is," I said. "Yes, we are."

Audrey stood to throw a stone into the water and, as if in answer, a fish jumped. She picked up several stones and threw them all at once using both hands, perhaps hoping for a dozen fish to jump. As the ripples receded she stood, a small, sturdy figure dark against a vast lake, waiting for that small miracle.

EIGHT

A DIFFERENT COUNTRY

·1967·

Slowly at first, and now in growing numbers, from Maine to Alabama to California, from ghettos, suburbs and schools, young Americans are coming to Canada to resist the draft. There is no draft in Canada. The last time they tried it was World War Two, when tens of thousands of Canadians refused to register. Faded "Oppose Conscription" signs can still be seen along the Toronto waterfront. The mayor of Montreal was jailed for urging Canadians to resist—and was re-elected from jail. No one expects a draft again.

It's a different country, Canada.

—from the *Manual for Draft-Age Immigrants to Canada*

WHEN JAMES OPENED his eyes the swirling shapes made no sense. Dream images flickered, then dissolved into themselves like spiderwebs, and he closed his eyes again, trying to reconstruct their tenuous patterns. Gone. Beneath him, the prickly

spring grass of a downtown park; above him, a flock of star-
lings. Nearby, quiet voices, the tentative chords of a poorly
tuned guitar, and the smell of weed. It was March, and
James was grateful for the sun; if he didn't move, but lay flat
where the breeze couldn't find him, he was actually warm.
When he'd crossed the border and arrived in Toronto two
weeks ago it had been snowing. He'd felt, then, as bleak as
the weather, but with the shift in temperature his spirits had
risen, despite a chronic feeling of disconnectedness, never
mind loneliness.

A shadow passed across his face. He raised himself onto
his elbows.

"Hey."

"Hey," said Myra, curling herself onto the ground beside
him in a fluid movement. Long brown hair, floppy hat. James
could smell patchouli and sweat, a pleasant, musty combination. Her arrival at his side, here where he knew almost no
one, felt like a miracle.

James had met Myra yesterday, when Fig introduced
them outside the Anti-Draft League office. Myra, framed in
the moment like a stray sunbeam against the bright yellow
office door, had surprised James by kissing him on the
cheek as if they were old friends, her hoop earrings sweeping his collarbone. Her proximity, now, brought with it a
pleasant rush. They didn't talk at first, but lounged together
in supine communion, enjoying the warmth of the sun, the
first real spring day. A hundred yards away a girl in jeans and
a suede jacket twirled on the grass to her own mental music,
leather fringes sweeping the air. To James it felt a million
miles—geographically and culturally—from Middleton,
Delaware.

"Where are you staying?" Myra asked lazily.

"I'm at Fig's for now. But there's a free house I'm going to check out." James raised himself up on his elbows. He felt conspicuous there in the park, where hair and mood seemed to flow equally; in preparation to cross the border he'd cut his own hair military short in order to make a better impression.

Myra lit a cigarette and tilted her long neck. "Fig's, eh?"

"Yeah. I was given his address by some people. Me and a girl, we came over together in a van. We pretended we were a couple, going to a friend's wedding. It was a Quaker group that helped us. They gave us three hundred bucks, a van, a suit, and a dress." Myra blew smoke, then offered the cigarette to James, who shook his head. "When we gave the van back, I was told to go to the address we'd been given to use for our 'friend' who was getting married. Whose name, it turned out, was Gerard Samson. Who turned out to be Fig."

Myra threw herself backwards on the grass, overcome with laughter. "*Gerard!*" she gasped, when she could speak. "Man, that's just too far out. He never told me his real name." She sat up and wiped tears from her eyes.

James found himself laughing, too. "So where did he get Fig, I wonder?"

"He told me once it had something to do with grad school. Fig's really smart." Myra paused to take another drag. "He dropped out in January."

"Smart," commented James, who had flunked out of his second year, hence his draft notice. Who am I to say? he thought.

"He dropped out so he could join the movement. So he could organize, you know?" She stubbed her cigarette in the damp earth. "And anyway, I heard something went down. Like maybe he was kicked out. I don't know; he doesn't really talk about it."

Myra lay down with her hat across her eyes, and after a while James thought she must have fallen asleep. But after a bit she spoke from under her hat, her voice sleepy, sexy. "Hey," she said, lifting the hat to expose one eye. "You want some Sunshine?" She sat up and, taking in the look of incomprehension on James's face, grinned. "You wanna trip?"

The day dissolved, then. James had tried pot before, plenty of times. This was new, the warmth of the day dispelling any apprehension. When Myra said "You can crash at my pad," it seemed so easy. About ten minutes after she'd placed the square of paper on his tongue, he thought wildly that he'd made some terrible mistake, that he didn't know Myra or Fig, really, and he briefly entertained the thought that they might both be agents working for the U.S. government. And then a wave washed over him—like sunshine, he thought—and separate colours became rainbows, each with their own distinct aura. He could feel his smile, and it felt larger than his face. He turned to look at Myra, and the colours of clothing of the people around him, the reds and yellows and blues, all followed along as if they did not want to be separated from him, he thought. His heart was pounding, he realized, and then Myra put her hand on his chest, sending butterflies swarming from her fingertips and into his bloodstream, where he could clearly see them coursing into all parts of his body.

"Oh, man," he said.

IT WAS DARK outside, while the inside of Myra's Scollard Street apartment was illuminated with candles. James had begun to come down a half-hour ago, but the effects still lingered: noises were sharp, and he felt vaguely uncomfortable, edgy.

"I know," Myra said, looking at him. She had made tea, and they sat on her couch, which was soft and springless and tipped them both into its middle. There was a stack of records leaning against the stereo, and James flipped through them absently: on an album simply called *The Doors*, Jim Morrison looked out, face bathed in darkness. He paused at the haunting image.

"I *just* got this," Myra said. "Listen."

Myra put the album on the turntable and set the needle. The strains of guitar and vocals seeped, dirge-like, from the speakers, then escalated into frenetic chaos. When Morrison began to sing *kill, kill, kill*, "Stop it," James said, willing the panic from his voice. He thought he might be sick.

Myra lifted the needle and slipped the record into its cover, leaning it back against the stereo, where Morrison glowered at James. "It's a good song. What he's really saying, I mean. Maybe later." She flipped through the record stack. In a moment James heard the lighter sounds of "Eight Miles High" and closed his eyes.

"I always feel sort of like an alien or something when I come down," Myra offered. She brushed his temple with a gentle finger. "Sad, like I don't belong anywhere."

"Yeah, that's me," James said, smiling slightly. "An alien for sure."

"Far out. From what planet?"

"Planet Delaware." He grinned, trying to relate Myra's apartment to his parents' rec room. Relief flooded in with the shift in music, and he felt as if he *had* touched down, like the song said. He felt unbearably sad, and he found himself fighting tears. It must just be the effects of the LSD, he thought.

He started to get up. "My stuff's at Fig's," he said.

"Why don't I run you a bath?" Myra asked.

It sounded to James like the kindest thing anyone had ever said to him.

LOUNGING IN THE clawfoot tub surrounded by candles, James felt, keenly, the surreality of displacement. Two weeks ago he'd sat down to a chicken dinner at the family table, his little sister chatting about something. He hadn't been listening; he'd been thinking about what he was going to say. He found himself looking around the house he'd grown up in, seeing each room in a different light. He caught himself watching his mother as she passed potatoes, caught the slight down on the edge of her jawline, and felt as if he was really seeing her for the first time. His sister Brenda laughed, and it sounded at once both achingly familiar and startlingly new, as if he'd never before heard it properly. The secret of his decision lay across his shoulders like something leaden: he would not be showing up for his pre-induction physical next week.

When he finally told them, the result was volcanic, his father apoplectic.

"No son of mine—!"

James tried to mollify his father. "Dad, you told me you fought in the last war so there wouldn't *be* any more." His voice was pleading; he felt like a little kid, and resisted the urge to cower.

"*Don't* tell me what I said—"

"Bob—." His mother, eyes wide.

His father continued, voice raised. "You have to stand up for something. What about democracy? What about freedom?"

"Dad, I *am*—".

"What am I going to tell the boys at the club? At work?"

"Is that what—?" James was almost speechless.

"How am I going to face Jim, for God sake?!"

"You'd sacrifice me to save face with the *neighbours*?" James said, and yet his father's last words jarred. Jim was Billy's father, and Billy had come back paralyzed.

"James, it's not that—" his mother began, but her words were cut short as his father left the room, door slamming behind him.

Brenda, who'd been looking at her plate, touched James's arm. James shook her off. "I'm going for a walk," he said.

Two days later, his mother and sister dropped him at the bus depot; his father was notably absent. His mother took his face in both hands. "I don't know when I'll see you again," she said. "You won't be able to come home."

Although James knew this, the weight of it sunk in then. "Mom, if I went to 'Nam, I might come home in a box," he said through a thick throat. He had held her, feeling like a small boy, then turned to embrace his sister.

"You're doing the right thing, Big Brudder," she whispered.

Feeling impossibly small, he watched the car recede from view until it rounded a corner and was gone.

"It'll be easy," Paul, the Quaker, told him in Buffalo. "We've done this a hundred times. Okay, maybe not a hundred, but a *lot*." And so James and Stephanie had driven in a borrowed van from Buffalo to the border in happy parody of a young couple off to wish some friends well who were getting married, that most respectable of institutions.

"How are your folks taking it?" Stephanie asked him as she loaded her stuff in the back, hanging up the borrowed dress and suit. "Mine threw me out when I told them." She spoke casually, but James detected a tremor beneath the words.

"Not too great," James said. "Why did your parents throw you out?"

"Because Alex is a deserter. And because we're not getting married. Who gets married these days?" She looked at the dress and gave a lopsided grin. "Except our friends in Toronto, of course. What are their names again?"

Most border guards were sympathetic, and in any case, evading the draft was no reason to be refused entry, James had been assured. Paul's group knew the best times to go, who was on shift when. So what went wrong? Maybe someone had called in sick. Maybe it wasn't the usual shift for the officer who took them into separate rooms and grilled them. James had felt himself falter—"we've known each other two—no, three years. We met at Penn State, she's taking, uh—teaching?"

James had no idea what checks and counterchecks might be in place, and whether the Canadian and American border patrols were cooperating. He could feel the sweat running down the back of his neck.

A tap at the door. "Call for you. Urgent," said another officer who, after the first had left, curtly told James he could go.

"Go?"

"Look," the officer told James, sitting down across the table from him. He ran his hands through pale hair, then placed them on the table, palms up. "I'm not going to turn you back."

James felt a shift, a tease of relief, but he remained wary. Was there an implied threat? Could it be some kind of trick? Good cop, bad cop? He peered at the nametag on the chest of the man opposite as he waited for the other shoe to drop. *S. Armstrong.*

"I fought in the last war," S. Armstrong told him.

Here we go, thought James.

"We thought if we did our job, there wouldn't be any more wars."

James willed his head to nod slightly.

"I was missing in action. Everyone—my father, my friends—thought I was dead. A lot of my friends already were." The officer paused. "I know why you're here."

James said nothing, afraid, even, to breathe. There was a moment in which their eyes met across the vast expanse of table.

"Welcome to Canada," said the officer.

"I THOUGHT WE'D be turned back," James said as he shifted into second gear, anxious to put the border behind him, but not wanting to appear too anxious. "And then I'd get arrested going the other way." It felt so close.

Stephanie exhaled, whistling through her teeth. Then she grinned. "Toronto, here we come," she said. "We're home free now.

"Hallelujah," said James. "Right on."

The van backfired, then picked up speed.

In Toronto a fellow named Bruce accepted the return of the van and the money and then peeled off a twenty for each of them, just to help them get where they were going. Stephanie offered to let James stay with her and her AWOL boyfriend, even though James figured it was probably the last thing she wanted to do since they had been apart for two months. James declined; he walked through the dark streets following Bruce's hand-scribbled map until he found the street and the brick walkup. It was late and the house was dark. Fig greeted James with a grasp of hands and a clap on the back and warmed up some leftover chili. After he had eaten, James had sunk gratefully onto the couch with a lumpy pillow and a scratchy Hudson's Bay blanket, and when he awoke it was to the smell of coffee and the voices of Fig and his roommates, and it had all seemed so friendly, so laid back, so *not* uptight, that he lay still for several minutes watching the pale sun make its way across the floor, not wanting to disturb a thing.

THE WATER IN the tub had cooled, and James ran some hot, finding the hot water on the right-hand side, wondering if this was a Canadian thing or just bad plumbing. He wished he had some weed to smoke to take the edge off, but this was a close second. He was stalling, he realized, hoping for an invitation from Myra. He sighed and slipped under, eyes closed.

As he came up, he heard Myra call through the door. "I'm going to bed," she said. "I put a blanket and pillow on the couch."

THE NEXT DAY they took a bus to the house on Baldwin Street, and Myra told James about the city. James, on the window side, rested his head against the cool glass and watched the Yorkville sidewalks full of people who lounged on porches or sat in groups talking or playing music. There were a few souls braving the spring air, selling jewellery on mats and blankets, all of it a rebellion of colour against a stone and asphalt backdrop.

"They're mostly weekend hippies," Myra told him. "They're not really living the scene. They leave mummy and daddy's house in the morning and go back at night."

"Really?"

"Baldwin's different. Lotta draft dodgers. That scene's really happening. The Village . . . the Village is changing. More bummed-out people just coming to hang out. They're not political. You can't *talk* to them about anything."

"What about you?"

"What about me?"

"I mean, were you born here? Where did you grow up? What do you do for bread?" It occurred to James that in all of the talk over their long, acid-insomniac night, he'd never asked her about herself. Instead, they'd talked about racism, feminism, socialism, communism, fascism, capitalism, milita-rism, and social justice, all of it through a surreal post-LSD haze.

"I used to go to U of T," she told him. "I'm taking a break right now. I'll go back, though—I needed some time, I guess. So now I work at a print shop. We just finished printing leaf-lets for TADP. And we do stuff for SUPA all the time."

James looked at her, a question.

"Toronto Anti-Draft Program. SUPA stands for Student Union for Peace Action. It's mostly guys, though, not enough women. Anyway, it's changing. A lot of people have moved over to the CYC." She took in his look. "Council for Young Canadians. They've got government funding."

It was too much for James to keep straight. He looked out the bus window. Someone had told him there were under-cover FBI agents in Canada, ferreting out draft-aged Americans by posing as hippies. Would Canada, with its liberal attitude, allow it?

"Here's our stop." Myra rose and pulled the bell. James stood, and let her slip past him. She swung down into the exit in a whirl of beads and feathers as the back door opened.

JAMES MOVED INTO the Baldwin Street house and found a job in a candle shop in the Yorkville area. It was part-time, under-the-table, and a start, at least. The Baldwin Street house offered free lodging for a while, but residents were expected to become self-supporting and move on.

"Wish I could give you more shifts," Ken, the shop owner, told him. "I got five working here, now, and there's not really work for five. But I like you, man. It's just, you maybe better look around for something else, too."

They were standing just inside the back door of the shop, keeping out of the spring rain while they shared a joint at the end of the day. "I'm short points to apply for immigration," he told Ken. "I heard it's better if I'm willing to relocate, right? To some backwoods place where they need workers." Ken passed James the joint, and James took it, then continued. "You know, I actually thought this place would be full of igloos and Eskimos and that Canadians were a bunch of poor frozen buggers."

Ken grinned. "You ain't been here in January. But yeah, I hear it's good if you're willing to move to the boonies."

"Any suggestions?"

Ken shrugged his shoulders. "Tuktoyaktuk. Kapuskasing. South Porcupine."

James took a deep toke, held it, exhaled, and handed back the joint. "There's a place called South Porcupine?"

"Got an aunt who lives there. We call her Aunt Quill." Ken snorted, laughing through the joint and blowing smoke and spit. He passed it to James. "Sorry, man." The joint, what was left of it, was a bit damp. "Got a cousin in Moose Factory, too."

"What do you call *him*?"

"Poor frozen bugger."

They were still laughing when the front door jingled. Ken stuck his head around the corner, then turned back to James, eyes wide.

"Cops!" he said.

James ran.

After several blocks James collapsed on a bench, hand against the sharp stitch in his side. "Just don't get arrested," Fig had warned him at the TADP office. "That's the quickest way to get sent home." He sniffed at his shirtsleeves, wondering if he smelled like weed, wondering if his paranoia was justified, or just an effect of the dope. Walking back along College Street, still buzzing slightly, he ran into Fig and told him about the cops coming to visit the candle shop.

"They just like to have their presence felt, man," he told James. "They don't actually do anything. Look, why don't you come by the office. Or go see Myra at the print shop. Stop hanging around looking nervous. Do something useful."

THE BELL ON the print shop door jingled when he opened it and Myra looked up from a long table where she was folding leaflets.

"James!" she said, smiling, and she leaned over the table and kissed him on the cheek. Sisterly, he thought, looking away from her low-cut tie-dye tank top.

"Here." Myra handed him a leaflet. *Spring Mobilization to End the War* it read. "In New York! We're going, Fig and me. Actually, I'm heading out in a minute to distribute these. Wanna come?"

As they walked down College towards the university they passed a street cop, and Myra gave him her disarming smile; the cop smiled back. It's a different country, James thought. Myra seemed to know everybody on the street, stopping to chat with an older Italian lady, then again to a tall black man with an afro. "This is James. He's from Delaware," she said more than once. Mrs. Gambini reached up to pat his cheek, telling him, "You get your girlfriend to cook for you, eh? Fatten you up. You're too skinny." Myra laughed, but didn't correct her.

Later, they came back to Scollard Street, and James sat at Myra's red Arborite table while she cooked pasta. There was an open bottle of Chianti on the table, and he sipped from a coffee mug, enjoying the tang of the wine.

"Mrs. Gambini would be pleased," he told Myra as she slid a handful of spaghetti into the pot of boiling water on the stove.

The room was full of steam. "Open that, would you?" Myra nodded towards the tall kitchen window, and James, with some difficulty, slid it upwards in its sash. He breathed in the late-spring air as street noises drifted up from below.

"Sometimes, it feels like I'll always be an outsider." He watched her as she moved from fridge to counter to stove with a dancer's grace. "I've been here a month tomorrow."

"Have you applied for landed? What do you need?"

"More points. First-year philosophy doesn't count for a college degree or a useful skill, even if I was willing to live in—" what did Ken say? "—South Porcupine."

"Where?"

"Never mind. I'm still way short."

"And?"

"And if I go back, it's Vietnam or jail. My only hope is to marry some nice Canadian girl."

Turning with two plates of spaghetti, Myra laughed. "Marriage. Now there's a dead institution," she said.

AFTER DINNER THEY sat in the living room where they listened to records, a different atmosphere from James's first visit; he appreciated the normalcy of it, and the easy conversation. "If I ever have kids, it'll be in a world where they can be free," Myra said. "Where the most important thing is love." She had her head on the arm of the couch and she stretched out her legs and put her feet in James's lap. "This is nice, just hanging out with you."

The words bolstered James's confidence. "So what's the story with Fig?"

"He's committed to the movement," she said, and James wasn't sure if this was a comment of relationship status or admiration, for there was clearly admiration in Myra's voice. "He's amazing. He knows more than anyone I've ever met. He understands the politics of everything, knows all the players. He can give you statistics on anything, remembers every date. I've never met anyone as smart as Fig."

In the wake of this, James could think of nothing to say. Myra tucked up her feet, and James reached for his wineglass.

"You're sweet, James," she told him after several minutes. "But you need to get involved. You can't hang back. There's a lot of changing this world needs."

The streets were empty as James walked back to the Baldwin Street house, but James felt the breadth of the city around him, the country, the world. So much world. He felt small in the face of it all.

MYRA CAME BACK from New York charged by the experience. "Everybody was there. Hippies. Old people. People in *suits*, doctors, and lawyers and things. Little kids. There were a hundred thousand people, James!"

They were sitting in the warm, late-afternoon sunshine of Queen's Park in roughly the same place they had taken the LSD. Myra played with a new blade of grass while she described the protest. "A whole bunch of draft cards were burned. Oh—hey, I brought you something." She sat up and rummaged in her bag, then pinned a peace button to his shirt. "There," Myra said. "Makes you look less straight." She ran her hand across his growing hair and smiled. "There was this one guy on crutches, a vet. He said some stuff about what he'd seen and—everyone just shut up and listened. I mean, he'd really *been* there, James. He was speaking the truth about what it's really like."

"I have a buddy who's a veteran," James told her. "He was in the action at Ia Drang, got a bullet in his spine. He came back in a wheelchair." Billy had opened up to James one night in the bar. He'd been graphic in his description of the villages they'd entered, the silence. The grimace of death, when, in a burned-out shack, he'd come across the body of a girl who could not have been older than himself. The memory of their conversation settled on him now, a hard and smoky weight. "Eleven guys from my grad class came back in boxes—that I know of. There were three funerals the week Billy came home."

"Maybe you should speak out, too, James," said Myra. "Come out to one of the rallies."

James lay back down. He turned his head to look at Myra, backlit by the sun. "I wish I could say I'm brave, or principled," he said. "I mean, I know it's an unjust war. I know it's morally wrong. But you know what?" He gazed up at the perfect, empty sky above him, thinking of Billy, and a dead girl in a burned-out shack. "I'm twenty-one, and I just want to live my life."

"But you care about the war," she said. It was a statement, not a question. "Agent Orange. Napalm bombing. Villages. Grandmothers. Babies."

In James's mind was the voice of Billy's father Jim, who had invited all of the neighbours for a homecoming all-American barbecue. "Civilians? Bullshit. They're all hiding vc commie spies. Our boys gotta protect themselves," he'd said, flipping steaks, while Billy, in his wheelchair, said nothing but knocked back beer after beer.

"Yes," James said to the sky.

WARM WEATHER CAME, and James found a room in a boarding house—clean, relatively cheap, and with a laid-back land-lady. Hanging around the print shop led to some part-time work, which helped since Ken had let him go. But the sense of disconnection, the loneliness, continued. Myra was often busy, working with Fig on the campaign to end the war, and when she and James worked together, it was all she talked about. James felt the implied rebuke.

"When I'm landed," he told her, "I'll get more involved. If I get deported—" The thought terrified him. Once, after most of a bottle of cheap red wine, he'd suggested to Fig and Myra and a few others that his father might even turn him in, something he had not wanted to admit to himself.

"Man, those American warmongers are really something," Fig had said, and James had felt absurdly defensive.

In the print shop, Myra told James she'd been thinking of heading west. "Vancouver is really happening," she told him. "And the winters aren't as cold." It was quiet, between jobs, and they were the only people in the shop. Sunlight filtered through the macramé hanging, with its asparagus fern, in the window. "I think I'm going to go," she said.

"What about Fig?" James asked.

Myra didn't look up from the papers she was folding. "I think you're my best friend, James. I'm so glad I met you."

James didn't press the point. Instead, he picked up the broom from the corner. Myra began stacking a pile of the pamphlets they had printed and folded that day, about the rally to "take Vietnam to Expo" in Montreal.

"Did I tell you we're going?" she said, tapping the top of the pile. "A whole bunch of us. Fig's got a bus rented."

With the broom, James nudged the sweepings towards the dustpan, bright bits of coloured paper trimmed from posters designed to change the world.

THE MORNING FIG and Myra were to leave for Montreal, James awoke late to a grey day. He was hung over; the three had been at the Riverboat the night before, where he'd felt like the odd man out. He'd spent the evening pressed to the pine wall under the brass porthole window smoking and listening to a blonde girl sing about clouds. He wanted to hear her words, he realized, but they fought for space with the fervent political discussions and heady plans for the rally. As he gazed at the stage through the smoky air, Fig's voice cut through the buzz of sound.

"We'll say hi to your buddy for you," he said.

"My buddy?"

"Yeah. At the U.S. Pavilion. Your buddy Lyndon. 'Course, you left. So he's got nothing to say to you, eh? You got a message for your president you want us to deliver?"

James wasn't sure what threat or criticism might be implied in Fig's words, or what expectation they held. There was a new hostility there, and James wondered if it had something to do with the time he was spending, lately, with Myra.

"Tell him to go fuck himself," he said, finally—the only thing he could think of through his beery haze. Who he'd meant, he realized, was Fig.

Fig laughed and pounded the table. "Right on, brother," he said, and delivered a punch to the shoulder that James could still feel this morning, as he lay on a rumpled sheet, feeling down. Outside, crows called.

In the fridge James found an egg and two pieces of stale bread. He fried the egg, toasted the bread, and put it all together in a greasy sandwich that seemed to James to hold the same approximate texture as the day. Although almost May, the air had turned cool again, and James remembered what Myra had said about Vancouver. By the time he'd washed down breakfast with the dregs from the coffeepot, he'd decided: he'd go to Vancouver, where the weather was warmer, and where Myra and Fig were not. He'd settle with the landlady, put out his thumb, and just *go*. But first, he'd leave Myra a note.

He took the bus to Scollard Street. He'd worked hard to assemble the words on the paper folded into a sealed envelope in his back pocket, attempting a tone of free-spirit carelessness while at the same time letting Myra know that he'd welcome her company if she cared to join him later. Alone. But as he steadied himself against the door while he slipped the envelope underneath, it swung open. A muffled sound came from inside.

"Hello?" James took a tentative step inside.

The sound continued; someone was crying. "Hello?" he called again.

"James?"

Myra lay curled on the bed, wrapped in a crocheted afghan. The room, which had looked tantalizing when he'd seen it in candlelight, looked shabby in the light of day. Plaster buckled and cracked on the walls, as if held together with layers of paint. There were clothes strewn across a scarred dresser. James stood in the doorway, frozen. Then, from the form on the bed came a wrenching sob, and James found himself on his knees, one hand hovering over her back.

"I lost the baby," she told him, her voice muffled by the afghan.

The day tilted. "What?"

"I had a miscarriage."

"Shouldn't—shouldn't you see a doctor?"

"No," Myra said. "Just lie here and hold me."

James pulled off his shoes and lay down, a tentative arm around her, as if she might be made of glass. They lay together not speaking, a hundred questions in James's mind. After a quarter of an hour he heard her breathing change, and knew she'd fallen asleep. He lay, afraid to disturb anything, for a full hour more, watching the light change in the room, listening to the sounds of the street below, footsteps on the apartment floor above, and Myra's gentle exhale.

Later, he made tea and they sat in her bed, backs to the wall, facing the window and watching the waning afternoon light.

"I told him I couldn't go to Montreal because I was puking all night," Myra said. "He thinks I have the 'flu."

"He doesn't know?"

"No. And don't tell him." She began to cry again. "You know, I wasn't even sure I was pregnant, not a hundred per cent. I thought—"

James didn't want to hear the rest. "Shhhh," he said. "It's going to be okay."

Myra rested her head on his shoulder. "I love you, James," she said. "It's like you're my brother. I can trust you."

TOWARDS THE END of July, all anyone talked about was the Detroit Riots—five days, forty-three dead, more than a thousand injured, seven thousand arrested, and all because of an after-hours bar raid in a predominantly black neighbourhood that escalated into full scale vandalism and looting.

"You should hear the stories Fig's been getting at the TADP office," Myra told James at work. "Once the National Guard joined the regular pigs, sounds like law enforcement had a police brutality field day." She looked at James as if he might be somehow responsible, by virtue of being American. "How could something like that happen?"

"It's more complicated in the U.S.," he said. How to explain in a country where race and social unrest didn't seem to be such a big issue?

In August, the Village planned a sit-in to take back the street. Attempts to get City Hall to agree to close Yorkville to traffic met with no success, but the residents felt that, this being their community, they should get to make the call. The plan was to disrupt traffic. "You should come," Myra told James.

At the print shop, Lou, the boss, let them print flyers for the sit-in after hours, just for the cost of paper. It was hot, humidity making the flyers limp, their underarms damp. While they worked they listened to The Beatles new album on Lou's turntable, the sounds of "Lucy in the Sky with Diamonds," a psychedelic backdrop to their work.

"It's going to be far out," Myra told him now. "Just people sitting together peacefully on the street. A be-in. Like San Francisco, or Greenwich."

As far as James knew, Myra had never told Fig about the miscarriage. He couldn't fathom why she didn't, but she had been adamant. "He's got so much on his mind," she had told James. "In Vietnam, babies are dying every minute."

Look for the girl with the sun in her eyes and she's gone, sang Lennon. James watched Myra's fluid grace as she worked, heard the enthusiasm in her voice as she chattered on about the sit-in, her laugh a slash of sunlight, and felt her slipping away from him. He couldn't see how the sit-in was going to make a statement about the war, and he told her this as the flyers rolled off the press.

"It's not about the war," Myra told him. "It's making a point. So they don't think they can push us around, like in Detroit. Fig says—"

"I don't want to know what Fig says."

James walked Myra towards Spadina, and the streetcar. Waves of heat rose from the pavement, causing small mirages. On the street, they would already be gathering for the sit-in. "James, you should come," she told him. "Did you hear about the guy who led the city hall protest last week? He's a U.S. Army deserter!"

"Good for him. He's probably landed. And anyway, I heard they picked a guy up the next day and threatened to deport him, just because he had some weed on him."

"So? They weren't going to actually *do* anything. Come with us. James, you need to take a stand."

"Who says?"

"Fig says."

Fig. "Says what?" It irked James that Fig had been talking about him with Myra.

"It's like, all these people are working to help you guys. You need to do your part, too. You need to get political."

James heard Fig's voice in Myra's words. "See you later," he told her.

IN THE END, James found himself standing at the corner of Bay and Cumberland as dusk fell and people gathered. The heat hadn't really abated, and it hung in the air, an invisible, malevolent presence. James couldn't see Myra or Fig, but then, there were a lot of people. The street was full of hippies, and James saw a number of burly guys with Vagabonds logos on their jackets. Outside the Riverboat he'd seen bikes parked, chrome gleaming. They didn't seem like people all about peace and love, and James felt uneasy, thinking about what happened in Detroit, aware of how quickly a scene could turn. A slight, bearded guy was speaking through a microphone, reminding people that there should be no violence and no drugs, but James smelled weed in the air. There must have been two hundred people sitting— even lying—on the street, chatting, laughing, smoking, playing guitar. On the sidewalks, hundreds more. He could hear car horns in the distance; clearly, no one would be driving down these streets.

"Damn hippies," said a man standing in a doorway. He spotted James. "Get a goddamn job," he muttered.

A commotion at the far end of the street, and James craned to see over the crowd, now several deep on the sidewalk. He heard shouts, and a scream. Cherry lights flashed on the sides of the buildings that flanked the street. He saw himself caught up in it, thrown in a wagon, deported. Heart pounding, James turned and pushed through the crowd, walking fast, willing himself not to run.

BY FALL, JAMES had been in Toronto for six months. One of the dodgers on the street, Gordon, was heading for a commune in northern Quebec with his girlfriend Cindy. "Come with us, man," he said. "They'll never find you."

They were standing outside Grossman's Tavern, where a sign in the window told James he could buy a hot hamburger plate for forty-five cents. With a beer, that'd be seventy. He was hungry, his under-the-table work not enough to cover rent as it was.

"You look like shit, you know? Come to Quebec, man. There's a few people there already, bought some big old farmhouse. Gonna get some crops in before winter."

"It's almost winter now."

"Suit yourself." Gordon wandered off to find Cindy.

James stood in front of Grossman's, hands in his pockets, hoping someone he knew would stand him a beer. Gordon had said he looked like shit, and the truth was, he felt like shit. Lost; empty.

He'd sent a postcard home the week he'd arrived, but of course he'd given no return address. What would his sister be doing now? Had his father cooled down? Did he regret his words? What about his mother? And here he was, in a different country altogether. He decided to go for a walk, think about things. He crossed Spadina and turned down an alley, head down, looking for solace in solitude. Five minutes with nobody telling him what he should do, where he should go, what he should say. A memory came to him: a day at the lake, fishing with his dad when he was twelve. When did everything become so complicated? He closed his eyes, saw the twist of a trout in the evening light, the brilliant arc of water, heard the whir of the reel as it spun. His father's easy laugh, paternal hand on his shoulder.

A horn, a squeal of tires, and a car bore down on him, a screaming blur of chrome and fins. There was nowhere to go in the narrow alley, brick walls on both sides, garbage cans. James leapt for a doorway.

"Fucking hippie!" someone shouted, and as he came up from his roll James saw a car full of leering faces, heard whooping and raucous laughter.

They had been aiming for him.

The car swerved, knocking over a garbage can before exiting. James leaned against the wall, gasping, sick. The palms of his hands were shredded from landing on glass and gravel, and his shoulder ached from where he'd fallen hard into the doorway of a loading dock. He stifled a sob. He had to pull himself together.

WHEN JAMES FOUND Fig and Myra sometime later at Grossman's, he'd resolved not to mention the incident in the alley. He felt pathetic. It didn't matter; they didn't notice his appearance, deep as they were in conversation, shouting over the din of people and music. Myra wore round tinted glasses James hadn't seen before, and he wondered briefly how she could see in the dim bar. She leaned in close to Fig, an occasional hand on his arm as they talked. James was too hungry to care; he asked Fig for a loan and Fig, distracted, had pushed a couple of bills across the table at him. James took them and went to the bar to order some food. If he could just sit for a while, feel the solid surface of a chair beneath him, eat a meal, and have people around him, he'd be okay. As he handed the barman the money, he saw that his hand shook.

After sopping up the last of the coldly congealing gravy with a piece of bread, James drained his glass and refilled it from the pitcher Fig had bought. Fig and Myra were talking animatedly about the next mobilization, organized by the Committee to End the War. Fig was planning to speak on behalf of SAEWV. As they talked, the two rattled off acronyms. James downed his beer and poured another.

"What's with that? SAEWV. SUPA. TADP, TCC . . . TCCEWV? Is this the ABCs of political activism or something? How the fuck do you keep them all straight?" James laughed, a half-sneer.

Myra glared at him; Fig looked unimpressed. "This is important, James," Myra told him. "We're doing this for you."

"We're doing this for Vietnamese civilians," Fig corrected. "They're the victims. They're why the war is immoral. You—"

Myra put her hand on Fig's arm, and James saw this as an intimate, exclusive gesture. "What *about* me?" he said.

Fig leaned across the table. "You're white. You're an American. You're so fucking privileged, you don't have a clue. What are *you* going to do to stop the war?" Fig's face was inches from James's.

A hundred possible retorts volleyed in James's brain, but what came out of his mouth was: "What's with the nickname, anyway, Fig? Are you some kind of fruit?"

The air was thick with tension, and then, abruptly, Fig leaned back. "You're not even worth it, man. Useless piece of American crap."

He got up and strode to the washroom before James could respond. On the stage, a young man with long sideburns settled himself on the stool, adjusting guitar and harmonica with the mics. Neither James nor Myra spoke while he began, in a quavering, haunting voice, to sing about lost childhood.

"What happened to peace and love?" James said.

Myra stared at the stage. The noise in the bar had risen, and it was hard to hear the musician's words. Finally, "He's had a rough week, James," she said. "First, TCCEWV doesn't want him to speak at the rally. I don't know why, it's some kind of inside politics. Then, this guy who came up from Maine about a month ago has been hanging around the office every day, getting weirder and weirder. Fig had to call the cops when he started smashing stuff, and you know they hate calling the cops; it just gives the authorities ammunition, like you're all undesirables. Turns out he's got some multiple personality thing. He'll get sent home, I guess. He'll get out of the draft, anyway." She looked towards the washroom, where Fig had gone. "And this other guy he was helping got busted for trafficking," she continued, running a finger through the wet ring from her glass on the tabletop. James watched as she made a series of lines imploding into the centre, then wiped it clean. She looked at James. "Are you okay? You look messed up."

"I'm fine," James lied. He peered at Myra. "Is that a bruise?" he asked.

"I tripped getting off the streetcar," she said.

All at once James's stomach lurched against dinner, beer, and the events of the day. He met Fig at the door to the washroom. "Fucking coward," Fig muttered. James couldn't tell if the shove Fig delivered was accidental or intentional, but he pushed past into the washroom, where he flung himself into the only free stall.

"Fucking asshole," James said when he came up for air. From the quiet of the washroom he could hear applause as the musician finished his song.

TWO DAYS BEFORE the October rally, James and Myra argued outside the print shop.

"Look, James, you have to get political *sometime*. This demo really matters: the more exiles that come out, the stronger everyone's going to be. There's a whole bunch from Baldwin Street coming. Yesterday there was a sign paint-in at the church."

James crossed his arms. "It's great for them. They're landed. I'm nowhere—and probably wanted. My time's up, and I haven't figured out what to do. I get arrested, I'm deported, and next thing you know I'm burning Viet Cong villages full of kids and old people. Or rotting in some prison."

"It's gonna be huge, James. You need to be there."

"I'll do it once I get landed. I'll march in every fucking demonstration. I'll be so political you won't even recognize me."

"Fig says you need to shit or get off the pot."

"*Fig* can go fuck himself."

"*You* can go fuck *your*self."

ON THE DAY of the rally, James couldn't keep himself from the street, but he hung back, out of the thick of the crowd, so he could make a quick exit if he needed to. The streets were choked with demonstrators, including, as Myra had said, exiles, identifiable by their "we refused to go" placards. The Yorkville residents had not been successful in getting the street closed to traffic, but nothing was going to be moving today.

The press had been less than positive in recent months, and there appeared to be antagonism on all sides. Draft dodgers were labelled cowards by the pro-war faction, and now Fig was calling James a coward for not speaking out as a war resister. *Was* he a coward? Standing now under the awning of a bookshop and looking across the sea of people, James didn't know. He could feel the anticipation and tension in the air like an animal presence. Anything could happen.

He looked for Myra, but with thousands in the street it was futile, and anyway, he hadn't seen her since their fight outside the print shop. The noise of the crowd—movement, voices, guitar, and, somewhere, a saxophone—swelled; he felt claustrophobic, and longed for open space. The pocket of sidewalk on which he stood was now filling. He found himself pushed against the wall of a building. A girl he didn't know grabbed his hand, pulling. "C'mon—they're starting," she said. He wrenched himself away and tried to move in the opposite direction, but the current was against him. The girl was gone, and around him was the press of bodies.

From somewhere down the street someone was speaking through a microphone, but he couldn't make out words, only an onslaught of disjointed, booming sound. He put his hands over his ears, and someone nearby said: "Hey, you trippin', man?"

The microphone sounds separated, and converged, and then became words, and through it James recognized Fig's voice. Moving forward on the tide of people, he was pushed towards the podium. *Fuck*, he thought. When he reached the stage, James saw Fig still trying to belt out his message. Clearly, he wasn't welcome: a scuffle had broken out, Fig shouting at the bearded man trying to wrestle the microphone away.

"Get the fuck off me!"

Fig kept his feet, and James, now at boot level, saw organizers arguing at the back of the stage. A voice said, "Just let him speak, man," and the bearded man backed off.

Fig's chest heaved, eyes wild; from where James stood, he could see the veins pulse in his neck, the sheen of sweat. Fig's gaze darted through the crowd, and then he saw James, and pinned him. He pointed. "There's the real thing, people," Fig shouted into the microphone. "We have here a bona fide American Vietnam Draft Dodger. Come up and say something, draft dodger."

There was a push from behind, and James was hoisted up and onto the stage. Fig shoved the mic at him; from the corner of his eye, James could see Fig surrounded, being encouraged off the stage. From somewhere in his peripheral vision he caught a glimpse of Myra pushing through the throng of people, but she wasn't coming towards James; she was trying to reach Fig.

On stage, with the microphone in his hand, James looked out at the crowd. The sea of people appeared to James like an uneasy ocean under a brewing storm. A weird silence had descended, vaguely threatening; James could not tell how to read it. He felt the suffocating crush of expectation.

The air stilled as the assembled protesters waited for the figure on the stage to say something. "Let him speak," came a voice from backstage, just as someone had said for Fig. James felt the thudding in his chest grow quiet. From somewhere in the crowd, a baby cried.

"I am a draft dodger," he began.

"Right on, brother," said someone near the stage.

"Speak up!" called someone else.

"Some might call me a coward," he continued, his voice rising. There were more shouts; James couldn't discern the words. "Others, an opportunist." He took a deep breath. A girl near the stage gave James an encouraging smile.

"But mainly," he said, "I'm just a guy who doesn't want to kill anybody."

A roar went up, the mic was handed to the next person who'd climbed the podium, and he stepped down. One of the organizers took the mic, but James no longer heard the words. His eyes were following Myra. At the side of the stage fists were flying, and within moments Fig's arms were pinned from behind. Myra was trying to reach Fig, James trying to reach Myra, around them the crush of bodies. James shoved, and someone shoved back.

Myra reached Fig as James tried to push through a half-dozen people in the way. A woman James had never seen before was already there, shouting at the guys holding Fig to "Let him *go*." Fig shook them free; from the podium, a new speaker had started a chant: *One, two, three, four! We don't want your fucking war!*

James watched as Fig turned to Myra, now at his side, saw rather than heard Fig's words, saw Myra's face as he said them. And then Fig, and the woman, were gone.

James saw Myra go down, then, pushed or simply fallen, he couldn't tell, and he shoved against the bodies in front of him to reach her.

"Let me through!" he yelled at the biker who blocked his path.

"No entry," said the biker.

James lunged. He saw the biker's fist like a cartoon, expanding as it came towards him. Then he saw legs, feet, pavement, nothing.

IN MYRA'S APARTMENT, James made tea and brought it to her in bed.

"You look like hell," Myra said as she took the cup.

"So do you," said James, climbing in beside her. It wasn't easy to smile.

He leaned against the wall, listening as she blew across the cup. The smell of oolong mingled with the patchouli scent she always wore and the must of sheets that needed laundering. The only light came from the lamp beside the bed. From the window's open half-inch a cool wind blew, bringing with it the smell of leaves and something else.

"How early does it snow here?" James asked Myra. "Can it snow in October?"

"I remember it snowed one Hallowe'en when I was a kid," she said. "You never know."

James thought about getting up to close the window, but he felt battered and weary from the events of the day, and far too comfortable beside Myra. "What was that you said about Vancouver?" he asked. "It's not as cold?"

Myra smiled slightly, but didn't answer. Her eyes were red. "Fucking Fig," she said. Then she began to laugh.

James laughed too, relieved by the sudden release in tension. "Yeah, fuck 'im," he agreed, but Myra put a finger to his lips.

There was no sound from the street below, the whole of Yorkville remarkably quiet. This, he thought, is peace, even if it comes at a price. He had seen the movement reduced to its parts. Now, in the slow-motion universe of the room around him, he felt a tentative solace.

Myra shifted beside him, then set the cup down on the blue plastic milk crate beside the bed. "It rains a lot," she said.

It came as a non sequitur, and James turned, an eyebrow raised. "Huh?"

"In Vancouver. It rains a lot."

He thought for a bit. "Do you think they need people to do stuff there?"

"What, now you like the mic?"

"It was—okay. It was even good. I don't know that being in the spotlight is really my style, though." James put a hand to his swollen lip. "Maybe something more behind the scene?"

"Right now, I think behind the scene is absolutely where it's at," Myra said.

She took his cup and set it on the table beside her own. Outside on Scollard Street, a gentle snow began to fall.

NINE

NORMAL

·1970·

HER NAME WAS Wanda Wysnowski, but we called her Wombat.

She was everything we weren't and nothing that we were: we all wore tartan skirts or the new polyester pantsuits recently allowed within the grade five dress code; she wore shapeless dresses that looked like they'd been scavenged from the Goodwill bin. Her leotards were pilled, covered in little balls of yarn that made them look diseased.

While we all brought our lunches in the handy zipper lunch kits with the matching thermoses, hers came in re-used brown paper bags. And her food: unidentifiable things wrapped in waxed paper. "Wombat's eating goulash again," we'd say, not really knowing what goulash was. We unwrapped our bologna-and-white-bread sandwiches, smug. Wanda would sit a little away from us on the school playground, intent on her lunch. And the way she said things, carefully enunciating, as if her words were fighting to get past her overlapping teeth. Why did she talk so funny?

"It's like she has rocks in her mouth," Donna Pistecky said to me as we walked home together after school. Donna's parents came from Czechoslovakia, but Donna was born in Canada. She knew what was what.

"Yeah," I said.

THERE WERE THREE neighbourhoods within our Ottawa school district. Ours was a pleasing labyrinth of crescents and cul-de-sacs, two-storey houses with long front walks and big backyards. All the streets were named after places in Britain. Even in 1970, with a modern young prime minister and real hippies protesting in Confederation Square, we were still children of the Empire.

My friends and I knew all the best places to hang around in the walking paths that bisected the neighbourhood. We knew the best coasting hills for our bicycles, and we knew where the dogs lived who sometimes gave chase when we tore around corners. We knew all the shortcuts. There were four of us: Andrea, Donna, Mandy, and me. "One-third of the Dirty Dozen," my dad joked.

The army kids who lived on the Base were a pack unto themselves, the constant shift of families who could be posted away at a moment's notice creating a special bond, more intense for its temporary nature. The army kids didn't mix with kids from our neighbourhood, and nobody mixed with the kids from Gilmore Park, which consisted of low-income row housing, faded Ontario brick with peeling white trim. Windows without shutters. Gilmore Park kids, our parents told us, had a reputation for being a bad lot.

WANDA'S FIRST DAY of school was almost three weeks after the start of the school year. Indian summer had made us all lazy that day, the boys shooting spitballs, the girls writing notes, all of us gazing through the windows at the playground bathed in autumn light. Wanda came to the classroom door with her mother. She knew enough to drop her mother's hand, but she didn't drop it soon enough for us not to see. We all looked at the newcomer, a short girl with mousy hair.

"What a baby," Andrea, sitting at the next desk, whispered. Andrea already had breasts, small buds that you could see poking out under the fabric of her ribbed turtleneck. This gave her a claim to maturity, as if she had graduated to a league far above the rest of us. She tucked her hair behind her ears and looked at me conspiratorially. I took solace, reassured. For the moment, I was still in the club.

Self-consciously, I adjusted my glasses. They were new, and they left painful red spots on the bridge of my nose that sometimes wept sticky fluid. At home I tucked tiny bits of toilet paper under the oblong plastic pieces, but of course I couldn't do such a thing at school. I was terrified someone would notice these sores, which in my imagination were enormous. I had learned that acceptance was precarious, something that could change in a heartbeat. I kept my head down and my glasses in place, smiling back at Andrea, who was watching the new girl with disdain.

"I'll bet she still sucks her thumb," I whispered.

My left thumb tingled as I said this. Another secret.

"Boys and girls," Miss McGrath began loudly. The new girl stood alone at the front of the classroom, her mother gone. "Attention, please. You have a new classmate. Please say hello to Wanda Wysnowski."

"Hello Wanda," we intoned. Two of the boys drew out the final syllable, so there was a baritone finish, like a dirge.

Somebody laughed. Wanda looked at her shoes. We all looked too. They appeared too big for her feet.

Miss McGrath was old, but she was on the ball, as my mother liked to say. She sized us up and then looked straight at me. "Meg, will you be Wanda's special friend for the first few days?"

I didn't want to look at Miss McGrath, who often singled me out for things. When I complained about it, Mum, who knew Miss McGrath from the Hospital Auxiliary, said that the teacher chose me because she sensed she could count on me. When my mother said that I had felt proud, but now I just felt self-conscious. I didn't want to be Wanda's special friend, and I didn't want to be singled out by Miss McGrath for anything.

"Margaret?" Miss McGrath prompted.

I could hear Donna snigger behind me. Andrea was grinning, looking straight ahead. Nobody called me Margaret except my mother when I was in some sort of trouble. Everybody called me Meg and although it sounded old-fashioned to my ears I liked it a whole lot better than Margaret, which was my grandmother's name. Granny, who lived with us, read *Winnie-the-Pooh* backwards or upside-down and embarrassed me when friends came over by saying things like "No flies on Charlie!" to nobody in particular.

I could hear Mandy, in the seat beside Donna, whisper "Go on, *Margaret*."

"Okay," I answered, not looking up.

I could feel my friends watching. I smiled at Wanda reluctantly, a flicker. She didn't smile back, but her eyes were hopeful.

THIS IS WHO we were:

Donna, large-mouthed and corkscrew-curled, lived in the row housing that perched on the border between our neighbourhood and Gilmore Park, a mini-neighbourhood of row houses in a horseshoe configuration. These were the nicer row houses. The yards were bigger. The trim didn't peel. There was a communal pool in the courtyard with a chain-link fence around it, just for the people who lived there, and if you knew someone you could go in. When the summer heat settled into a ceaseless swelter, Donna was everyone's best friend. You didn't want to fight with her and lose access to the pool, and so Donna managed extraordinary arrangements during this time: loans of favourite shorts sets, just purchased in Ogilvie's and hardly even worn yet; the *Archie Super Summer Digest*, the one you wanted to read over again, even though Veronica always won and you liked Betty better.

Mandy had three younger brothers whom she called, collectively, the Brats. They were all blond, as was Mandy, who had an elfin face that freckled so much in the summer the spots all joined in places like a tan. Her spritely personality matched her short, bouncy physique, and this endeared her to teachers and parents who could not see her devious nature under her perky demeanour. She could be your best friend or your worst enemy. Mandy lived in a two-storey two-tone house on Essex Avenue. She had an English Setter called Polkadot. Her parents, she told us, were once tennis champions.

Andrea had straight brown hair and a tall, solid build. She had an older half-sister who came from her mother's previous marriage, and that made her mother seem slightly dangerous, a Woman with a Past, which in our neighbourhood was a strange and exotic thing. Andrea's sister Gina still lived at home and went out at night to bars and sometimes, when we'd all sleep over in a tangle of sleeping bags on the rumpus room floor, she would come in late at night and flop on the leatherette couch, not yet ready to sleep herself after a night on the town. She'd sit and smoke and tell us things that sounded scary and sexy. I learned new words, things I would never, ever, hear at home, things that surprised me but didn't seem to surprise Andrea at all.

I was the youngest in my family of four, a late child. By the time I was in kindergarten my eldest siblings Anthony and Eleanor—twins—were already in university. By the time I was in grade three, Janice was gone, too, and it was just me at home.

"She gets *everything*," Eleanor would say when she'd come home for the summer and see my new green five-speed bike or hear I was going to summer camp. She hated that I got my own room while she had always had to share with Janice. Still, my mother never quite got over the lean years of raising the first three children while Dad was working his way up the company, and she was always telling me how much things cost, and what we couldn't afford. I had a keen sense that I could not expect to get the things my friends had, and felt guilty when I did get the bike or two weeks at camp.

I looked nothing like my siblings, fair where they were dark, myopic when their vision was perfect. I had buck teeth I hid behind my hand when I smiled. Once, I overheard Andrea and Mandy speculating as to whether I might have been adopted. But when I asked my mother, suddenly suspicious, she reassured me. Eleanor, home at the time, said: "Did you think they'd have taken you on by choice?"

But if I enjoyed the benefit of being the only one left at home, as Eleanor complained, it was not so beneficial at school. There, I felt the difference of older parents who were not as interesting as those of my friends. They didn't go to Puerto Vallarta in March. They never had cocktail parties. When we went to Ogilvie's, my mother chose the conserva-

The first catseye succumbed to the cant of the pavement, rolling sideways and into the waiting palm of the grade five girl, who scooped it into her purple Seagram's bag. The second, shot so as to compensate for the slant, missed the mark as well. I took a breath, and decided to go for the other beauty in the back, inching my knees across the pavement for a better angle. I used my best pitch, the gentle thumb flick that always, always, won for me. There was that angle again, a dip in the pavement I didn't see and wasn't expecting. My fourth catseye also missed the mark.

I rubbed my beauty, my last marble, my favourite marble, between my palms. I was sure now that my initial assessment must have been wrong, that the front beauty was the easy shot. How sneaky to make the one that looked easiest the one that *was* easiest, a brilliant strategy. I blew into my hands.

The bell rang.

"There's no time," I said, relieved.

The grade sixer eyed my orange beauty. "Yes there is," she said.

"Not for three shots."

"Okay, one, but if you hit it I'll give you *six* beauties," she said.

It was a good deal, and if I was right, the front beauty would be the easy hit after all. But what if I was wrong?

"Do it," whispered Wanda. She was looking at me in admiration. The schoolyard was almost empty, and the wall yawned between us and the door. The recess teacher was waiting, holding the door open for the stragglers.

I blew on my marble again, rolled it between my thumb and index finger, and shot. Missed. My orange beauty disappeared into the purple Seagram's bag, and the bag disappeared with the grade six girl who ran into the school before I had even stood up.

"Sorry," said Wanda. "If you come over to my house after school, I'll give you one just like it."

I didn't believe her. After all, it was obvious she didn't even know what the game was. "I have lots more at home," I told her. But I didn't have another beauty like the one I had lost, and I didn't wait for her as I ran towards the door.

After school, Wanda came up beside me as I got my lunch kit from the cloakroom. She didn't say anything, just stood there. Did she think I was going to walk her home?

"I don't live near you," I told her. I was sure she didn't live in my neighbourhood. She didn't say anything, just stood there with her pilly leotards and her big, scruffy shoes. I noticed for the first time that her mousy hair was held back with two barrettes shaped like kittens. Baby barrettes.

"I have to go," I said, seeing Donna, Andrea, and Mandy gathering at the end of the hall. We always walked together. As I moved away, Wanda moved with me. I could feel her presence as she walked beside me, but I didn't know what to say. Miss McGrath had asked me to be her Special Friend, and Miss McGrath was counting on me. As we approached, my friends turned to meet us.

"Hi Wanda," Mandy said in a tone I knew. "It's neat that you're in our class. Where do you live?"

"Gilmore Park," said Wanda.

Andrea rolled her eyes. "What does your dad do?" Her own father was a lawyer.

"I don't know."

"You *don't* know what your dad does?"

Wanda appeared flustered. We waited, one beat, two.

"He's away a lot," she said finally. "On business trips."

We waited again. "But what does he *do?*" asked Donna.

"He can't tell us. It's top secret."

"Like a spy?" Andrea looked around at all of us, a smile playing on her lips. There had been a show on television last weekend in which a girl's father was a spy, and the family didn't know anything about it. At first you thought he was a spy for the bad guys with the accents and then you found out he was really a double agent working for the good guys, the ones who talked like normal people. It was likely that Wanda had seen the show. Everyone had.

Wanda nodded earnestly.

We split up at the corner of Avon and Cambridge, Wanda walking towards the busy road that she'd have to cross to get home.

"See you tomorrow, Wanda," we called.

There were four blocks to go before we would begin to split off towards our separate homes. Mandy was the first to speak.

"She is so *weird*," she said.

"Yeah, as if her dad's really a spy," offered Donna.

"Weird," Mandy said again. "Weird Wanda. Wanda Weird."

Andrea laughed, and I joined in. "Her name sounds like *wombat*," Andrea said.

"What's a wombat?" I asked.

"Some kind of animal. In Australia. They're really ugly, with piggy snouts." She pressed her thumb to her nose, pushing it upwards, and snorted.

IT STARTED OUT just between us, the jokes about Wanda. The way she talked, what she ate, the way she wore her clothes. The way she followed me around, even when the few days during which I was supposed to be her "Special Friend" were long past. Andrea teased me about it: "Wombat likes you. You're so lucky to be her *Special Friend*," she said.

It was one day when Andrea and I were walking across the school field to the big maple tree, Wanda trailing behind us, that Andrea said over her shoulder, "This is private, Wombat." I didn't look behind, but I could sense her stop where she was. As if it was me in her shoes as they stood, unmoving, on the scuffed earth.

After that, Wanda left me alone. She left all of us alone. As she did, we grew bolder, talking about her when she was not quite out of earshot. We never called her Wanda anymore, only Wombat.

"I'll bet she never washes," Donna would say. "I'll bet they don't shower where she comes from."

"Yeah," I said. Then: "Where does she come from?"

"Somewhere in Europe." Donna said vaguely.

"Yeah, somewhere where they don't shave their pits," Andrea snorted with laughter, and we all joined in. Andrea, who had sprouted several hairs under her arms and shaved them off weekly, was an expert in armpits and all bodily functions. This made me nervous, me without hairs at all, and so I laughed louder than I meant to, a barking laugh that drew their attention.

"Hey, Meg, you're her Special Friend. Ask her." Mandy grinned at me.

"Ask her what?"

"Ask her if they shave their pits where she comes from. I double dare you!"

WHEN I APPROACHED Wanda the next day, my tone friendly, she was suspicious.

"You want to play with me?" she said, unsure.

"Yeah," I said. "Let's walk over to the big tree."

We walked together to the maple tree, feet crunching on dry leaves, their smell earthy. Once I was alone with Wanda I had no idea how to ask her where she was from or what their hygiene habits were there, even with a double dare behind the question. Instead, I asked about where she lived before Gilmore Park.

"The west end," she told me. "But my mum's job moved over here. She works for a big company. It has offices all over the place."

"What company?"

"I doubt you've ever heard of it," she said, sounding snobby. She was looking up into the branches of the maple, most of the leaves gone, now. The lower branches had been cut off so we wouldn't climb the tree, something that was forbidden anyway. I thought of the marble I had lost thanks to her, and the teasing I got about being her Special Friend.

"Want to climb up?" I asked her.

"Are we allowed?"

"Sure. Here, I'll give you a leg up."

"Then how will you get up?" she asked me.

"I climb this tree all the time. It's easy for me," I said. She looked at me doubtfully. "C'mon," I said again. "Are you chicken?"

She put her shoe in my clasped hands. The sole was worn smooth. Her clothes smelled of dry leaves. She didn't smell bad, like I thought she would. She pushed up to reach the lowest branch, didn't make it, and fell back against me, her arm around my neck, knocking off my glasses.

"Sorry," she said. Over her shoulder I could see Donna, Andrea, and Mandy grouped together by the corner of the playground, watching. I cupped my hands for her foot and she tried again, this time catching hold of the branch with her right hand. I could see her underpants as she swung her foot free.

"Where do you come from?" I asked as I watched the grey underpants swaying above me.

"I told you," she grunted. "The west end."

"*Before* that."

"Yugoslavia," she said, one leg braced against the trunk, the other flailing in the air. "But we moved when I was seven because we're Croats."

"What?" It sounded like Crow-rats. My father always said that crows were just rats with wings, and that's what I was thinking about as I stepped back, watching her scramble up the trunk. I knew I was supposed to ask her if they shaved their armpits in Yugoslavia, but I didn't know where that was, and suddenly that mattered. I tried to find the words to ask, to make good on the dare, in a mental scramble that mirrored Wanda's struggle into the tree.

She had both hands firmly on the branch and was working her feet up the trunk, her smooth soles slipping on the bark. I watched, the question temporarily forgotten. She was more agile than I thought she'd be. I had never been able to climb this tree. From the corner of my vision I could see my friends approaching.

"Do they shave their armpits there?" I blurted suddenly as she hooked one leg over the first branch.

"What?" she asked. And then she fell.

WE WERE NICE to her for a little while after that. We all signed her cast, drawing hearts and peace signs from her wrist to her elbow. We wrote Flower Power in bubble letters. The *a* in Mandy was replaced with a big pink daisy. "Get well soon,

Wanda," she wrote. But when the excitement died, Wombat was back.

That October, Ottawa was frozen in the spell of the Quebec crisis, beginning with the kidnappings of James Cross and, later, Pierre Laporte, names I'd never heard before but that now appeared everywhere. When Prime Minister Trudeau imposed the *War Measures Act*, "Good for him," my mother said. My father, a Conservative, didn't comment. All of Ottawa was in the grip of tension, every family transfixed by the newscasts. "These terrorists. It's awful," I'd hear my mother say almost nightly to my father as they watched the CBC news. "They have to be stopped, or they'll just think they can get away with anything."

ON WEEKENDS WE gathered in one of our four houses, although less frequently in mine, where Granny was apt to say anything at any time. If we did, I carefully steered my friends past her, where she sat in the flowered chair in the living room, to the basement, where we had the old black-and-white TV, the brown hide-a-bed couch, the orange shag rug, and the African-print curtain that divided our hangout from the part with the furnace and the washing machine. That was where, one Saturday afternoon, Andrea lifted up her shirt and showed us her breasts, so the rest of us could see what we were in for. They looked like little mounds of soft whipped cream, the nipples pale pink. Donna and Mandy lifted their shirts, too, in front of the old mirror in the corner, checking for signs. I didn't want to.

"My mum might come down." I said.

"Chicken," said Andrea. "It's just your body. It's natural, you know. Here, feel," she took my hand and began to guide it towards her chest. Mum's step on the stairs as she descended with a load of laundry caused a flurry of movement as shirts descended.

"What are you girls up to?" she asked cheerfully. Fully clothed again, we giggled, falling against one another like puppies.

WHEN WE RETURNED to school on Monday Wanda was absent. "Where's Wombat?" asked Donna, and we all giggled at the double *W*s. Each day she was absent, one of us would ask the question, dissolving into fits of laughter over the alliteration. When Wanda returned after two days, we could barely contain ourselves.

"The Wombat Weturns," whispered Andrea, sounding like Elmer Fudd. Wanda, in the desk on the other side of me, looked up. She had heard.

Later, in the cloakroom, I asked her why she had been away.

"My dad died," she told me. I didn't know what to say.

But after school, Mandy snorted. "She doesn't even *have* a dad," she said. "My mum says Wanda's mum is a single mother."

I had heard the term but couldn't quite grasp the circumstance, so different from my own. Didn't you need two parents to make a baby? I wondered. I didn't realize I'd spoken out loud until Mandy rolled her eyes.

"You're so stupid, Meg. Of course there were two parents. They had to have sex to have Wombat, didn't they? They had to make Wombat Love." She drew out the last words and we fell into fits of laughter, my own a little forced. I was happy to hide my embarrassment in the hilarity of the moment.

"He probably left them," offered Andrea after a minute. "He probably took one look at Wombat and ran."

I BELIEVE IT was then that I really began to feel sorry for Wanda, who had begun to be absent for a day here and there, always returning with a little folded note for the teacher. Not that I became her bosom buddy or anything, but I began to look for moments in which to offer a few friendly words here and there when I thought nobody was looking. Miss McGrath noticed and took me aside.

"Good for you, Meg. I know your friendship means a lot to Wanda," she said.

Andrea overheard. "What are you, teacher's pet?" she said later.

From then on I did my best not to invite any comments from Miss McGrath and I avoided Wanda, but when I found Wanda standing alone in the cloakroom after everyone had gone, I told her I liked her jacket. I didn't—it had two sets of big ugly round buttons down the front—but I did like the colour, which was a deep blue. She was struggling into it at the time, trying to pull the wide sleeves over her cast. As she looked at me I noticed for the first time how black her eyelashes were, and how perfectly they circled her eyes, almost without stopping at the corners.

"Thank you," she said. "My dad bought it for me."

"I thought you said he was dead."

"I mean, he bought it for me before he died." She turned away, as if she couldn't bear to talk about it. Mandy came in to the cloakroom.

"What are you two talking about?" She asked.

When we replied, it was in unison. "Nothing," we lied.

THE DAY THE news announced the execution of Pierre Laporte at the hands of the terrorists, our kitchen radio was cranked up to full volume as I ate my cornflakes. The morning was cold and wet and I walked to school feeling the weight of something I did not understand wrapped around my neck like a scarf pulled too tight. When I stepped from the slate grey morning and into the reassuring yellow light of the classroom I found on my desk a small white envelope. There were similar envelopes on the desks of each girl in the class. Thirteen envelopes. The boys were curious.

"Wouldn't *you* like to know?" Andrea said to Maurice Landry.

My envelope contained a small card with a picture on the front of the Eiffel Tower. It wasn't like most party invitations, with balloons or birthday cakes, but looked like part of a set of hasty-notes, like the kind my mother used. Inside it said:

> *You are invited to a birthday party*
> *Saturday, October 22, 12:00 – 5:00*
> *#4 627 Thornstone Rd.*
>
> *Wanda Wysnowski*

"SHOULD WE GO?" Donna asked at lunch. "What if she feeds us some kind of goulash cake?"

Andrea laughed. "Wombat stew," she said.

"Let's ask her," said Mandy, and I followed as my friends approached Wanda where she sat in the corner of the lunch-room eating a sandwich that, remarkably, looked just like ours. Bologna. White bread.

"We're going to McDonald's," Wanda told us through her sandwich. Andrea raised her eyebrows. McDonald's was new. It had just opened downtown a few months ago. We'd heard all about it, but none of us had been there yet. "And we're going to see *The Aristocats*." The new Disney movie. We hadn't seen that either.

"Neat," I said. My friends looked at me.

"Yeah, that's really neat, Wanda," Mandy offered.

"So you'll come?"

"Of course we'll come," Mandy said again, and we all gathered around her, fawning. Our new best friend.

WE WALKED TOGETHER to Wanda's home, a narrow townhouse with a paved frontyard.

"Maybe they don't believe in grass in Yugoslavia," whispered Andrea.

"Shhhh," said Donna as I reached forward and rang the bell.

Wanda answered the door, Mrs. Wysnowski hovering behind her. Wanda was wearing a brand new pantsuit with gold buckles. "Welcome," said Mrs. Wysnowski in an accent I supposed was Yugoslavian. She was round in shape, with a big bosom and dyed red hair and hoop earrings.

The narrow hallway opened into a small living room. The furniture looked different. Old-fashioned. On the end tables were round white mats with lace edges and embroidery of flowers and birds. In a glass cabinet in the corner stood ornate brass jugs and painted china plates. There was a piano, with framed photographs on the top. I wanted to look for Wanda's father, to see if he looked like a spy, or dead, but before I could approach, Wanda's mother began to speak, and I listened, transfixed by her deep voice and the way she pronounced different words. *Darlings*, she called us, the *a* elongated, the *g* hard. She sounded like an actress.

We would go to McDonald's, she explained, and then to the movie. We would take the bus. Since my parents had a car, a Ford station wagon with green leather seats, I had never taken the bus, and I was excited by the prospect.

"I bet they don't even have a car," said Donna in my left ear, but I pretended not to hear her.

"After the movie we'll come back here for presents and birthday cake," said Mrs. Wysnowski. I had placed my present with the others on the table in the hallway, and now I felt bad about my choice. My mother had asked me, when we went shopping at the mall, did I want to get her the Nancy Drew book or the plastic troll necklace set. Trolls were the newest thing, squat dolls with pug noses and coloured hair. We collected them, but I didn't yet have the necklace. "The Nancy Drew," I had said.

There, in that small townhouse, I thought suddenly about what thirteen McDonald's lunches and thirteen movie tickets must cost, imagining my mother's voice in my ear. When I had asked her if we could go to McDonald's she had said it was too expensive. But our house was a lot richer-looking than Wanda's.

"How can they afford this?" I asked Donna. She looked at me like I was crazy.

"Who cares?" she said.

McDonald's was everything we hoped it would be: perfectly formed patties completely unlike our backyard barbecue hamburgers, French fries shaped like small square pencils. We thought the little packets of ketchup and mustard were cute, and we tucked some away in our pockets. We didn't really speak to Wanda but talked and laughed among ourselves. Still, as we walked the two blocks to the Elgin Theatre and nudged and jostled one another, she walked in the thick of us, smiling, and stood beside me while her mother paid at the box office.

"Thanks for coming," Wanda said to me as we waited.

Wanda sat beside me in the theatre. When the movie drew to a close, she took my hand and gave it a squeeze. "You're nice to me," she said.

Back at the Wysnowski's, Wanda beamed as she blew out the candles, the flames reflected in the decorative buckles on the front pockets of her pantsuit. We ate chocolate cake made from a cake mix, and stirred our melting ice cream into the crumbs as we sat crowded around the dining-room table. We played Pass the Spoon, a game in which each girl would put something from her plate—ice cream, cake, candles— on the spoon until it was piled so high that it spilled. The girl holding the spoon when that happened had to eat everything that had dropped, candles and all. Just before it got to Wanda, one girl reached for the salt and pepper in the centre of the table and dowsed the pile liberally. As Wanda took the spoon, the inevitable happened.

"That wasn't fair," I said to the girl, and everyone looked at me. "It's just supposed to be stuff from our plates." The table was quiet.

"That's right," said Mandy after a moment. "You don't have to eat it, Womba."

That's what she said: Womba. She had begun to say Wombat, she told me later, then caught herself and tried to change it to Wanda. I looked at Wanda, still holding the spoon. She was smiling, frozen. Mrs. Wysnowski came in from the kitchen, then, wiping her hands on a towel. She wore an apron that was embroidered like the doilies on her coffee tables.

"Ready for presents?"

We left the shambles of the table and tumbled into the tiny living room, a tangle of elbows and knees as we all found places on the floor. I tried to peer up at the photographs on the piano again to find out what Yugoslavians looked like, especially Wanda's father, but I couldn't really see. The presents were in a pile in the centre of the floor. It took a little while to open so many presents, and, as we had been taught, we all said things like "wow" and "neat-o" as each was unwrapped. When Wanda opened *Nancy Drew and the Secret of Shadow Ranch*, she held it to her chest.

"My favourite," she said.

"I hope you haven't read it."

"No, but I really want to. Thank you, Meg."

THE FOUR OF us walked home from the party in relative silence. We were full of hamburgers and popcorn and cake. I was feeling queasy.

"She's not so bad," ventured Donna.

"Nah," agreed Mandy.

"Did you really call her Womba?" Donna looked at her sideways, suppressing a laugh so that it exploded into a snort. The others started laughing then, the way we often do, sometimes close to peeing ourselves before we manage to stop. I laughed a little, but my stomach didn't like it. As I turned off to my own street, I thought of Wanda and the way she squeezed my hand in the movie theatre. I rubbed the hand against my pantleg.

When I came home Mum was in the kitchen, Dad drinking a rum & Coke and watching the news. The reporter was talking about the FLQ, and whether James Cross would be freed. A photograph released by the terrorists showed a balding man bound with his hands behind his back.

"Wanda called you," Mum called as I stood in the doorway to the den, watching Dad watching the television. "Hi dear," he said, not turning to look at me. He didn't ask me if I'd had fun at the party.

"Did you hear me?" Mum called again.

"Yeah."

I wondered why Wanda would call me. Maybe I forgot something at her house, I thought. I had to look up her number, and to do that I had to be able to spell Wysnowski. I tried a few possibilities before I found the number and began dialling. It seemed as if the dial had scarcely completed its final rotation when the receiver at the other end was picked up. "Hello?" came Wanda's voice.

"It's Meg. You called me?" I may have sounded short, impatient. I could hear her voice falter.

"I just wanted to say thank you for coming. It was really . . . nice to have you." She sounded formal, foreign. I thought of the embroidered doilies, the photographs on the piano.

"Sure," I said. There was silence, the telephone wire thick between us.

"See you tomorrow at school?" She sounded hopeful.

"Sure," I said again. When I hung up the phone my damp hand had left a mark on the handle that evaporated as I gazed at the silent telephone.

On Monday I walked to school as usual with Donna, Andrea, and Mandy. We talked about *The Aristocats*. We discussed McDonald's, and how they said that soon there would be one in every country in the World. It seemed impossible to us.

"Even in Yugoslavia?" I asked, and although I meant it, my friends took it as a joke about Wanda.

"They could call it McWombat's," laughed Andrea.

Around the room were tacked last week's art projects, put up on Friday, I supposed, after we'd gone home. They were wax and paint pictures, Hallowe'en scenes drawn in crayon painted over with black paint so the wax came through.

Wanda's scarecrow looked happy, a big smile across its yellow face. At the bottom of the picture she had written her name in black magic marker. *Wanda*.

When the bell rang and we took our seats I sat, as usual, at my desk between Andrea's and Wanda's. As I looked at the board I could feel Wanda's eyes on me. After a moment I glanced at her and smiled, then looked quickly down at the open reader in front of me. I kept my eyes on my work until the morning recess bell rang.

It was a beautiful day, a last gasp before November would take hold and the sky would descend into a relentless grey winter. I left the classroom ahead of Wanda, running slightly to catch up to my friends, who were discussing Hallowe'en. Wanda was behind us somewhere.

"I'm going as a hippie," Andrea was saying. "My sister's got all the clothes."

"You're supposed to go as something scary," Mandy protested.

"What about going as a *wombat*? That's really scary!" Andrea said. I turned to see Wanda behind us. She brushed past us, running.

I walked with my friends to the maple tree, from which point we could see into the boys' yard, another reason why the tree was a favourite spot. There, we speculated on who was cute and who wasn't. We accused one another of liking a boy, or being liked.

"Maurice Landry likes you," Donna said, planting an elbow in my rib cage.

"No he doesn't," I said. "Besides, he's short." They waited. "And he looks like a retard," I said, pushing up my glasses, and Andrea nodded approvingly.

As the bell rang Andrea ran ahead, followed after a moment by Mandy and Donna. I didn't feel like running, my feet heavy in my shoes. Wanda was walking from the other side of the playground, alone, and I entered the classroom before she did. I sat at my desk, Andrea grinning beside me, but I couldn't figure out what the joke was. Wanda came in and sat down.

I could hear a few of the boys begin to laugh, then a small commotion as people turned in their seats. I turned as well. Under Wanda's scarecrow someone had crossed out *Wanda* and written *Wombat*.

Miss McGrath didn't notice; I almost wished she would. I didn't look at Andrea or Wanda or anyone for the rest of the morning. At lunchtime I ate my sandwich in the lunch-room and then went straight outside, the way we were supposed to. Wanda was standing by herself watching the Double Dutchers.

". . . if it's Wanda let her in, and we'll sock her in the chin . . . "

But Wanda wasn't skipping. She was just standing there. When I approached I saw she was crying.

"Hi Wanda," I said, quietly. I don't know what I thought I would say. I just wanted to be with her. I was not prepared for what she did next.

She hugged me.

I stood, arms straight at my sides, not moving. Maybe that's what they do in Yugoslavia, I thought as I waited to be released. It was certainly not something you did as a ten-year-old in our neighbourhood in 1970.

"Meg, what are you *doing*?" came Andrea's voice from behind me. She said it like she had just caught me eating slugs. Wanda let go of me, stepping away.

"That's really gross. What are you, lezzies?"

I didn't know for sure what a lezzie was, but it sounded like something I didn't want to be. I thought I might have heard the word from Andrea's sister, but I couldn't remember exactly, and I thought it might be when two girls got married, and I knew that this was something that was not normal. I knew that being normal was the most important thing.

Then I looked at Andrea, and knew suddenly that it was Andrea who had crossed out Wanda's name on the drawing.

I might have stood up for Wanda then, might have stood by her and told Andrea I thought she was mean. I might have made excuses to my friends: she was upset, that's all, I might have said. But then Wanda reached out and took my hand in a gesture that was complicit. Her hand felt warm, sweaty. I felt their gaze on our joined hands and pulled away.

"It's just that she was crying," I said, too late. Then: "I don't even like her."

I walked away. I walked away from Wanda, who, the day after James Cross was freed by the terrorists, would change schools, taking two buses to get there every day. And I walked away from Andrea, who later became my main tormentor when I got fitted for braces, an abuse that continued through junior high.

I walked to the maple tree and leaned against its trunk, my right hand pressed against its bark. I was trying to lose the tingle of warmth from the hand that had been held in Wanda's. The bark was rough and cool, but the sensation remained.

TEN

THE LANGUAGE
OF BONES

·1985·

THE WIND IS always present. It blows across the shifting plates of summer ice, slate and cobalt and the many shades of white; it sweeps across the tundra of Herschel Island, laying flat Arctic lupine, lousewort and vetch. Terns ride its currents or let the wind hold them, motionless, in the air. A polar bear lifts its nose, trying to discern the scent and sound of ring-necked seals through the steady blow off the Beaufort Sea.

I walk under the high distant sun of a Northern evening, the wind flattening my clothing against my body. When it blows like this, the mosquitoes are gone, at least. I am wide awake, despite the long day of sifting soil and cataloguing tiny fragments at the excavation site, and insufficient sleep. Barry, my supervisor, says it's hard for any Southerner to adjust to twenty-four-hour Northern light, and I've felt eerily awake most of the time since I got here. It's wearing, though; I can feel it fraying my edges, this wakefulness, and light and wind.

Ahead is the Inuvialuit graveyard, my destination. The wind, undulating across tussock and scrub, looks as though it might blow away the weatherworn pickets that surround the knot of graves. I put my head down and push against it, moving forward towards the past, and it pushes back as if to say: who are you to go digging things up?

BEFORE I LEFT for Herschel Island, I took the ferry from Vancouver to Victoria to see my folks. As soon as I arrived, "Nina—I was getting worried," my mother said, hugging me briefly. "We were waiting for you. Drop your things—there's just time to get to the graveyard."

It was the anniversary of my younger sister Lucy's death, and I had forgotten. How could I? A hot wave of guilt washed over me, and I mumbled apologies for being late. I didn't tell my parents the truth: that in my excitement, I had imagined a family dinner in which we'd talk about my upcoming summer dig up north; my dad would be proud, I'd thought, my mother anxious, both of them excited with me. We'd get out the atlas and I'd trace the route north to the top of the Yukon. Now, in the shadow of Lucy's sad anniversary, my own impending departure to what was merely a different geography seemed unremarkable.

Lucy had been the bright spark: imaginative, emotive, dramatic, and talkative. She was also the pretty one: raven hair, big eyes, in contrast to my mousy appearance. Where I was tentative, she was forthright; where I was shy, she was outgoing. By the time she was twelve, boys were drawn to Lucy like moths to a flame; they ignored me, three years older. Her life cut short before her thirteenth birthday, Lucy was the daughter who didn't grow up, and so she would always be the shining potential of a future she didn't get to live.

Being top of the class had nothing on that.

When Lucy died, my grandmother took me aside, perhaps worried that I'd burden my grieving parents with my adolescent outbursts; I was still a teenager, after all. "You'll need to be strong," she told me. "You'll have to grow up."

I took her at her word.

BACK IN VANCOUVER, I scrambled to find a car I could afford. I'd been so busy with school, I'd left it late. But I'd seen an ad tacked to the bulletin board in the laundromat on Commercial: *Car. Cheap, or trade for truck. Quick sale, good Karma.* It made me laugh; it didn't even say what make or year, but I figured cheap was good. I don't know what I thought about the karma part. I pulled off the number in an act uncharacteristic for careful, practical, no-nonsense Nina. Maybe things were changing.

James and Myra arrived in a rusty '75 Civic, hand-painted flowers across the hood. James unfolded himself from the driver's side and gave me a laid-back grin. As Myra awkwardly disengaged herself from the passenger side, I saw she was pregnant.

"Two reasons for selling, the car," he said. "That's one of them."

"Hi," said Myra, hand up, palm out.

"What's the other?" I was waiting to hear the bad news about the car's mechanical condition.

"We need to get a truck instead. We've decided to head for the Kootenays, find some land. Live a healthier life. Settle down." He nodded towards Myra, who was leaning against the car, hand moving in rhythmic circles over her belly. "We have a kid coming. Been trying forever—we were ready to give up. I'm thirty-nine this year; figured it might be time to grow up. What about you?"

"What about me?" Was he asking about my reproductive status or my maturity?

"What do you need the car for?"

"I need to drive it to the Arctic Circle," I said. "And back."

James seemed to take this in stride. He patted the closest daisy. "No problem. She's been around the block a few times, but she'll get you there."

After the papers were signed and the keys tossed into my hand, I had to empty my new used car of the detritus of someone else's life—one wholly unlike my own. I shovelled out pamphlets, books, cassette tapes, odd articles of clothing, food wrappers, and other miscellany. The irony that it was an archeological dig of sorts—garbage being a telling indicator of what life may have been—wasn't lost on me, heading as I was to a real dig of my own. I was Nina-turned-adventurer. I left the daisies.

After I'd packed my tent, sleeping bag, bug spray, boots, and field guides, I tucked into the glove compartment the journal I've kept with me since Lucy's death. When I write in it I'm never quite sure if I'm writing to myself or to my sister. Maybe I'm writing to the person I'd be now, if Lucy were still alive.

The Civic behaved remarkably well on the long road north. Three days after I left Vancouver I pulled up at the Whitehorse address my supervisor had given me: a small house with a low roof and missing siding. When I knocked, a tall, freckled guy opened the door, hand outstretched, a big, friendly grin on his face.

"You Nina?" he asked, and I nodded. "Stuart McKinnon. Glad you made it." He looked past me. "Interesting car," he added.

Stuart was just back from Herschel, where he'd been setting up, arranging supplies, and scoping out the accommodations. After dinner we sat in his low-ceilinged living room, the stove going against the chill in the air, even though it was the beginning of June. I was warm and comfortable and happy not to be driving.

"Who else is there?" I asked Stuart.

"There's a couple of guys from U of T studying warming trends," Stuart told me. "They're presenting a paper on climate change for an intergovernmental conference next year. Man, if Herschel is anything to go by, something's gotta happen quick." He took a swig from a can of Canadian. "That's it for people, except for the Lapierres. White guy and his Inuvialuit wife, four kids. They've been on Herschel for years, but I hear they might not be much longer."

"How come?"

Stuart shrugged his shoulders. "Things are changing, I guess. It's slated to become a territorial park, but I don't think that's the reason. The ice isn't what it used to be; hunting patterns have shifted. It's gotta be lonely. Who knows? Anyway, it's good you're going. I don't think the Washout excavation site will be there much longer. It's eroding so fast you can almost watch it go. This is probably the last chance."

Before bed I stood on the porch marvelling at the light, wide awake, listening to coyotes call and answer across the bluffs.

I SPENT THE next day picking up supplies and got back on the road late in the day, energized by the daylight. As I pushed north I could feel the breadth of the land like a presence. When I pulled into Dawson City it had to be well after 2 a.m., but there was a soccer game in progress in a playing field near a school, and an old guy was riding an older bicycle, wobbling down the middle of the road as if it were the middle of the afternoon, the sun just above the low mountains to the north.

The next morning the Dempster Highway was a mine-field of mud and potholes, but the land opened up, a vast canvas of open space and light. I crossed the Peel River on a cable ferry, drinking in the scent of water, running on little sleep but with the heady excitement of the shift in light and landscape and the adventure ahead. Here, the boreal forest gave way to the scrub of the Mackenzie Delta, a wash of subtle colour and texture. On the ferry across the great, swollen Mackenzie River I stood on the deck and thought about the Mackenzie Valley Pipeline proposal, still in its ten-year moratorium. I closed my eyes and imagined a pipeline running like a scar across the land.

At Inuvik I took a late room at the Eskimo Inn and ate in a bar filled with men, sitting on a tall stool facing a wall of bottles, feeling conspicuous. The blind was broken in my room, and I slept with the covers over my head, trying to shut out the light.

The next day I found my way to the airport, bleary from lack of sleep, but the flight woke me up. From my bird's-eye view in the Twin Otter, hundreds of lakes and ponds below looked like puddles nestled in foliage of green and russet. I wanted to look, and at the same time I wanted to put my head between my knees as the bumpy ride played havoc with my stomach, and my nerves. Jerry, the pilot, yelled soundless words over the roar of engine and wind, once pointing at a pair of Tundra Swans on a pond below, and I took a deep breath and looked. In turns fascinated and terrified, I managed to hold it together until we landed on hardpacked beach at Pauline Cove, the Otter bumping to a stop a reasonable distance from two figures: Barry and Andy, I guessed.

As I emerged from the plane, the wind took my breath away.

HERSCHEL ISLAND IS not the sort of place where you can sneak up on a person; as I stand in the graveyard I see the woman and two kids approach from well in the distance. She appears to have a level of comfort with the blasting wind, or at least she doesn't seem to be fighting it like I am. She's wearing a light summer parka, and her features tell me she must be Inuvialuit. With her are a boy and a girl, perhaps seven and five.

I stand up from where I've been examining a grave. I feel guilty, caught poking around here. This grave likely belongs to a person held in living memory, unlike the thousand-year-old Thule house we're working on at the Washout site.

"Hello." I smile at the approaching woman. The boy regards me with that disarming stare some children deliver so well, but his sister tucks herself behind her mother's legs. "Hello," I say again, directing the greeting at the girl. In an odd way, she reminds me of Lucy, the way she was when she was small. That black hair; those eyes.

"This is Pauline," the woman tells me, then points to the boy. "That's Luke. The other two are fishing with their father."

"Nina," I offer. "I'm working with the group on the Washout site."

She nods. "Annie."

Luke pokes at his sister, who hangs back further. "I don't bite," I tell her.

Annie lays her palm on her daughter's black hair, and the girl breaks into a smile. Luke reaches around back of his mother's legs and gives her another poke. The smile broadens, rosebud lips in a round face and dark, shining eyes.

"You remind me of someone I know," I tell her.

"She's quiet now, but she likes to talk," Annie says. "We saw you walking here." She follows my eyes, seeing the lop-sided fences, I suppose, as I'm seeing them. Suddenly I feel like a tourist.

"I'm sorry," I say. "Maybe I shouldn't be here. Are some of these your relatives?"

Annie doesn't answer directly. "This grave belongs to Kudnalik." She nods at the grave in front of us, fragile in its precarious grip on the shifting earth. "He was in a fight with a whaler who ran away from his boat. This happened a long time ago. It was a big storm. Kudnalik and his wife and boy, they were inside their igloo, waiting for the storm to pass. And their dogs started to bark and a man came out of the snow. Maybe he got lost because of the storm. He said he had been travelling for two days, but he was not so far from his ship, maybe a few miles."

"And he was killed? Kud—"

"Kudnalik. Yes. And later his wife died. The whalers brought all kinds of diseases."

"And the boy?"

"The boy grew up." She turns to the kids, who continue to poke one another, giggling, and speaks to them in Inuvial-uktun. They scamper off towards the gravel beach.

"How do you know all this?" I ask.

"Kudnalik was my great-grandfather," she pauses: "Come to the house." Annie points over the dunes, but I know where it is. Andy pointed it out a few days ago, a square house built of driftwood logs. "I'll make tea," she says.

"How about tomorrow? I still have some things to write up."

Annie nods and calls to the kids, who hear her despite the wind. "We don't get many women here," she says, then: "My grandmother believed that if you touch the possessions of a dead person, you'll be cursed." She shades her eyes and watches Luke and Pauline playing tag, taking their time returning. "These are old beliefs. She would not have liked to see me here, even, near this burial place. I don't think it's bad to be here, but right now I can feel her beside me, telling me to go."

She calls the kids again. Her words sound like the clatter of beach rocks in a receding wave, a pleasant sound, a mixture of granite and sand.

Tomorrow I'll ask Barry about these graves, and about the whaler's graveyard. I know there are plans to try to move some of the buildings farther from the shore—there's the Hudson's Bay Trading Post, Anglican Mission, the RCMP detachment, the warehouses, all of which eventually may be washed away—but I've heard of no plans to move the graves. In most graveyards, people remain safely underground. They won't come up to remind you that life is, after all, a fleeting and tenuous thing.

The Washout site is clearly threatened. The first half of my day today was spent constructing a berm to keep out the sea, which, at high tide, threatens to compromise the first house site; maybe not the next tide, or the one after that, but all it would take is a high tide or a good storm to wash away a thousand years.

I can feel it now in my shoulders, the hard work of earth-moving followed by the small, constricted movements of delicate excavation work. I watch the receding figures of Annie Lapierre and her children, then turn, the wind now comfortably at my back.

IN THE SEMI-DARK of the RCMP barracks, Nina sleeps. She's alone; Barry and Andy are visiting the climatologists who are staying in one of the warehouses. She met John and Frank on the first day. Both had been interested to find out there was an unattached female working on the island, and John had asked her several questions about herself. She'd answered awkwardly, later consoling herself that she was there to work, after all, and had since declined enough invitations to socialize that they had ceased to be offered. After several days Barry and Andy had opted to sleep in their tents, giving Nina the barracks to herself at night. Nina was grateful; this way, she might eventually get a good night's rest. Now, she sleeps fitfully, her breathing shallow.

ARCHIE GORHAM, BARELY backlit against the point of light creeping from behind the covered windows, shifts in his seat. There is still a small amount of tobacco in the tin he carries, and he pinches it into his pipe and lights it, observing the form of the girl asleep in the bunk as he does. He's dressed in caribou hide, fur turned in, as if for winter; even in the mild temperature, he appears cold. His skin has a blue cast.

From the other side of the dim room comes a cough, and Archie looks up.

"What, you back?" he asks through the pipe which is clenched in teeth the colour of old piano keys.

"I am back." The words are spoken in Inuvialuktun.

"Talk English," says Gorham. "Goddamn Eskimo."

"You should learn our language. You should know my name. Kudnalik."

"I know your name."

"You come and you buy our meat, we teach you how to hunt, our wives make your clothes, you take our wives and sometimes even our daughters—"

"I never took anyone's daughter!"

"—and you don't learn a single word. I've heard you are all thieves and murderers where you come from. That's what your captain Bodfish said. That every one of you should be dead, hanging."

"He was drunk when he said that, which was something for him, I'll allow. None of those officers was supposed to be drinking, that was the rule. You know why he was drunk? Because it was Christmas, and we got him to have a little glass just for a toast. Shamed him into having a toast with the men for once, and then kept topping up his glass. So then he started telling everyone—even you Eskimos, because by then the party was pretty big, and the bonfires and all, and the dancing—"

Kudnalik smiles. "I remember. It was a good time."

"—that we're all a bunch of scoundrels, when he's got a past, mark my words."

"And you?"

"Some petty thievery. Nothing serious."

Kudnalik rises and picks up the straightback chair, moving it closer to Gorham so they sit with just a small table between them. "You got some tobacco?"

"You know I don't have much left." He looks across at Kudnalik, the whites of his eyes glinting in the diminished light. "All right." He pulls the tin from his pocket and hands it to Kudnalik, who sniffs at it.

"Smells old," he comments, but he takes his own small pipe from his pocket, similar to Gorham's but carved from antler. "When you robbed that hunting camp, that was not a small thing."

"No," Gorham admits.

"White men, no guns, no food, no dry clothing. They had to come after you or die." Kudnalik draws on his pipe several times until the tobacco glows.

"But they didn't die."

"No, because you did."

Gorham snorts. They're both quiet, regarding Nina as she shifts, rolls, and sighs.

After a while Gorham taps his pipe on the metal tabletop. "Anyway, that Christmas night? That was the first time we made a break for it. If it wasn't for the cabin boy spilling the beans, we'd have made it. Too many people knew. We'd been hiding food, so the cook was in on it. We promised to pay him once we made it."

"It would have taken many days, even with good dogs. And you were on foot."

"Of the three of us, I was the only one who kept all of my toes. And Barclay lost his whole foot. Bodfish was heavy-handed with that saw. And he put the cook in irons." Gorham rolls his eyes. "We were never going to make money on those boats. Not that whaling wasn't profitable. But by the time it got down to us—*we* weren't getting rich. And it wasn't like the beginning, when we were taking hundreds of whales—"

"Whale heads, you mean. You take just the baleen and throw the rest of the whale in the water. Inuvialuit would never treat the Bowhead with such disrespect. Or any animal. That is why we can live here, and you freeze to death."

"Not all of us. My point is that by the end of the season some of us wound up *owing* money, and that's after risking our lives in the killing boats. Two drowned on our boat alone that season. In the Gold Rush we could really make our fortunes. We'd have made the cook and that damn cabin boy rich, too."

Kudnalik stands up. "I need to see to my dogs and get back to my wife."

Gorham shrugs his shoulders. "They're not going anywhere."

"No," Kudnalik agrees. "But I will go now, anyway." He steps through the barracks door and out into the hard, flat light.

I WAKE UP and clutch at the fading ghosts of dreams. I can't quite pin down the images, which dissipate even as I try to grasp them. Such is the nature of dreams, but it's frustrating. On the other hand, if I dreamt it means I must have slept. I look at my watch: seven o'clock.

At the excavation site Barry and Andy are discussing the damage. The tide has receded, but at its highest point it washed away most of the berm we built yesterday. If we can't keep the water back, we'll have to do our best at low tide. This site is closest to the shoreline. Barry begins to carefully excavate the gravel we had excavated yesterday, while Andy and I work on a new berm. That work takes us well into the morning. At lunchtime I stretch, every muscle aching from too many hours hunched over.

"I got lunch," says Andy, and I stretch out on the ground, letting the sun warm me, while he trots back to the barracks, and our stores.

Barry flops down beside me and scratches at his beard, then rubs his hands over his face.

"This afternoon we'll be able to start sifting," he says. "As long as we don't get a serious storm, we'll be okay. You can still get a blizzard this time of year."

"It would be awful, wouldn't it? To lose everything before we've really started?" I'm up on my elbows now, squinting across the surface of the sea. There's a rise in the water in the distance, then a blow. Once, whales here were "thick as bees," according to historical records, and the area remains a favourite of Bowhead and Beluga. Closer to the shore, a flock of black guillemots bob in the water.

Barry follows my gaze and watches for a moment before replying. "Hard to say which would be worse: losing every-thing now, or losing everything after we've finished. You heard about what happened in '73?"

I shake my head. My stomach growls, and what I'm most thinking about is lunch, to be honest, although I'm looking forward to getting back into the dig.

"What happened?"

"A group spent all summer excavating two house features at Pauline Cove. It was an important collection: aboriginal artifacts from the 1880s, when the Cove was almost a city, full of whalers and Inuit. There were some trade items there, too, so it was a good indication of relationships between the two. The collection was stored at Newport House, an old whaling warehouse. It's gone, now," he says. "Fire."

"Fire?"

"Yep. Kids with matches. I guess kids will be kids, any-where you go. There was nothing left."

"Nothing—?" In this climate, with little opportunity to spread, I'd have thought fire would be easy to put out. The permafrost is right there, too, the reason why artifacts are so well preserved on Herschel.

"There were also twenty-four drums of helicopter fuel stored there."

I wince.

"It's a good thing the kids didn't go up with it, too," Barry says.

My first thought is the Lapierre kids, but they'd have been too young or not yet born. Maybe Annie, her brothers and sisters? I can't tell how old she is.

Andy comes back with a knapsack and starts hauling out a big thermos of tea, some hardtack, peanut butter, and dried fruit. He spreads his big hands and grins.

"Dig in, grunts," he says, and Barry raises an eyebrow.

"Okay, grunts and bosses," Andy amends. He holds up a package. "And," he adds, with a flourish. "Tuktuk! Ray gave it to me. He was over at the other camp last night." He looks at me. "Dried caribou to you, newbie," he says.

I put a piece in my mouth. It tastes leathery and rich and strange.

The afternoon is spent screening earth through three-millimetre mesh, and for the most part we turn up bone fragments—the remains of Thule dinners, most likely—and an excellent harpoon head. Andy's attention is on construction, primarily: analyzing the remains of the once sod-and-driftwood structure with its square pit and log floor.

Residents of Herschel have always been happy recipients of the driftwood bounty spilling out from the Mackenzie Delta and washing up on the island's south shore. That same driftwood kept the whalers alive in the late 1880s and early part of this century—that, and the help of the residents themselves, who provided meat and replaced the whaler's heavy wool clothing with pants and parkas made of hide. By the height of the whaling era, these "Eskimos" were people from Alaska, Siberia, and the Yukon North Slope, coming to trade or to work on the boats, all living in tents and igloos and driftwood dwellings at the relative metropolis of Pauline Cove.

I measure, weigh, and catalogue the fragments we find. Late in the afternoon a piece of baleen turns up, the bony plates of the Bowhead whale's filter system. This house pre-dates the coming of the whalers by hundreds of years, of course, but the discovery of the baleen fragment—likely used as a flexible scraper—brings to mind the real reason for Herschel's version of the Gold Rush: the wasp-waists that were popular with "civilized" women of the time, and which necessitated corsets—constructed of baleen. I can't help but feel insulted on behalf of these mighty beasts.

I quit at five with Barry's blessing; they'll work a while yet, but I want to keep my appointment with Annie and her family, not that we had any sort of time set. I'm told that things are not so precise in the North, which makes sense to me. What does it matter when the day just goes on and on?

I'm excited; this visit could develop into an important element for my thesis. I set off across the tundra. In this light it's hard to imagine winter, how long and quiet that must be. For the Inuvialuit, winter is a part of life, but for the whalers a hundred years ago, it's no wonder they might go mad with drink or fear or boredom, and bolt. Months of isolation and lack of light would push dark emotions to the surface like bones from the ground. For some, there may have been a point where risk no longer mattered, never mind that others had tried and failed, been put in stocks, lost limbs to frostbite, died; a run for civilization, as a deck hand or boatman might see it, was worth it. I close my eyes, try to imagine day after day without a sunrise.

I open my eyes and blink. Ahead of me, an Arctic fox stares, interrupted in its hunt for a shrew or lemming. We look at one another for several moments and then it moves on, and I exhale.

I stop at the whaler's graveyard on the way to Annie's house. These wooden headboards will be restored this summer. The Inuvialuit graves, respecting belief and tradition, will not be touched. I pause at the grave of Archibald Gorham, who died in 1896. Barry told me that the melting permafrost is having the effect of pushing these graves up to the surface, and that some, close to the shore, have actually been washed away; between this and the erosion of wind and rising water, I half expect a bony hand to poke up and give me a wave.

The kids run towards me as I approach the Lapierre house, a large structure made of driftwood logs. One of the older boys I didn't meet yesterday is pushing a wheelbarrow with his small sister Pauline bumping about inside. They're good-looking kids, grinning and laughing. They don't seem bored, in this world without electricity.

"One of you must be Luke," I say. I look at Pauline in the wheelbarrow. "Have I met you before? Are *you* Luke?" My uncle used to play this game with Lucy and me, mixing us up. Pauline giggles and the boy pushing her laughs.

"*He's* Luke," the boy says, pointing at his younger brother.

"So you must be Pauline, then," I tell him, and I make a point of not looking at Pauline, who's beside herself with barely stifled laughter, or at Luke, who's tugging at my arm.

"I'm George," the boy at the wheelbarrow grins. "That's Albert."

"Ah!" I say, and now Luke is pulling me towards the house, where Annie stands in the doorway smiling. Beside the house five huskies are also smiling, but not barking. With a full escort, they must figure I'm okay. Ray doesn't appear to be around.

"He took some people on a hunting trip," Annie tells me.

"Tourists?" It seems ridiculous even as I say it, but then Herschel is slated to become a park. I suppose it stands to reason.

"Pipeline people. I guess they have some time off."

Annie tells me that Ray was a commercial pilot, flying between Inuvik and Sachs Harbour. He grew up in Tuktoyaktuk, where his father ran the Hudson's Bay store.

"How did you meet him?" I ask.

"One time he landed here. He was picking up some people. This was at the beginning, when they were first talking about the pipeline. The weather turned bad, and Ray stayed with my family." She smiles, almost girlish. It's infectious: I smile back. "He started landing here more often after that."

The house is a clutter of bins, buckets, and tools, all of it useful; there are no knick-knacks. There are three rooms, two clearly for sleeping. We sit in the main room, light pushing through the panes of the big front window, the ceiling low. Clothes hang drying above us. On the woodstove, a pot sits, and from this Annie pours tea into mugs, adds powdered milk and sugar. The kids still play outside, but I catch Pauline periodically peeking through the window.

"Are you happy about the island becoming a park?" I ask Annie. The tea tastes as if it's been steeping for days; with the milk and sugar, it's surprisingly good, and I close my eyes for a moment to savour it.

Annie sips from her own cup. "It's good, I think. But we will move."

"Because of the park?"

"Because the children should go to regular school. Because it's better, maybe, to be in Aklavik. More people. But we'll always come back. This is our place."

"You never said if you have other relatives in the graveyard."

Pauline bursts in, and Annie pulls her up onto her lap. "My mother and my grandmother are here. Maybe I'll be buried here. Do you have children?"

I smile. "I'm only twenty-five."

"I had three children by the time I was twenty-five. A boyfriend?"

I shake my head. I don't say that I'm too awkward, too shy, too unapproachable in social situations. Other girls had boyfriends; I had school.

"What about your family?"

"My parents live on Vancouver Island. I had a younger sister." Annie's gaze contains the question, and I find to my surprise that I don't mind answering, here amid the happy clutter of the Lapierre home. "Meningitis," I tell her. "It happened so fast."

"My grandmother had eight kids," Annie tells me. "Five grew up. My mother had six, but my little brother drowned. So far, I've been lucky."

Before I can respond, Pauline slides from her mother's lap and climbs into mine, as if it's something she's always done. It warms me—my lap, and my heart—as she holds up a toy to show me, a small figure carved from some sort of bone. I take it and turn it around in my hand.

"She's nice," I say to Pauline. "Does she have a name?"

Pauline utters the first words I've heard her speak. "Nina," she tells me.

Annie laughs. "She likes you," she says.

I sit with the little girl on my lap. Outside, a dog barks, and I can hear shouts of the boys in play. "I like her, too," I say.

AFTER THREE WEEKS on Herschel Island, sleep for Nina is still fraught. Often, she wakes exhausted. It's only the half-remembered ghosts of dreams that tell her that she has, indeed, slept. Tonight she came back to the barracks after a dinner with Ray and Annie and the kids, her first dinner with them. Nina found Ray Lapierre friendly and talkative, a self-styled ambassador for Herschel; she liked him. John

McGrath, the climatologist from the other camp, had turned up as well, having been out with Ray examining shifting shorelines, listening to Ray's recollections of changes within the sands and the seasons.

Dinner had been challenging: raw seal meat and Beluga whale blubber, cut up with an ulu on cardboard that had been spread on the floor. Nina, kneeling with the others, had taken a deep breath and joined in. John caught her eye and gave her a complicit smile that told her he had eaten this way before, and she found she watched him more than she watched Ray and Annie, following his lead. The blubber surprised her with its taste, which she found almost pleasant, but the texture, she thought, would take some getting used to.

Ray nodded at them both approvingly. He clearly enjoyed eating in the tradition of his wife's people, but told her he was pretty happy for a restaurant meal in Fort McPherson, too. It's a rare Southerner, he told Nina, who can chow down on a traditional meal. Pauline had spent most of the evening close to Nina, bringing her small things to look at, chatting non-stop as, indeed, Annie had warned Nina she would.

Nina walked back full of raw meat and personal pride. John walked her as far as the barracks, the two of them discussing the meal.

"You dug in like a *Kigirktaugnuit*," John said. She raised her eyebrows. "I was impressed."

"Thanks," she said. "I liked it."

Nina declined John's offer to play cards with the others at the warehouse, preferring some quiet time to digest the evening—physically and intellectually—sitting on the front step of the barracks and writing in her journal.

Now, Nina tosses in a sleep as light as the sky outside, pillow over her head to shut out the fingers of light that creep from behind the blinds.

SOMETIME PAST MIDNIGHT the scent of tobacco smoke and drying caribou hide overtakes the smell of socks drying over the stove.

"There's a storm coming," Kudnalik comments after a while.

"Well, you'd know," says Gorham. "You Eskimos always seemed to know. It's downright spooky."

"It's not so hard. You watch the colour of the water, the movement of animals. You listen, and you hear the birds are no longer singing. Even the dogs are smarter than you. You should have paid better attention."

Gorham grunts in agreement. "All that planning we did. I didn't like it that there were twelve of us when the time came. I thought we'd have better luck with fewer people, but then one found out, and another, and another. We broke into one of the warehouses that the Pacific Steam Whaling Company kept under lock and key—to keep out the Eskimos— and stocked up on food and guns and ammo, so that when Bodfish and his party went after us, as we knew he would, we could keep them at bay."

"The one you killed first was Kiogiak. He was my cousin."

"Well he shouldn't have been there," Gorham says dismissively, but he pushes the tobacco tin across the table to Kudnalik in a conciliatory gesture.

"What was he to do? The captain says go search, he goes. He left behind a wife and a daughter on the boat, where they sewed the clothes for the white whalers. Too many of our women were on those boats. Some for the captains—some young ones, too. Some to make parka or mukluk. Kiogiak's wife probably sewed the clothes you were wearing when you shot him!"

Gorham, ignoring him, continues. "I felt bad about ransacking that camp. I knew a couple of those men, even though they weren't from our ship. But what could we do? We needed those supplies. But I'd have come after us too, I warrant, if my supplies were gone. Still, we'd have escaped if it wasn't for that storm."

"Like the one that's coming now," says Kudnalik. "Can you hear my dogs whining?"

Gorham listens, head cocked. "That's just the wind," he says.

"No. My dogs know. It's a long way off, but still they know."

"It was the storm that did it. Six were captured. Simpson was shot, and Morgan's knee was shattered. Three got away, and for all I know, made it out."

"Maybe."

"The storm confused me. All that white; I couldn't see. I shouted for them. I walked circles looking for tracks, but they were gone. The wind was howling; I'd never felt anything like it. I couldn't feel my hands or feet or face. After a while I prayed to see anyone, anyone at all—even that goddamn joker Bodfish."

"You saw me."

"Actually, I tripped over one of your dogs. They were all just lumps in the snow, but he came up all teeth." Gorham shakes his head at the memory and rubs at his ankle. "There I was, drowning in snow and wind and fear and then there was this goddamn thing tearing at my leg."

"You shot my lead dog. He was sleeping." Kudnalik nods at the figure in the bed, as if the sleeping young woman and the long-dead, sleeping husky have something in common. "She wants to know about the people who were here a long time ago. Maybe she digs up our past so she doesn't have to dig up her own."

"That's awfully philosophical of you."

"Being dead makes you see things differently," Kudnalik says. "Anyway, I think it is better to leave bones lie."

"As long as mine don't get chewed up by some damn Eskimo dog," Gorham tells Kudnalik as he rises from the table, "it doesn't matter to me."

IN THE MORNING I'm tired, still short of sleep, and making tea when I hear the sound of voices. It's Sunday, and our day off. I was planning a hike around the island, perhaps another visit to the graveyards. For some reason I feel drawn there.

John is here, with Pauline and Luke. Pauline is talking a blue streak, and I feel suddenly jealous that she should be as comfortable with John as she's become with me.

"They tagged along," John explains when he walks in the door without knocking. "Sorry; I'm looking for Andy. I was thinking of a hike—with anyone other than Frank," he laughs.

"You two have an argument?" I ask him. Pauline wraps her arms around my leg and I rest my hand on her head, my jealousy abated.

"It's just a lot of time to spend with one person."

"I know what you mean."

John and I eat breakfast while Pauline and Luke wander around the barracks, looking at my things, mostly. Pauline puts on my sunglasses and grins. Before long both kids are decked out in my clothes. When Luke holds up my bra, I take it away, embarrassed. "That's about enough," I say. "How about we walk you home?"

We find George pitching a ball at Albert, who swings at it with a solid piece of driftwood. "Want to play baseball?"

Albert asks John, but he shakes his head. We've decided to hike across to the north shore and then circle around to the graveyards. We leave the kids and strike out across the tundra. It's a grey day, fog drifting, but it's all we have, and it's enough.

John tells me about his course of study. "Right now, people are just beginning to discuss the possibility that the earth is warming up. You wait: another ten years, it will be an accepted fact. In a hundred years Qikiqtaruk may even be under water," he says, using the Inuvialuit name for Herschel Island. "The life Annie grew up in, that her ancestors knew, it'll all be gone."

"It's not the same now," I allow. "Everything changed forever a century ago. Earlier, really. Since Franklin. There's no going back."

"No," he agrees.

We walk companionably, not speaking. It's nice to be with someone and not have to feel like there are silences to be filled. In the afternoon we see figures in the distance, west of the cove.

"Some of Annie's relatives are here," John explains. "Ray told me they were going out to net seals today."

"They net seals?" I ask, but it occurs to me I never really had any idea.

"In the spring, before the ice breaks up completely and when the water is muddy from the Mackenzie runoff," John explains. "They set these big square nets across an open lead in the ice. Ray sells the pelts he gets, and his dogs, mostly, eat the carcasses. He stacks them up in winter like cordwood."

The figures move in the distance, and we head toward the whaler's graveyard. John squats to read a marker, clearly as interested as I am.

"Archibald Gorham," John reads. "He was on the *Mary D. Hume.*" He looks up. "I wonder how he died. At sea? Disease? Frozen to death? He was only twenty-five."

"I'm twenty-five next month," I say, thinking aloud.

"And remarkably well preserved," John grins, and I find myself blushing.

I look out across the graveyard. The graves here belong to such disparate groups: Inuvialuit, whaler, and Royal Northwest Mounted Police, all of them bonded by this place. In the distance, the sea sparkles under a finger of sunlight that breaks through the clouds, but there's an odd quality of light that makes me uneasy.

"There's a storm coming," John says. "Maybe we'd better skip the Inuvialuit graveyard and just head straight back."

I shake my head. "I just want to look at one, just for a minute."

When we reach Kudnalik's grave it appears oddly fragile, but perhaps that's just the strange light, the bruised-looking sky, and way the wind has come up, causing the remains of the weathered fence to rattle like bones.

Andy, Barry, and Frank are all inside the barracks building when we drag open the door against the rising wind. The air has turned cold, and I believe I can smell snow. Frank and Andy are playing cards at the table, while Barry's got something cooking on the old stove.

"There you are, you two," he says as we walk in. Frank and Andy exchange looks, which I ignore. "Big storm coming. We'll all be bunking here tonight."

Everything from both camps is piled in the corner: tents, sleeping bags, equipment. The barracks is the most substantial building. I notice something resting on top of my sleeping bag and pick it up.

"The Lapierre kids came by a while ago," Barry tells me. "The girl wanted to give that to you."

"Nina!" I say, picking up the carved figure.

"That's your name," John agrees.

"It's what Pauline named her doll." I don't know what to think.

John looks at me kindly. "I expect it's a compliment," he says.

AT THE TABLE, Kudnalik works on a piece of bone, scraping at it.

"What are you doing?" Gorham asks. He's sitting at his usual spot on the other side of the table, packing his pipe and scratching at his head. "Damn lice," he grumbles under his breath.

"Making something for the boy. I think he'll like this." Kudnalik holds up a small human shape. "A hunter. I'll give him a harpoon."

"I saw the boy in the doorway that night, didn't I?"

"I don't remember. He was probably there. After my wife died, he went to her family. It was a sad life for a small boy, but he made out okay."

"How do you know?"

Kudnalik makes a gesture that Gorham can't read. Instead, "My wife lived only a few more months," he said. "They said it was smallpox. So many died, when lungs filled up, or fever took them. Sometimes it happened very quickly, alive and then—" Kudnalik looks up from his work, "—dead. Some with the smallpox would roll in the snow, and the snow would be red."

Gorham winces. "Do you have to talk about these things? Why don't you talk about the good times?"

"There were good times," Kudnalik acknowledges. "There was good trade, and some of the whalers treated us well. The best times were when we would meet relatives and go out on hunting parties. Or sometimes we would all come together and tell stories or dance. We laughed a lot. Sometimes we played sports."

"Go on," Gorham says. "It's going to be a long night with that storm outside. Can you hear it?" He looks around at the dark forms, sighing and tossing. "It's getting crowded in here. Bad as the hold of the *Mary D.*"

Kudnalik scrapes some more at the bone he holds, then pauses to run a finger over its curves. "I remember one storm, when we were two families together. We ate good food. We played games. Games of strength, or skill. The little ones and the women watched. It was a good time."

"Before the community house was built at Pauline Cove, we did everything on the ship. You'd get a good blow and there'd be no fresh meat, just salt beef and potatoes and beans. And each other, farting away. One time a mate disappeared after acting strange for a few days. You know what he did? Tried to freeze himself to death. They found him, but he lost his feet to frostbite. Scared the rest of us, that you could go crazy like that."

"You should have stayed home. Left this place to the *Kigirktaugnuit.*"

Gorham ignores him. "We had to start organizing more to do. We made skis and sleds from barrel staves. And baseball! We had teams: the Herschels, the Arctics, the Northern Lights, the Eurekas, and the Pick-ups," he says, his voice warming. "Used ashes to mark the baselines and a sail for the backstop. Did I tell you I was number one hitter for the Arctics?"

Kudnalik doesn't look up from his work. "Yes," he says.

"The crack of the bat, when it's thirty below, it's a whole different sound than on the ballfield where I grew up. It was great fun, until that one game—you remember?"

"I wasn't there, but it was told to me. The blizzard came up very suddenly."

"It sure did. Hey—I thought you said you could tell when a blizzard is coming."

"Even *Kigirktaugnuit* are sometimes surprised," said Kudnalik. "Especially in Amaolikkervik."

"Didn't I tell you to speak English?"

"March. A storm can come up out of nowhere."

"Well, it did. And after it passed, there were five found, frozen to death. One was only a hundred yards or so from shelter." Gorham shook his head.

"There were six," Kudnalik said. "You white men only count your own corpses."

"The point is, it's a cruel world in which you live, Kudnalik," said Gorham, "where a man can freeze a hundred yards from his own front door."

"And yet you thought you'd walk two hundred miles to Fort McPherson with a few guns and some stolen food." Kudnalik holds up his carved figure. "I'm almost finished. He just needs his harpoon."

IN THE CLAUSTROPHOBIC confines of the barracks, wind and snow lash the plank siding while we try to pass the time. With five unwashed bodies and piles of gear everywhere, the air becomes close by the third day of the storm. I think about the whalers in the hold of their ships, day after day of one another's company, while winter storms raged. There must have been more than a little madness, emotions close to the surface. I'm not much of a drinker, but all of us get into the rye whisky Frank brought. I let myself slip into the feeling, relaxing for what feels like the first time in years.

"Hey," Frank says as I laugh at a particularly racy joke. "Is that the real Nina coming out?"

When I stand up to go and pee in the bucket we've put in the back room, I realize the walls are moving. I make it, though, and weaving back resolve to stick to my bunk, where I pick up my pen. I've been writing most of the evening, the whisky loosening my hand, secrets spilling out onto the page.

We're well into the second bottle when what begins as a friendly game of cards disintegrates into a nasty argument between Andy and Frank that is barely pacified by Barry. I look up from my journal; I've missed most of what was said. The atmosphere is suddenly thick as smoking seal oil.

"Okay. Truth or Dare," Frank says into the toxic air.

Barry's voice is serious. "Time to shift gears."

"What are you writing?" John asks me from across the room, trying to lighten the atmosphere. Andy is shuffling the cards, but they splay across the table, and he swears.

"Nothing," I say. I close the book.

"Truth or Dare," Frank says again. His words are slurred. "How about Little Miss Nina over here?"

"Aw, leave her alone," says Andy. Barry moves to twist the cap back on the bottle, but Frank reaches over and tops up his glass again. "Okay. You then," he says to Andy, gesturing with his full glass, sloshing a bit.

"Dare," says Andy guardedly.

"Right." Frank thuds over to the corner, boots hard on the cold floor, and from his duffel hauls out a bottle we haven't seen before. "Picked this up in Whitehorse. Dare you to eat the toe."

We all lean forward and look. Sourtoe whisky is a Yukon legend, but there's no way Frank would have a bottle of his own complete with human appendage.

"No, it really is," says Frank. "I got it off a guy who got it from an emergency doc at the clinic. It's a real honest-to-god amputated toe. He was selling shots for five bucks. I bought the whole bottle for fifty."

I get up off the bunk to look. We all peer into the amber liquid in the bottom. "God," I say after a few moments. "I think it really is." Barry starts to laugh.

"Whatever," says Andy. "It's a stupid game." He's looking a slight shade of green, but it may be the shifting light as the wind screams around the building.

"You can take dare number one," Frank says, holding up the bottle. "Or dare number two."

"What's dare number two?"

"Go outside and walk once around the building." We all stare at Frank. "Without touching the walls," he adds.

We all know this could be suicide. You could walk two feet and lose yourself in something like this. The two stare at one another. There's something else here, something besides just the cards. Stuff can happen over a few weeks of isolation; this life isn't for everyone. It's one thing for Annie and her ancestors, quite another for Herschel's temporary immigrants, past and present.

Andy looks as if he's actually considering it. His jaw is set, eyes narrow. John's watching him, glass poised near his lips, waiting.

"Frank," I say, scrambling to diffuse the situation. "You asked me first. I'll play. I'll take Truth." How bad can it be?

Frank looks at me for a long moment. "Okay, Miss Cool-As-a-Cucumber Nina," he says. "Read us what you just wrote."

He gestures at my journal, which I hold on my lap. I feel the heat rise, a nauseating combination of alcohol, and embarrassment. What had I been writing?

In the embrace of my alcohol haze it had flowed onto the page: horrible, embarrassing, adolescent words about John, about attraction and about hope, and now I can see the ridiculousness of that, the impossibility, my words maudlin and juvenile. Not a grown-up at all, more five than twenty-five, mousy and boring and pathetic. Nothing at all like my beautiful sister.

As Andy lunges for the book, I suddenly see my colleagues as they are: men, sure of themselves and stupid with drink. These are the whalers who came with their alcohol and their diseases and their opportunistic, murderous, lecherous ways, to change irrevocably everything that was perfect.

Because everything perfect dies.

The air becomes thick, the walls close, and I hear the moans of ghosts from the walls around me, or perhaps from inside my own head, the roar of emotion and alcohol, or perhaps it's the wind—before anyone can stop me, I take the dare: I throw on my parka and push through the door, my journal clutched to my chest.

Instantly, the cold wind reaches down my throat and seizes my lungs in an icy fist. I can't breathe. A gust nearly picks me up and I stumble a few feet and turn to see the building I left has disappeared completely. All I can see is white; all I can hear is wind. In the maw of the storm I can't tell which direction is safety, which direction death. I am nothing at all in the face of this.

The sound that comes from my throat can't possibly be mine.

In a moment John has hauled me back inside and he wraps his arms around me while I sob. I am terrified, and ashamed.

"She's just had too much to drink," Barry says. "I mean, she's just a kid. I shouldn't have let this happen."

"None of us should have," I hear Andy say, but I have my head down, not looking at anyone, weeping and weeping like a small child.

"Shhhh," says John. "Shhhhhh."

"IT'S NOT FOR everyone, the North," Kudnalik says. "And drink is the worst. It brings out the devil." He waves his hand at the empty liquor bottles on the table.

"You've been listening to that preacher," says Gorham.

"I've been spending too much time with you," Kudnalik answers. "Look. I have finished my little man. I'll give it to the boy as soon as the storm passes. Do you think he will like it?"

Gorham picks it up and squints at it in the dim light. "He'll like it," he tells Kudnalik, his voice soft. "Give it to him tomorrow. The storm will be over by then."

They sit, backlit, observing the sleeping bodies, the air permeated with sweat and alcohol. In one bunk, two are intertwined, still bundled up against the cold. The fire has almost died.

"I'm sorry I killed you," says Gorham after a while. "I couldn't see. I had all those people after me, Eskimos, the god-damn lynch mob from the *Mary D.* I was scared. I thought you were going to kill me."

"I *was* going to kill you." Kudnalik turns his head to look at Gorham, and the pale light catches his eyes. The storm is abating, the sky brightening. "I was protecting my family."

"But another bullet killed you, first."

"Yes."

"It was supposed to be for me, but you had already shot me from behind."

Kudnalik doesn't answer.

"And then later, your wife died. She got sick."

Kudnalik, turning over the figure in his hands, nods once.

"I'm sorry," Gorham says. He turns to fully face Kudnalik, and the two regard one another across the table. Around them is the gentle breathing of the sleepers, and outside, the quieting air. "What about the boy?"

"The boy grew up."

AT THE WASHOUT site, the first house is gone completely. There's no sign of the berm we made, or the pit or driftwood remains. The sea is wild, the waves sweeping up, and over, and out, and with each receding wave I imagine it takes with it more of the past. Barry is emotional, pacing and swearing.

"There are still two more," offers Andy.

For John and Frank, the storm has been a disruption only, and after the fact presents an opportunity to measure its effects on the shoreline, an unexpected windfall in a way. They stand back, keeping a respectful silence as if at a funeral. John catches my eye, and there's a silent agreement between us. We'll go see how the graves have fared.

Archibald Gorham's wooden marker has blown over. I right it, and pile stones around the base to hold it up for now. The wind has calmed slightly as we walk to the Inuvialuit graves, but it's cold and damp as if making sure we won't soon forget the force it can be.

Annie and Pauline are there, checking the damage. We join them at Kudnalik's grave, and I can see as we approach that the storm has taken a greater toll here, blowing away sand and soil, ripping up the cover of grass and lupine. Inexplicably, I want to pick up some of the flowers and put them there, but it's not my place. A crevasse has opened up along one side; it feels as if I could reach into that shallow, frozen grave and for a moment hold hands with the past.

Some day in the future the earth will heave, and the wind will blow across Kudnalik's bones.

Pauline runs up to me, holding something out. It's a small figure.

"I found it there," she said, pointing, and we all look at Kudnalik's grave.

"Pauline! You have to put it back." Annie's eyes are wide.

Pauline grips the figure more tightly. She wants to keep the little man. "You should do what your mother says," I tell her. In my pocket, my fingers close on the carved doll, the one Pauline named Nina. "Here," I give it to her. "So he won't be lonely."

WE ALL WALK back to Annie and Ray's to sit in their bright and cluttered home, drink tea, and talk about the storm and the damage done. John holds my hand as we walk, and I catch Annie smiling at me.

The house held up well, but around the house tarps and boxes have blown around. The boys come around the corner pushing the wheelbarrow, now full of driftwood. The storm has delivered a fresh batch of firewood. Pauline runs ahead to meet them. We've all been through something, but these kids seem to take it in stride.

"It's hard to believe such calm could exist after that," I say.

"This place sees a lot of weather," John agrees. "It's too bad about the Washout site."

We pause at the door. "My ancestors saw the sea give birth to Qikiqtaruk," Annie says. "We will be there, watching, when the sea takes it back."

If there's a note of regret, I can't discern it. Annie makes tea while Ray and John talk, and I watch through the window as the children play.

ELEVEN

RIVER RISING

·1999·

Brigitte

PLEASE. I NEED to get home to my children. Can you help?

They say I am here for my own good. They say now it is my turn to be looked after. But they don't understand. I must go—the children are alone.

Oh, I know. You will say what they say over and over. Don't worry, Brigitte, everything is fine. And they put on me the silly hat and they say: Look! It is a new year coming. A new century. We will have a party, they say. But it is no time for a party.

What is the world coming to? So many changes, I don't understand them all. And young people who are not family should not call their elders by the first name. Mme Gauthier, they should call me, but *non*, they say Brigitte this and Brigitte that. My own children would not treat adults with such disrespect.

Sometimes I am forgetting. They tell me I forget. But you must understand: the children are at home, they are alone, they are waiting for their *Maman*. And they might be afraid!

Oui, there is Lucien, who is *dix ans* and very good at taking care of his brother and sister, but still, he is only ten years old. And there is Benoit, he is eight and—what is the word?— impulsive. He does things without thinking about them, like the time he pulled out all of the pillows and quilts onto the lawn and then climbed up on the roof thinking they would make such a nice, soft landing, and if Lucien had not seen him—

I was out back, hanging laundry. I had the baby with me, Emilie. She was playing in the empty laundry basket with her little doll MouMou, and Ami, our spaniel, was lying beside her with his head on his paws. And all at once here was Lucien, running around the side of our little house, yelling and wav-ing, pointing up, and I looked but the sun was in my eyes at first, so I couldn't see. Ami was barking by now, and Emilie started to cry, and I was about to scold Lucien for all the noise when I saw little Ben—*mon Dieu*, he was only four at that time—on the peak of the lower roof with his arms stretched out like Our Saviour. I told Ami to stay with the baby and I ran—oh, how I ran!—up the two flights of stairs to the attic, and I saw the open window under the eaves and the chair pushed up against it. From there I could see to the roof over the summer kitchen, and it was on this roof that Benoit had edged his way along to stand at its end, ready to dive headlong into all of our bedding, piled on the ground below.

There I was, hitching up my housedress and straddling the roof, inching my way to my baby, coaxing, coaxing. What a sight I must have been! Oh, I can laugh now, but then I'll tell you my heart was in my throat with fear; I could feel it pounding in my chest like *une bête*. As I drew closer to the edge I could see Lucien below on the lawn standing beside that pile of bedding with his mouth open. Emilie had stopped crying; I could always trust Ami, and I knew Emilie was safe in the laundry basket with the dog standing guard.

I coaxed Benoit back along the rooftop, while my mind it was scrambling for the promise that would return him safely to my arms. I promised him a trip to town for ice cream, even though we could scarcely afford it. When I reached him he turned and hugged me with his arms and legs and buried his face in my chest and began to cry. He knew that he had done something wrong.

I can't remember how I got him back along that roof and in the attic window. But of course we did get safely back, because I remember we all had ice cream: Lucien had chocolate, and so did Ben, and I chose strawberry for Emilie, who had never had ice cream, and then, even though I hadn't planned to, I bought vanilla for myself!

Because it was a celebration, after all, with everyone safe.

Daniel

I SHOULD GET home to the kids. Probably nothing is going to happen, but I should be there. They are my children, after all, and Chantal is my wife. It will be midnight soon, celebrations across the country—and maybe that's all that will happen. Still . . .

Late as it is, Mémére is still up, talking, sometimes to herself, sometimes to me. I can't always tell what she says, but I hold her hand, and around the two of us the nurses and care aides come and go. Somebody turned off the big TV awhile back; nobody was watching. Here and there, old people in their chairs have nodded off and most have gone to bed. I wonder what Chantal is doing now.

My dad still talks about the year the Red River flooded, how much snow they had. He was the oldest, and he felt a great sense of responsibility, I know. Mémére has always talked about it, but lately she's been getting confused, and then the Home calls me, asks me to come and see her. And I know I should try to convince her it's 1999, and sometimes I do try, and sometimes I just listen to her stories. Sometimes she knows it's me, sometimes she doesn't. It's like a switch on the wall, with a loose wire. When she worries about her children, I try to tell her: It's okay, Mémére. Everyone is okay.

It is the role of the mother, isn't it? to be concerned with the safety of the children. It's what I keep telling myself, these past months with Chantal becoming more and more obsessed. She's home now with the kids, Marcel and Josslyne. She's got the generator and the back-up generator primed and ready to go, and if those fail she's got candles and the propane barbecue and enough food to keep us all for a year.

The other day I came home to find her unloading cases of soap. Soap! "If the world ends, Chantal," I told her, "at least we'll die clean!" She gave me that look she's been giving me more and more—like *I'm* the enemy, instead of a bunch of digit-challenged computer programmers—and said: "When the grid collapses, all the shipping routes will be compromised. That's if there isn't total anarchy. You want me to make soap out of ashes and lye, like the grandmother who you're so fond of?"

Chantal never really liked my grandmother Brigitte. That's because Mémére never liked Chantal. She didn't approve of the way Chantal raised the kids, for one thing. Marcel has always talked back to us, from the time he could say *non*, and Chantal says it's good, that he's learning to assert himself, but when he tried it with Mémére—

Boy, I remember it clear as day, and it must've been a few years ago because Marcel is seven, now, and Josslyne's nine. We were at the dinner table, and Marcel—he must've been a toddler, still—was fighting with his sister over something, I don't know what. Mémére was visiting—she wasn't in the Home yet. She still lived in St. Vital. For her, it's still a separate village, with Winnipeg the big city. It's a big thing for her to come to our house; distances are different for old folks.

At least we are here. The rest of our family is scattered across the country. My aunt and her family live in Rivière-du-Loup and my uncle and his partner are in Toronto. My mother is *Anglaise*—she'll correct you and say her ancestors were Irish, but it's all the same if you're French—so when Dad retired she talked him into going to B.C. She said it was for the mild winters on the coast, but Dad says you can't take the Anglophone out of the girl, no matter how fluent she is. As for us, Chantal and I settled here after college, so we're the closest to Mémére. Before she moved into the Home, before she became confused, she would come over to see the kids. She certainly didn't come to see Chantal!

Anyway, I was trying to settle the kids down that night, because of Mémére, mainly, and Chantal was going on about letting the kids freely express themselves, and then, whap! A handful of mashed potato goes flying across the table, right across Mémére's face! Well, okay, my first instinct was to laugh, I'll admit, but I jumped up to help Mémére, who was flapping her hands and trying to clean potato from her glasses. I thought Chantal would look after reprimanding Marcel, but what did Chantal do? She told him: "You must eat your food, *mon ange*, if you are to grow up to be a strong boy!"—and she wiped off his hand and put the spoon in it!

Mémére got up and left the table, closing the door of the guest room, and she didn't come out all evening. Chantal and I had words after the kids were in bed, you better believe it, but she didn't listen, and anyway, the damage was done.

She's still not listening, not when I tell her this millennium computer-bug thing is overblown, that January 1st, 2000, will be no different from December 31st, 1999, except we'll all be a little older, and some of us will have hangovers. And when I say we should join the neighbours—there will be a bonfire at the park with games for the kids, a party to bring in the new millennium—she tells me: "This is no time for a party, Daniel. This is about keeping the children safe."

Brigitte

MORE THAN ANYTHING else, we need to keep our children safe. And you, do you have children? Of course you do, of course. I am forgetting. I have become so forgetful! Josslyne, yes, such a lovely girl; she looks like her father. And Marcel, yes. A rascal, but a good boy underneath. So like his uncle Benoit.

Ice cream was always a rare treat for us. Oh, Henri worked hard, but it was never enough with three children needing so many things. Still, I managed to save a little each month in a jar I kept at the back of the pantry. I thought if I saved enough that we might someday go, as a family, back to Quebec to see my parents, my brothers and sisters.

Foolish.

So: there is Lucien, and Benoit, and Emilie. All born in Winnipeg, so very far away from my home in Rivière-du-Loup. I met Henri there, in the town where I grew up. He was working as a millwright for the Canadian National Railroad. It was his hands I first noticed. I was shopping for my mother at the grocer, and I had dropped my glove. Oh, how I loved those gloves! You should have seen them: pig-skin, with tiny white pearl buttons. My father had given them to me for my eighteenth birthday. They were not the sort of gloves a young lady would normally wear to the gro-cers, but you see my birthday had been just the week before, and I wanted to wear them all the time. Just between us— you won't tell, will you?—I wore them when I went to sleep that first night, wore them right to bed. I wanted to smell their sweet leather smell, and to feel their softness against my face. I woke with the round buttons pressed into my cheek, three small indents I tried my best to rub away before I came down to breakfast.

I don't know where those gloves have gone. I think per-haps someone has taken them. Mme Sinclair, down the hall, she is always saying someone took this, took that. She says there are thieves here.

But yes, I was telling you, wasn't I? About Henri. About his hands. Henri had the largest hands I'd ever seen, and when he picked up my glove from the plank floor of the grocer's it was almost lost in those long, wide fingers of his. He held it out so gently! He was always a gentle man, my Henri. Soon after we were courting, and then married, and then the CNR offered him work in Winnipeg for twice the pay. I did not want to leave Maman and Papa, but Henri was my husband, and so I went. And then the children, first Lucien . . .

THE CHILDREN! I must get back to the children. Please. They are alone, and the river has been rising for days, now. We are so close to the Red where we live, and there was so much snow last year. Lucien, he is such a good boy, but will he know what to do?

SO MUCH SNOW this past winter! We made paths to the root cellar, to the mailbox, to the outhouse, which we had to use for a few days when the temperature dropped low, before the pipes thawed again. It did not snow, while it was so cold, but the snow that was on the ground squeaked underfoot, like we were stepping on frozen mice, and it was necessary to have a scarf over your mouth and nose or the cold would burn your throat. And then, when the cold snap broke, then came the snow.

The banks on the paths we dug were so steep it was like walking in a white tunnel. And Lucien, after a while he couldn't throw the snow as high as the banks. Ben would pull Emilie on the small sleigh fast, fast through the tunnels and she would squeal when they came around a corner, Ami running behind and barking, and Lucien angry when the sleigh dislodged snow into his carefully cleared pathway.

Sometimes I think Lucien is too serious, now, since his father has been gone. He feels he needs to be the man of the house. A child should play, should be a child. Should not have such worries.

We had settled in St. Vital, which made me happy because of so many French. Our neighbours, the Bouchers, were very kind to us. Henri worked long hours, and sometimes travelled for the railway, staying away for days. In fact, when Lucien was born—he came early, almost two weeks—Henri was away and if it wasn't for Mme Boucher, I don't know what I'd have done. When my waters broke—

OH, MON DIEU, the children! Who is with them? Will they know what to do? The water is rising. It's been on the news; we must all evacuate. I need to go home—

No, I said. I said no—I will not calm down. You must listen, it is important. I don't care what is the date, what is the time.

Daniel

WHAT HAVE WE come to? We live in such a world of fear.

All Chantal has been doing these days is talking about the time. She's been watching the calendar, and now, for sure she's glued to the clock, like that doomsday clock the anti-nuke freaks had going during the Cold War.

I took a look in the cupboard the other day, and I couldn't believe it! There were seventy-two cans of tuna. Seventy-two! "It's good protein," Chantal said. "And those ships all rely on computers these days. Do you think all those foreign shipping companies will be on the ball? I doubt it. Besides, there'll be riots in China. I read it on the Internet."

Which for Chantal, is the gospel truth. Cans of pears and peaches, because "when the grid breaks down, we won't be getting food from the States, and Canadian farmers won't be able to meet the demand. They'll be patrolling their orchards with a shotgun!"

Okay, so I admit I don't know everything—I mean, I only have a hardware store, I'm no computer expert—but I can't see it that way. Humans were smart enough to invent computers, right? They should be smart enough to fix them.

Still, it's good for business. We've sold thirty-seven generators since November, and they're not cheap, those things. I had to put a sign up saying that we'll only take returns for malfunctions, because otherwise everyone'll be wanting to return them January 2nd. And candles? Can't keep 'em in stock. Other stuff, too: flashlights, batteries. Hurricane lamps. Propane, coal oil.

And string. Ha! I suppose we can tie the string to all those empty tin cans and make telephones between our houses for when the lines go down. Been selling barbecues of all kinds, not exactly a big seller in December most years. Usually, it's snow shovels, but what are they buying? Barbecues. I guess that when the system breaks down and anarchy reigns, there'll be no city bylaw officer around to tell us to shovel our walks. Maybe we should be thankful for small mercies.

When I told Chantal I wanted to spend New Year's with Mémére, she let loose with her own flood of words.

"Daniel—you're going to abandon us? Are you crazy? There might be riots! What if something happens?"

"Nothing will happen, *cherie*," I told her. "And Mémére is old, she's confused. She needs someone to reassure her, especially with New Year's and everything." But the truth is, I don't think I can bear to be with Chantal as the clock ticks down. The kids will be asleep; they'll be fine. Chantal can call some girlfriend to stay with her, and I told her so. They're understaffed at the Home, I said, and Mémére might become agitated with everything that's going on.

"I'm the only family she has here," I told Chantal. She gave me a look that could freeze every computer on the planet.

"*We're* your family, Daniel."

I DON'T KNOW why they even bother to celebrate at the Home, since most of the residents don't know today from yesterday. The TV's on again, with the sound turned down, and some guy with a party hat is talking. Nobody's watching.

I felt bad as I walked out into the snow earlier this evening, eight inches since yesterday. There was almost no traffic as I drove through the big, fat flakes across town to the Home. I felt torn, you know, but the kids are asleep anyway, and I can't spend the evening with Chantal while she counts candles and cans of tuna. I just can't. And Mémére won't come to our house anymore.

Outside the snow is still coming down. Nature doesn't care about calendars, dates, or computer digits. If it wants to snow, it snows. If it wants to rain, it rains. We are not so important, not really. The world keeps turning, and we just turn with it.

Brigitte

THERE WAS TALK, you know, of flooding after all that snow, but nobody expected so much water. If Henri were here, I am sure he'd have been sent to go and work the pumps, to keep the water down. Millrights, machinists, skilled workmen from all over have gone to help. People with no skills fill sandbags. Everyone has to be there, to stop the water. You must help me. Lucien is a smart boy, but sometimes Emilie runs away, she thinks it is a game, and what if she is hiding somewhere when the water comes?

Yes. Yes, Lucien will keep everyone safe until I return home. He is a good boy, so much like his father.

Lucien, when he was born, came in a flood of water, my water. It was there, suddenly, in a pool at my feet on the kitchen floor, my hands dusty with flour. I was making *tourtière* for Henri. I was so tired in those days, when I was big with the baby. Henri, when he was home, would laugh and hold me from behind and try to make his arms meet in front, over the baby, and of course they wouldn't. *Petite baleine*, he called me. *Ma petite baleine.*

But Henri had been away five days in Fort Garry installing new switches for the railway. He would be home tomorrow, and I thought: if I make the dough today and keep it cool in the ice box, then tomorrow I can make the spicy pork filling. A bit at a time, that was the way, because I would get so tired. I imagined Henri, he would come in the door with snow on his cap and coat, and stamp his boots and say "ahhhhhh" when he smelled the salty, savoury smell, and he would hug his arms around himself like he had been cold for a very long time and now wanted to wrap himself in that warm, warm smell like a fat blanket. And then he'd wrap his arms around me and make me feel safe, and so happy to have him home.

Yes, I was making the dough for the *tourtière* crust, and at first I thought I had—well, I am embarrassed to say I thought I had gone to the toilet right there in the kitchen, and then came a tightening all over, and I held onto the table with both my hands, watching my knuckles go white. And there was just me, and no phone, yet, and all of that space between our small house and the Bouchers' much bigger one. The Bouchers had nine children. Mme Boucher had said to me: If you need anything, come and get me.

When the first pain stopped I took several steps to the door and managed to put my feet into Henri's extra pair of boots, which were so big I could step right in. I could not close my camel coat, which Henri had given me for Christmas, over my big stomach. I started across the dry grass, because it was November, before the first snow but cold so that the grass crunched under Henri's big boots. It was strange: the ground looked very close, as if I were crawling, and yet I was up on my two feet. And the branches on the trees looked sharp, like knives. And the sun, too, broken the way it looks through the crack in the windshield of our Ford truck, the one we drove west in with all of our things from Rivière-du-Loup piled in the back just seven months before. I was wet where the water had come, surprising and warm when it did, but now cold, clammy, a big patch on my dress and I felt ashamed to be arriving at the Bouchers' like that. What if M. Boucher came to the door?

Another pain came, so hard that I fell to my knees in the sharp grass, and then I didn't care who might answer the door so long as somebody did, and that I managed to get there. It seemed so far away! But then I saw little Solange running towards me. She had been playing outside, and so her cheeks were bright with cold, and her hands, when they touched my own cheeks were like ice, for her mittens swung from their strings inside her sleeves. Do all children not notice the cold, and let their mittens dangle, forgotten? Solange, only five, put both of her cold, small hands on my cheeks and said to me: *Jouez-vous au chien?*

She thought I was pretending to be a puppy! I suppose I must have been panting like a dog. My mother, when she told me about these things that happen to women, said that sometimes a woman will labour many hours, sometimes days, a thought that frightened me when I was fifteen years old. But how much more frightening was this, so fast?

Solange had stepped back, looking at me with wide blue eyes. I gripped both of her elbows, unable to speak at that moment, and I suppose I frightened the poor child, who wrenched her arms from my grip and spun away to run for her mama.

Of course, Mme Boucher quickly guessed the story and ran to meet me, and I'll tell you, I never felt such gratitude as I did at the sight of her running across the grass towards me, growing bigger in my vision as she came nearer until she was there and I was crying and she said: Come, now, it will be fine. And I knew it would.

Lucien was born two hours later; Cecil Boucher, who was the oldest, had gone on his bicycle almost a mile to get the midwife, and she came just in time. All of my children came like that, so fast. No time to prepare, each one took me by surprise: a rush of water, me submerged in the birth so all I could do was swim or drown. By the time Emilie was born, I was a good swimmer! If things had been different, I might have had as many children as Mme Boucher, bang-bang-bang.

There was no way to reach Henri where he was working. Henri arrived home to find the house cold, and my half-made dough a shrivelled, floury ball on the table. What might he have thought in that moment? That I had run home to my parents in Rivière-du-Loup? Or been swept away by some *force de nature*? Of course, he found me at the Boucher home with Lucien swaddled at my breast, the two of us surrounded by the noise and commotion of a house full of children and merriment, with talk and laughter and play, and the smells of cooking.

I always wished our home had been more like the Boucher home. Loud, and happy, and full to bursting with children, and with M. Boucher always home after work, not like Henri, who was gone so much. The Bouchers' home was like my own home when I was growing up. Did I tell you? I had seven brothers and sisters myself: Adele, Alain, Anne-Marie, Armand, Antoine, Aurélien, and Andrée. I was the youngest. Brigitte. My parents, they ran out of names beginning with *A* when they came to me. Later, when I told my mother that Henri and I were moving to Manitoba, she said: "That's because you have a different letter. If I'd thought of Anouk or Aurelie or even Anastasie, you wouldn't be leaving me now." Making me feel terrible, of course. It is always hard to be away from your children, no matter if they are grown up and have children of their own.

THE CHILDREN. I must get back. It is terrible to be away from the children, especially now. Because the water is rising, the Red is already overflowing its banks! The St. Vital Firehall, that is where we must go. Please. Ben doesn't always listen to his older brother. Emilie, she might be hiding. Lucien is a good boy, a smart boy, and so much like his father. Will he know what to do?

And Henri, Henri is gone.

Daniel

CHANTAL AND I weren't always like this. We met at a Rush concert in '86. She was beautiful, and charming, and when the band played "Closer to the Heart" she looked at me and said something, and of course I couldn't hear one word, so I just nodded. And then she kissed me, and I guess that's when I fell in love. I don't know; now, I wonder what she did say. Or what I agreed to.

Once I heard my mother tell my father that "Daniel's girlfriend is a little—foolish, don't you think, Lucien?" But it was way too late by that time: I loved her, everything about her, especially her laugh. I don't hear her laugh so much, now, but she is still beautiful, and sometimes I look at her and see the girl that she was.

I'll be the first to admit that I haven't been perfect. I drink too much, and I've put on a little weight. There were times I could have asked what was wrong, and I didn't. Times I should have stayed to talk things out, and instead I met a few buddies at the bar. They seem like small things at the time, but I suppose they add up.

What is it about a New Year that makes us dwell on past regrets? Twenty-twenty hindsight makes everything so clear, but it wasn't clear when I met Ginette. Josslyne was two-and-a-half and Marcel just a few months, and it seemed to me it was all about the children. Don't get me wrong: I love my children. But there was always someone crying, always the house was a mess, and Chantal was tired all the time, and bitchy. I'm not kidding you, from the moment I came in the door she was at me: "It's so easy for you, you just go to work and you play with your staple guns and tell your staff how high to stack the paint cans. And here I am—" but I didn't get the rest, I remember, because she stomped off to our room, leaving me with Marcel, who was smearing mashed bananas all over his high chair and himself, and Josslyne, who was whining for attention.

And so Ginette, when she came looking for a job, well of course at first I was just happy to have such a smart young girl want to work at the store, and I put her straightaway at the till. And then came the day Sandy went home early and Joe and Brent gave me a wave and locked behind them, and Ginette was still trying to balance the cash, and almost in tears because she couldn't get it to balance. It was her first time, she said; Sandy had shown her how but she'd never done it on her own. So we went up to the office with the cash sheets and the drawer and I showed her how. And, you know, one thing led to another.

I am still an attractive man at thirty-four, even with a bit of a belly, and I was not thirty, then—and Ginette, she was not so much younger really. Maybe twenty-two? Twenty-one? I don't remember. But for a little while, she made me feel like I felt at that Rush concert, you know? When I was young, and the future was this big blank slate. Anything could happen.

My dad used to carp about how hard things used to be, and how easy kids have it now. My mum never forgot the story of her ancestors—the potato famine, the trip over in steerage—and she never let us forget it, either, especially at dinnertime. And when I was a teenager I didn't care, I'd just tell them yeah, yeah, and I'd go out and listen to music with my friends. I remember I told my father once: "Isn't that the point, Papa? The older generation works hard so the next generation has it easier, and then what does the older generation do? Complain we have it too easy!"

He just looked disgusted. "You have no idea," he told me.

We have never been so very close, my father and me. But I think I'll call tomorrow. Just to wish them a Happy New Year. It's good for families to stay in touch. You never know what might happen, they're not so young, and then—

I should have stayed with Chantal and the kids tonight. I was going to, even though I'd told her I was going to see Mémére, that the Home had called to say she was upset and confused, that she wouldn't settle down. What am I to do? I'm her only family here. This turn-of-the millennium stuff is all in Chantal's head, just like the flood is in Mémére's. Still, I think now I could have been a little kinder, a little more sympathetic.

It was because Chantal pulled the Ginette card that I guess I just snapped.

"Sure, you'll see your precious Mémére and then you'll go meet up with that woman—"

"Chantal, that was over *years* ago. It was nothing. I swear—"

"You think I can just forget? You think I can trust you now? I hope the riots do come, and they call out the army, and you both get run over with a tank."

I started to laugh, then, because it *was* ridiculous. There was a time when Chantal would have laughed with me, and then we'd kiss and make up and maybe go to bed. But not for a long time, and not this time. She said: "I've got news for you, Daniel. When we get through this, I want a divorce, and you can bet I'll be bringing up—" Chantal's pretty mouth turned ugly, "—*Ginette*. The kids and I, we're going back to Ste Agathe—"

"Over my dead body, Chantal!" I told her, but she just looked at me, her face contorted. She didn't look like the girl I knew in college.

"I fucking hope so," she said, and if she said any more I missed it, because I was out the door and in the car and when I turned the key in the ignition the radio was blaring some stupid rock station Chantal likes, and do you know what they were playing? That song by REM, "It's the End of the World as We Know It."

. . . *and I feel fine*, I joined in, singing to the dashboard, and then put the car in gear. As I hit the gas the loose fan belt screamed, which was pretty much exactly how I felt.

Brigitte

WHEN THE TELEGRAM came about Henri, about the accident, I stood at the door in my housedress and I screamed. Because a telegram, it can only mean bad news. Do you remember in the war? Everyone was afraid of the telegram.

The poor man in the blue uniform with the cap, he stood not knowing where to look. After a while Lucien came and said to me: *Maman*, come, and the man at the door turned to go, but I clutched at his sleeve. Wait, I said. I must know more. Tell me.

But the man shook his head again. I just deliver the telegrams, ma'am, he said. I don't write them. I don't even know what's in them. And then he was down the walk, and Lucien was pulling at me, with the cold air blowing in through the open door.

I sat on the couch. It was like a dream; nothing seemed real. Lucien closed the door quietly, as if something would break, and stood with his hands at his sides, as though he didn't know how to move, what to do. I can still see his face, too serious for his years. Ben curled up next to me and put his thumb in his mouth, even though he was too old for such a thing. Emilie, she climbed up into my lap and touched my tears when they ran down my face, and said: *Maman pleut*.

Mother is raining.

Daniel

WHEN MÉMÉRE TALKS about my grandfather Henri, I think: that's the man I'd like to be. Or at least, I'd like to be the man that Mémére thinks my grandfather was. Because who's to know, really? Every family has its secrets. My grandfather was often away from the family, working. A lot of men did that in those days. Sure enough, there's been more than a few times I've wished for a bit of road time. Just for a break, you know? But the kids. How could Chantal even *think* of taking the kids back to her hometown?

I think about Marcel, what a little imp he is, with his mother's dimples and those black, black eyes. He has every toy truck we carry in the toy section we introduced last year, and he knows the names of all of them. For Christmas I gave him a big book of every working machine, and he already knew most of them! I promised him that for his birthday in May he'll get to ride in a real front-end loader, and get to work the controls. I have a buddy down at the public works yard. That's if Chantal will let him.

That's if the kids are here.

I think about Josslyne, what a beautiful girl she's becoming. At nine, she is so much more sophisticated than I remember girls being when *I* was nine. She has this way of saying Dad-*dy* in this affectionate way when she thinks I'm being ridiculous, and it breaks my heart.

Brigitte

EMILIE, SHE LOVES to hide, and after a while we have come to know most of her places. She gave me a fright more than once, when darkness would fall, dinner growing cold on the table, and where was my little girl?

Once, when Henri came home late and I had been calling Emilie for an hour, myself sick with worry, and she ran to him as he came up the walk, I told him: you must spank her, Henri. She must learn to come home when she is called. But Henri, he is such a soft man, so tender. He could not strike a child. The boys, maybe, but never Emilie. But Emilie, that day, he swung her up on his shoulder and she laughed and put her fingers in his ears, and over his eyes, and he staggered towards the house pretending to be blind, one hand in front and the other clutching her stockinged foot. She'd lost a shoe somewhere. She was always losing things, that girl.

If Henri had punished Emilie that day, or if I had, with my wooden spoon the way my mother did with my sisters and brothers and I, perhaps she wouldn't have played by the river one day a few weeks later, towards the end of summer. It had been a hot day, I remember, and the cicadas had sung into the evening, so loud I thought maybe they had multiplied to become thousands in the trees, ready to take over the whole world.

Even when the sun fell the air was still thick, sticky. It was dusk and there were fireflies out, and Lucien and Benoit were trying to catch them in jars, but the flies were faster than the boys. Still, they ran around the yard shrieking, the neighbourhood filled with their childish voices, and it was a nice sound. I remember I wished Henri had been home to hear it. I knew he would be out there too, diving for fireflies, like a big child himself.

I was listening to the CBC on the radio, and they were broadcasting a concert of the Winnipeg Symphony Orchestra. Here was the sound of violins and cellos inside, and outside, the voices of children, and I remember thinking that those people playing those instruments had no idea the places their sounds might be heard, and what other sounds might become part of the music they played. It seemed as though, as the music got louder—crescendo, it's called—the laughter of Lucien and Ben, joined by some of the Boucher children, got louder as well, and as the cymbals crashed I thought: *Emilie.*

When had I last seen Emilie?

I rushed to the door. I could see the shapes of my boys, and Solange and Mathieu from next door, four shapes running across the lawn. Is Emilie with you? I called. Solange called back: No, Mme Gauthier, she said. We haven't seen her.

Emilie was small enough, then, to hide under a bed or in a closet, where she would make up games about caves or haunted castles. It was past her bedtime, I had lost track of time. I ran through the house, looking: inside the doors of the wardrobe, behind the curtain, under all of the beds. With each empty space my panic rose. It felt like moths in my chest fluttering, then swarming, hammering against my breastbone. Emilie! I called. As my cry became louder the children must have heard me, because when I ran to the door they were all standing, staring.

We spread out, running down the street, calling. It was becoming darker, now, but still light enough that shapes could be seen under bushes, beside sheds. At the bottom of the street was a dead end, and then a park where I would sometimes take the children, and then the river. I always told them, don't play at the river. It was August so the river was big, but slow, not like now, a wild thing it has become. Every spring the Red floods, but this year—

She had never gone so far by herself, but my Emilie is an adventurous girl, and she doesn't think, just like her brother Ben doesn't think, except that with Emilie, she will be following a story in her head about dragons or fairies, or she might pretend she is a rabbit running from a fox or who knows what? And then she is far from home, her small, sturdy legs taking her through her story to happily-ever-after and then when we find her she is in a tree, or behind a woodpile, or once perched on someone's freshly painted bench as if it were a throne and she a queen.

We are all running, now, down the street, calling. Myself, Ben, Lucien, Solange and Mathieu, and now M. Boucher, our voices small against the big, big night. Even the fireflies seemed to have fled.

I run to the river. I told her: don't play near the river, but somehow, I just know. I stumble as I run down the path, because I can't see the rocks under my feet, and once I fall and I can feel blood running warm down my leg as I pick myself up, all the time calling: Emilie! I hear nothing, not even the water, for the roar in my ears, and then I feel two big hands on my shoulders. I want to scream but there is M. Boucher's voice in my ears: Shhhhhh. *Arrêtez; écoutez.*

There is the sound of my breathing, fast, with the fear, and the beating of my heart. Then the sound of the river, moving through the dark like a large animal. And then, a small sound, like the mewling of a cat.

We found Emilie on a large rock very close to shore. She had crawled across a tree limb to get there, and when she had reached the rock the tree had fallen away and she was too afraid to get back. M. Boucher took one step into the water right up to his hip and snatched my little girl in his big arms, and she buried her head against his shirt. I cursed Henri for being away, for not being there, so that it was M. Boucher instead of Henri saving Emilie. It should have been Henri.

Oh, I should not have cursed my husband. It was a bad time, I was upset and relieved and angry, all at once, but who knows what fates are unleashed when you utter a curse? If I had known what would happen . . .

But my Emilie was safe, and that was most important, with everyone else running up as M. Boucher gave Emilie into my arms. *Maman!* she sobbed. *J'ai peur du monster qui vit dans le fleuve!*

The monster that lives in the river.

And now the monster is again here, only bigger, much bigger, and more fierce. It swallows up the river bank and farms and homes. It drowns cattle. The things swept down in its huge, gobbling mouth, as if it is hungry for everything: animals, outhouses, chicken coops, washing lines.

Daniel

CHANTAL JOINED A group last year, a Y2K Preparedness Group. I'll admit that when I saw the list she brought home of "things every home should have," my first thought was what a great time this is to own a hardware store! First aid supplies. Toilet paper. Duct tape. Wire. Tinfoil. Rolls of plastic. Batteries, all sizes. Manual can opener. Gas. Cash.

Chantal told me that ATMs probably won't work, and if the system breaks down there will be uncontrolled inflation. A loaf of bread could cost five dollars one day, a hundred the next. She wanted to take our money out of the bank and buy gold, but I put my foot down.

There might be no airplanes, trains, Chantal says—they all run on computers. Television won't be able to broadcast, and probably radio, too. The government might have to get the news out using old-fashioned megaphones, with soldiers broadcasting from the tops of tanks driving through the streets.

It's important not to be in an elevator at midnight, Chantal warned me. Now why would I be in an elevator at midnight? I asked her, but she went on with her list.

"We should have some plywood on hand," she said.

"Plywood?"

"In case we need to fortify the house against looters," she said.

Now, we have extra locks on all of the doors, so that when all hell breaks loose, we'll be safe in our own private hell. I don't even know where the keys are to most of them.

Brigitte

I MUST GET home. Help me, please. Why won't anyone help me? The door is shut. There is a way to get out, but I don't understand. I see people push the buttons with the number, dit-dit-dit. We never had such things. We didn't often lock our doors—who would steal from us?—but when you did lock a door, there was always a key.

I WILL NEVER forget the day we were locked out. We had come home from town. I had the children all with me, Lucien pulling a wagon on which was piled the groceries I had bought.

Because whatever happened, we had to eat, didn't we? Before any bills—and there were so many, on our hall table, I had stopped opening the envelopes, because what was the point?—we had to eat. You can't eat heat. You can't eat light. You can't eat payments to the bank.

I can remember what I bought, exactly: flour, because with flour I can make bread. Split peas, for soup. Pork bones and onions, because with these, and the peas, I can make a soup to fill our bellies and the house with a good, warm smell as if we are rich. Milk and tea. Some sugar. I had apples from Mme Boucher, from her tree because it was autumn and she said I could have the fallen ones. I had potatoes and turnips from Mme Garneau, who said she had planted too many in her garden, even though they will keep through the winter. From the spinster Mlle Laurent, I had eggs.

I could see the notice as I came up the lane, fluttering in the wind. It was fall, but still mild, which was good because Lucien had grown out of his winter boots and I did not yet know what I would do about that. His shoes were tight, but they fit him still. I wondered what the paper was, at first, and thought perhaps a kind neighbour had left me a note, but then Ben ran ahead and came back to say: *Maman*, the door is locked! There is a lock on our door!

I have never read English very well, but I could understand it. Foreclosure, it said. There had been letters, but this sort of thing was something Henri had always looked after. I suppose I just didn't want to see them, like the bills, and so I didn't.

But now, there is a new lock on our door, a padlock. And I have no key.

We found our dog, Ami, around the side. Perhaps he had tried to bite the man who came with the lock. He was such a faithful dog. I told the children he did not suffer, that it was quick, but how could I know? Lucien, such a good boy, dug a hole in back of the house that was no longer ours.

How can we ever really know the suffering of another?

Our new house was at the back of M. Laurent's property, near the river. It had been empty for a long time, but I scrubbed every room, and our good neighbours in St. Vital brought us furniture and other things. M. Laurent said he would not charge us rent; instead, I would clean the house of the Laurent family, a big house, a large family. So if I am careful, Henri's pension is enough for food, for Lucien's winter boots, for coats for Ben and Emilie.

M. Laurent worked for the railway, but not like Henri, not with his hands; M. Laurent worked in an office and made decisions for the Western Line. Why did he help us? I suppose he felt badly, because of Henri.

BUT THE NEW house, it is so close to the river. We are to be evacuated, to the firehall. We must go at once! Lucien won't know where to go. Ben and Emilie, sometimes they don't listen; they think everything is a game. Poor Emilie, she's so afraid, now, of the monster in the river.

We must go. Will you take me?

IF HENRI WAS here we would be already safe. Even though Henri was away so much, working, he always looked after us. Always. The children loved him so. Lucien adored him, and looks like him, too. Those big hands. Lucien is good with his hands, like his father. He made the wagon, the one we use to carry groceries. He made it himself, with wheels from a baby carriage he found thrown away, and two apple boxes, and the handle of a broken shovel.

Henri was a good husband. A good father. It was not Henri's fault. Henri would have wanted to make sure everything was working on the line. Perhaps he knew something wasn't right. Perhaps he went out with a lamp to make sure everything was right at the switch, so no more accidents would happen.

They blamed Henri for the derailment. But what happened to him later, it was because he was just making sure. Because you would be afraid, wouldn't you? That after a mistake like that happened, even if it wasn't your fault, that it might happen again.

I am sure he slipped, caught his foot. Could not get out of the way. Yes, they said they found a bottle, but Henri would never drink when he was working, of that I am sure.

They said it was quick. That he did not suffer.

I don't like to think of it.

ALL I MUST think about now is the children. I have to know they are safe. The river is rising; we must get to the firehall. We can't wait any longer! Please. My babies.

The water.

Daniel

BY THIS AFTERNOON Chantal had candles and camping lanterns in every room, ready. She had extra blankets out and folded at the ends of the beds. Marcel thinks it's a big adventure. He made a fort out of chairs and sheets in his room, and he has it stockpiled with Cheetos and comic books. Josslyne, though, was invited to spend New Year's Eve with her friend Annette, but Chantal wouldn't let her. Josslyne looked at me, hoping I would intervene, but I shrugged my shoulders and winked, as if to say: this is Mummy's game, and we'll just have to go along for now. She stomped off to her room. Why didn't I bring her with me to see Mémére? I don't know.

Maybe when midnight comes and Chantal sees that nothing has happened, we can talk. Maybe I can convince her to get some help—or maybe both of us will go. These things don't start all at once, do they? They build and build, like the flood Mémére is always talking about, and then whoosh! The dam breaks.

The main thing is the children.

When I left this evening, Chantal had every container we have in the house full of water. She had me bring four-gallon containers from the hardware store, everything we had, and these are stacked up in the basement for drinking water. Then she started filling everything else: buckets, garbage cans. To drink? I asked her, but no, she said. Was I nuts? To wash, to flush the toilet. The kitchen counter is lined with pop bottles full of water. If the Y2K apocalypse comes, we might drown anyway.

Brigitte

I WILL NEVER forget.

The water it came higher, higher. They said, you must be out by the first of May, and at the beginning I thought, no, it would not ever come so high. M. Laurent, Mme Laurent, they have gone to stay with relatives in Portage la Prairie. They wanted us to move, but we have only the house, and if the house was washed away, where would we go? So we stayed, because we had made a wall, yes? A wall of earth.

Lucien and Ben, two brothers, they were outside every day, digging and piling. M. Archambault came with his tractor, and soon there were more and more people, and then came big machines, and then the army! Everyone worked, and the dike we built, it was called the Carriere Dike. We filled sandbags—so many sandbags. Two working together, one to hold, one to fill. Emilie would hold the bag open and I would shovel, and sometimes we sang a little song, to the tune of *"Frère Jacques."* I will sing for you, listen:

La pluie, la pluie
Les nuages, les nuages
Le tonnerre et les éclairs, le tonnerre et les éclairs
L'arc-en-ciel, l'arc-en-ciel

YOU LAUGH! BUT I had a very nice singing voice, and it helped to make the work go easier, especially for Emilie. There were no rainbows, of course, just more and more rain. We would fill the sandbags, and then the men would form a line and toss them one to the other, and up onto the top of the wall that grew higher and higher. But so did the water.

The noise, *mon Dieu*. Lying in our house in the night, Emilie with me in one bed and the boys together, and in the dark I knew we were all awake and listening to the roar of the water as if it would come right in our door, in our windows, at any moment. How can I explain? I would lie there with the sound all around and think and think how I could protect my children and our home, and I would talk in my head to Henri. Sometimes I would curse him for being dead, and sometimes I would plead with him to tell us what to do. Because if we left our house, as they wanted us to do, would it be there when we returned, and if not, where would we go? But if we stayed, then we could keep piling high the sandbags.

And all the time the water gets higher, and I would dream of waking up to find it swirling around our beds. And of course it would have, except for the dike. But would it hold? We went every day, the neighbours too, to make sure, and every day the water was higher. Emilie began to have nightmares, she would wake us all up: *Maman, Maman, il vient!* Of course, she was afraid of *le monstre dans le fleuve.*

The Seine and the Red Rivers, they met like two huge *serpents de mer*, and when the dike broke there went Marion Street, and St. Anne's Road.

So much water.

I GO TO see M. Archambault, to say yes, we will go to the St. Vital firehall, we have our things we will take. We would not stay any longer. To ask: will you take us? In his truck, Emilie and me, we could sit in the front, the boys in the back with our things.

But the Archambaults have gone. I walk through their house. Everything has been moved—table, chairs, rugs— upstairs, and the downstairs, it is empty. My heels sound hollow on the linoleum as I walk across, calling, although I know there is no one there. It is like what they say is the eye of the hurricane, because there in the Archambaults' house it is still, nothing, while outside is the roar of the water. It seems louder than before. Is it a trick of the empty rooms? *Alors, mon Dieu!* I know it is the sound of the river with nothing to hold it back.

I run across the field to our house, but it is so far away! I can't run fast enough in these shoes, with this mud! I am slipping, falling, my heart is pounding and in my ears I hear Emilie's voice as if she is here with me: *Maman, il vient!*

Where are my children? I told them, stay upstairs. You will be safe if you stay upstairs and wait for me. Will they know to wait? *J'arrive!*

What is that sound? Is it the water, at last, breaking through the dikes?

NO, NO, MÉMÉRE. It is just the fireworks starting. See, they have turned the lights off so we can see out the window better. For a moment I thought—but never mind, everything is fine. No one was washed away. We are all safe. Chantal and Marcel and Josslyne. Papa and Maman. Uncle Benoit and David. Aunt Emilie and Didier. All of your grandchildren!

Everyone is celebrating the New Year, Mémére. It's a new millennium.

Look out the window. Here, I'll push your chair.

Aren't they beautiful?

YES. YES, THEY are beautiful.

TWELVE

ACROSS THE ATLANTIC

·2012·

Day 1

THE WEATHER'S FINE as we leave the Halifax port behind us, and before us, the open sea. It's going to take a bit of getting used to, the movement beneath my feet, but it's nothing compared to what my great-great-grandmother, who came from Ireland in 1847, endured. Her ship was a sailing ship; she didn't have the small, efficient cabins we have, and she certainly didn't dine with the officers. We are the only paying passengers on this voyage, while on Mary's ship almost two hundred people travelled crammed together in steerage.

My granddaughter Josslyne turns from the rail and grins at me. For Josslyne and her brother Marcel, after a gruelling year of university, this is a great adventure. For their father Daniel, it's a concession—it was hard for him to take time from expanding his hardware business. For my husband Lucien, it's a celebration, because I'm still here, after all.

It took a fair bit of research to find a cargo ship that would trace the same route, more or less, as Mary and her family took, but I insisted. I wanted to cross the Atlantic as my ancestors did, and I didn't want to travel in some fancy cruise ship. I wanted to sail from St. John's but we had to settle for Halifax and this freighter, which is transporting Eastern White Pine among other things. We'll dock in Liverpool, and then we'll take a ferry across the Irish Sea to Dublin.

Lucien puts his arm around my shoulders. He's still protective, even now that I'm well. I lean into him, sheltered from the wind by his familiar body.

"Did you know there was another family on that crossing?" I ask, and Daniel turns, humouring me.

"I imagine there were a few."

"I wasn't finished," I say, and give him a playful slap. "The McGraths and the Murphys became friends on the crossing. Mary McGrath was a Murphy before she married Daniel— your namesake—and so afterwards, when her younger sister Catherine married Paddy Murphy, Catherine got to keep her last name."

This revelation is lost on Josslyne, who is getting married next month, but who will still be Josslyne Gauthier. "Different times," I add, catching her eye.

"Hmmph," grunts Marcel. "She should have hyphenated it. Then she'd be Catherine Murphy-Murphy."

They're all humouring me. I think it was this research into family history that pulled me through recovery, giving me a different focus, and by the time my hair had grown back and I'd gotten used to the absence that was once my right breast, I knew I needed to go, and I needed my family with me, as many as would come. I wanted to complete the circle.

Marcel faces the wind, eyes closed against the sun, arms outstretched in parody of that scene in the *Titanic* film. Josslyne, hamming it up, joins him. I plant my feet on the deck and spread my arms, too, letting the wind press my clothes against my body, outlining the parts that are there and the parts that aren't. Rooted this way, I can't help but think of the family tree that we are: great-great-grandmothers behind us; great-great-grandchildren yet to be born.

Day 5

THERE ISN'T MUCH to do on a ship like this, which is fine by me. I love the day stretching before me, with time to read, or think, or talk with Lucien, who still follows me about like he might lose me. My energy is returning, and yesterday I played table tennis with Marcel, and won. There's a weight room, a day room with a tiny library, a small swimming pool, dining room, and an officer's bar. This ship has only three passenger cabins, and so Lucien and I are in one, Daniel and Marcel in another, and Josslyne has the third all to herself. Last night I joined her there for a bottle of wine, which we drank like sneaky teenagers; since I've been healthy, nothing feels out of character for me. I want to know my children, my grandchildren, all of the people I love in this way: as themselves, no expectations, no judgments. I want to meet them on their turf; to remove any constructs of distance or separation. There is nothing like facing death to make you want to take down walls.

When I was in chemo, I met a woman, Allison, in the waiting room. Enough of our appointments coincided that we became friends. It's such an intimate thing, sitting together in that vulnerable state. It was Allison who got me tracing my roots, herself in the process of digging up her own.

One day when I arrived she was sitting in the corner chair by the lamp with a folder open on her lap. She looked up and raised the area where her eyebrows used to be.

"Mary!" she said, "Look at this. I just got my grandfather's military records. I knew he was in the air force, but I didn't know he was a navigator. He never talked about the war."

Allison had recently subscribed to an online genealogy service, and had quickly become immersed in her family history. I sat down beside her. "A lot of men didn't. My father was the same." I looked closer. "Your grandfather was in 160 squadron in Vancouver. That sounds familiar . . . "

Allison looked up. "Really?"

"Well, who knows? This course of treatment is messing up my memory, I think—that, or I'm just getting old." Allison grinned, nodding, but she's thirty years younger than I am— far too young for this.

"Look at this." She handed me a photocopied page. Under the name Robert Handley the citation read:

THIS OFFICER'S SKILL, courage and devotion to duty as a navigator have contributed much to the success achieved by the squadron. As navigation leader he has done exceptionally good work and has set a splendid example of efficiency both in the air and on the ground. His repeated development of new ideas, modifications, and training schemes have been of exceptional value in bringing the navigation in his squadron to its present high standard.

"HE MUST HAVE felt proud when he read this. I'm proud of him, reading it now. I wish he were still alive, so I could tell him," she said.

The receptionist called Allison's name, and she packed up her folder and left. That evening, flattened as I was from the chemo session, I lay on the couch looking through my own folder of family records, passed down to me. Lucien was reading the paper, but he looked up when I made a noise of surprise.

"Same squadron!" I said. I explained about Allison. "Not only that, here's a postcard Dad sent home; Mum kept everything. He mentions his friend Bob. What are the chances . . . ?"

"Common name," remarked Lucien from behind the *Globe and Mail.*

But it wasn't. Over the weeks of our treatment, Allison and I grew closer, and started digging further. My father and her grandfather *were* friends, although it appears they lost touch after the war.

"It's that six degrees of separation thing," Allison said. We were having lunch, our friendship having moved beyond the waiting room. I hadn't heard the term. "It's based on the idea that everyone is, on average, six steps away from any other person on Earth. Everyone's a friend of a friend—if you follow the chain, six steps like that should connect any two people. I don't know if it's really true, but how many times have you caught yourself saying: small world?"

"A lot," I admitted.

ALLISON DIDN'T MAKE it. Her cancer returned, aggressively. At her funeral, a childhood friend of hers approached me and asked if Allison and I were related, assuming, I guess, that I was an aunt or something.

"Yes," I told her, after a pause.

Day 9

IT'S HARD TO hold the scope and breadth of a family tree in your head when you really start to think about it. There are the matrilineal and the patrilineal aspects. There are second and even third marriages. There are adoptions. But I like the idea of having this web of branches and roots, supporting me. With all of this, how is it possible to fall?

With all of the space and time on this voyage—which will take less than a third as long as Mary's was—there is time for all of us to think. Josslyne has been thinking about her upcoming marriage to her young man, Adam. She loves him, but she saw her parents' marriage break up, and I can see why she might be wary.

"Have you ever talked to your dad about it?" She shook her head. "He might have a bit of advice. You might be surprised."

She shook her head again, but this evening I see them talking earnestly, leaning on the guardrail against a technicolour sunset. Marcel is on his way to join them, but I head him off.

"Crib?" I ask. "I think you owe me a game. It was best two out of three, remember? We haven't played the third."

We sit in the day room, the board between us. Marcel draws high card and shuffles the deck the way I taught him: shuffle, riffle, tap down, repeat.

"Thanks for taking us on this trip, Gran," he says, dealing. "Joss and I haven't spent this much time together since before high school. And even though we saw Dad most weekends and summers, it's different as adults."

I toss two cards in the crib. "Huh. What about your grandfather and me? Isn't it good to see us, too?"

"Well, yeah—of course. It's great to spend time with you. I guess all we're missing is Aunt Elizabeth." He lays down a seven of clubs.

My smart, serious girl—okay, middle-aged woman—is a full professor now, teaching in Paris. It would not be possible to get away, she told me, even in June.

"Well, we could never have brought everyone—there are your aunts and uncles and cousins. Great-uncles. Second cousins." Marcel rolls his eyes. They're all a little tired of the subject, I think. "Besides, a lot of them will be there, at your sister's wedding; it will be a bit of a reunion." I put a seven of hearts on top of his. "A pair for two," I announce, moving my peg forward. "My mother always said there should be more reasons to get together than weddings and funerals. This is good."

"And seven makes twenty-one, for six," he says, grinning. "The more, the merrier."

Day 12

SOMETIME IN THE night I'm awakened by a change in the motion of the ship. A ship this big isn't at the mercy of the waves like Mary's was, so the swells out there must be pretty big. Without waking Lucien, I put my warm jacket on over my pajamas and slip out to go above and see.

It's beautiful: the stars are out, although far on the horizon I can see a black presence where the stars stop. The pitch and roll must be from a storm far away from us, I think. The roll seems diminished, now that I have the sky and deck as reference points, and I lean on the rail, enjoying the space. I can hear movements of the crew somewhere on the deck, but I've found an out-of-the-way place. It's good to be alone. My family doesn't say as much, but I feel them watching me carefully, as if I'm still fragile. As if I could be snatched away from them at any moment.

We'll be in port sometime late tomorrow. It was such a journey to get this far. There was the journey of my own recovery, of course, but I prefer to think about the journey of discovery that began in earnest when I found Mary's diary in the provincial archives in St. John's. It felt as if a familiar hand had reached out to grasp my own. It was then that I decided that, when I was strong enough, I would make this trip.

My mother gave her first baby up for adoption, and then found her much later—giving me a half-sister I never knew I had. We have the same laugh; it's our mother's laugh. Lucien's mother raised her children by herself, kids who learned to look out for one another, who raised their own kids to do the same. We don't all behave the way we should all of the time, but these basic things are rooted deep. What came to me, as I pored over ship's lists, and birth, marriage, death, and military records, is that people, circumstance, place and time vary through generations, but the themes do not. Our stories are all about desperation and courage, hardship and hope. They're about keeping the people you love safe, and sometimes, leaving them behind.

I'm so busy thinking about this that I don't feel the wind come up, sheltered where I am behind the lifeboats, and I don't see that the stars have gone out. The rain, when it comes, is hard and cold, as if the heavens are hurling down pebbles. I turn to head back to the cabin, but as soon as I step away from my shelter I'm met with a horizontal wind so fierce it pulls me off my feet. I'm sliding across the wet deck with the tilt of the boat, grasping for something to hold onto, finding nothing. I cry out, but the wind takes my words away.

And then Daniel is here. He grips my arms, the rain pelting down around us. I can barely hear, over the roar of the wind, Lucien's shout: *Mary!*—a wail of fear. In a scrambling moment they have me back into the shelter of the narrow stairwell where I sit on the top step, shivering as I gasp for breath.

"Gran, what were you thinking?" says Marcel, while Josslyne puts her sweater around my shoulders. I look up to see them around me, faces shifting in emotions of fear and relief. Lucien is crying.

Later, warm and safe in my narrow bed, I hear him whisper into the dark.

"If anything happens to you, my heart will break."

Day 13

THE INCIDENT WAS not reported to the crew. I've had about enough attention, I told them, and I've learned my lesson. The day dawned fine, and we all agreed to let it go. But I woke thinking of the McGraths and the Murphys, pitching about in the hold of that ship. They must have wondered, more than once, if the choice they had made might be their last. Sometimes you see death coming, and sometimes you don't.

And now we can see Liverpool, the Royal Liver Building with its beautiful towers dominating the waterfront. *Land.* There are ships on all sides as we approach, the air full of engine noise, clangs and clatters, and above that, the scream of gulls. They fill the air with sound and motion.

Now there's another sound, one that seems out of place. It's Daniel's cell phone.

I peer over his shoulder to read the text message on the screen. Who would be calling him here? Now?

"Meet you dockside," the words on the screen say. "Don't tell Mum."

"Who—?"

"Elizabeth!" Daniel says, grinning. "I didn't know, either. I guess you'd better pretend to be surprised."

I lean on the rail, letting the sun wash over me, the wind now a gentle presence. A seagull lands nearby and cocks its head, considers me with a black and beady eye. Then it spreads its wings to join its family, circling above in the cloudless sky.

AFTERWORD AND
ACKNOWLEDGMENTS

IT WAS AN ambitious project to try to capture a century of a country's history through a selection of moments in this novel. I wanted to illustrate Canada's geographical scope, to offer a sense of her social and cultural diversity, and to suggest that—young country though we may be—there's a rich history here. I tried to choose both the familiar and the unfamiliar from among the almost overwhelming possibilities of historical topic.

For every event that makes the history books there exist people for whom those events form an unavoidable backdrop to a personal story. It is my hope that this narrative embodies an emotional universality, revealing similarities that compress time, geography, and cultural difference.

More than anything, I wanted to tell a good story, and I hope that I did.

Each chapter in this book owes something to somebody, a cast of real-life characters to whom I am deeply grateful.

My writing group is an insightful bunch full of goodwill and humour, and they saw me through every one of these stories. They are: Antonia Banyard, Vangie Bergum, Sarah Butler, Jennifer Craig, Kristene Perron, Rita Moir, and Verna Relkoff. A million thanks to all of you.

Deryn Collier offered another set of eyes for the majority of the stories, setting me straight on Montreal geography for *Angel* and asking all the right questions for everything else. Katya Maloff weighed in on a sensitive topic for *To Be Like You*, and found additional readers for whom forced residential school was a reality. Tom Wayman, author of *Woodstock Rising*, weighed in on the times for *A Different Country*.

For *The Language of Bones*, retired Yukon wolf biologist Bob Hayes was a great help, as was Yukon College biology instructor Dave Mossop; Jacqueline Cameron was worth her weight in gold as usual when it came to critiquing, particularly on the subtleties of Northern culture. Kirsten Smith at the Yukon Archives really went the extra mile for me. Thanks to Pat Rogers for her suggestion on how to marry past and present in that story, and for keeping me on the historical straight-and-narrow generally.

Static owes a chunk of its authenticity to Mary Audia, who wrote out her mother's jigs dinner recipe and told me all about Deadman's Pond. Steve Thornton offered insights for *All of the Colours*, Michael Chapman and Francyne Laliberté corrected my French in *River Rising*, Stephanie Fischer checked my German, and children's author Cyndi Sand-Eveland advised on the youthful voice of my protagonists in *Static* and *Home Girl*.

To my agent Morty Mint, one of the more colourful characters in my life, thanks for holding me up and watching my back. Thanks to Kim McArthur for the extra push towards a narrative link, and to the talented team at McArthur & Company who continue to have faith in me.

Finally, thanks to my kids, Alex, Tam, and Annika, who are my constant inspiration, and my partner Phillip, who is unfailingly there for me, and who gives a great foot rub.